EXQUISITE
CORPSE

EXQUISITE CORPSE

Robert Irwin

THE OVERLOOK PRESS
WOODSTOCK & NEW YORK

This paperback edition first published in the United States in 2003 by
The Overlook Press, Peter Mayer Publishers, Inc.
Woodstock & New York

WOODSTOCK:
One Overlook Drive
Woodstock, NY 12498
www.overlookpress.com
[for individual orders, bulk and special sales, contact our Woodstock office]

NEW YORK:
141 Wooster Street
New York, NY 10012

Library of Congress Cataloging-in-Publication Data

Irwin, Robert.
Exquisite corpse / Robert Irwin.
p. cm.
1. Absurd (Philosophy)—Fiction. 2. Missing persons—Fiction.
3. Surrealism—Fiction. 4. Artists—Fiction. 5. Typists—Fiction.
6. Europe—Fiction. I. Title.
PR6069.R96 E97 1997   823'.914—dc21   96-47788

Printed in Canada
ISBN 1-58567-386-2
1 3 5 7 9 8 6 4 2

Dedication

For Oliver Sorge who taught me all I know about writing.

'Books have their destinies.' The first edition of this memoire, or rather it should be anti-memoire, was published only last year. What need for a second edition so soon after the first? The answer is that within a few months of the publication of *Exquisite Corpse* and in response to its publication certain things happened which forced me to re-examine the events it described and to look on them in a new light. When I look back at what I first wrote, I laugh, though really I should weep. I thought that I could look back on the past as if through a window, but what I was actually looking at was only a painting of a window ... Illusions of the heart and the eye ... When I was last in Brussels, René Magritte showed me one of his early paintings, 'Human Condition I', in which we see a picture on an easel standing in front of a landscape and obscuring part of that landscape. The picture itself shows a landscape, but it is doubtful whether the landscape it shows is really the same as the one it obscures. I have only recently become aware that the version of the past which I present in this book is somewhat like Magritte's puzzle painting. I now have a very different idea of what happened so many years ago and would not now write what I have written here. Neither the manner nor the content would be the same. Nevertheless, I have not changed a single word of the text. Only I have added an additional chapter at the end, a chapter which changes the meaning of everything which comes before. Now it occurs to me to wonder if, in a year or two's time, I may not be drafting a prefatory note to a third revised and expanded edition ... I hope not. There has to be an end to all this.

London, December, 1952.

Chapter One

1951

I rarely dream of Caroline. However, I dreamt last night that we were walking round Battersea Funfair. She wanted to be a milkmaid. I promised her a miniature Trianon. Then I was on my knees before her. She was impatient to go back to her office, but she condescended to feed me coughdrops.

Where is Caroline? Where has everyone gone? I walk up and down the old familiar streets of Soho and Bloomsbury without encountering anyone. And not just Soho and Bloomsbury, for I venture further – to Ealing, St Albans and the Faubourg St Germain – but the streets are always empty, empty save for the regiments of City men in bowler hats and suits, of spivs and street traders in trilbies and demob suits and the soldiers and sailors on leave. But these are dead people. Only the women seem alive. My eyes are always on the women, looking for Caroline, or if not Caroline, then for some other woman, in the hope that studying her may help me to understand Caroline better.

No Caroline. No Ned Shillings. No Oliver Sorge. No Jenny Bodkin. No Mackellar. No Felix. No Jorge. Even Pamela, who used to draw hundreds nightly to hear her sing, has vanished. Where have they all gone? While my back was turned, did they enter into a secret pact to sign up as lighthouse-keepers, nuns or foreign legionaries? It may be that they have settled down in quiet suburbs and have found employment and contentment as town clerks, insurance salesmen, jobbing decorators and so on, but that is hard to believe.

I have a photograph of some of the group in front of me now. It was taken in 1936, a couple of months after the

Surrealist Exhibition at the New Burlington Galleries closed. We are assembled outside Winkelmann's Gallery, just off Regent Street, all squinting into the sun, all save Ned, who from the centre of the group gazes fearlessly into the camera. The brilliant whites of his eyes always used to make me think of a raptor. Most of us are smiling sheepishly. Jenny Bodkin in her striped sailor's shirt is brandishing that preposterous glove puppet of hers, the one shaped like a voracious cunt fringed with pubic hair. Jorge, kneeling in front of us, wrestles unconvincingly with a concertina. Glasses and cigarettes are much in evidence and some of the glasses are raised in the direction of Ned, whose show this is. Felix sits at his feet and lets an exploring hand stray mischievously up his trouser-leg towards his groin.

I am on the edge of the group in the shadow of the Gallery's awning. Looking at myself now, I know that I was preoccupied that day. I wanted to talk Winkelmann into agreeing to an exhibition of my illustrations to Mackellar's *The Girlhood of Gagool*. I never had much chance of that. Oliver has one arm flung round my shoulders while with the other he cradles Monica. Caroline does not appear in the photograph. '*La femme trouvée*', she was never regarded as part of our group. But she was the one who took the picture. Later, much later, after the war, I used this, her photograph, as the basis for a retrospective portrait of the group. I changed nothing except that I painted everyone with their eyes tightly closed, so that they appear to sleep, propping each other up in a collective dream. In this version, it is only I who is awake and who stares wide-eyed out of the canvas. The painting has passed into the hands of the National Portrait Gallery and I believe they keep it stored in some basement as part of their reserve collection.

There were about twenty or thirty of us, members of the Serapion Brotherhood, plus hangers-on and admirers. In the years before the outbreak of the War, I could walk into the Dead Rat Club on any night and find half a dozen

8

of them at least. It was even unusual to walk any distance in central London without encountering one or other by chance. Indeed, it seems to me that chance operated differently before the War. We in the Brotherhood were so sure that we would change the face of art, literature, politics, everything. Now Soho's bars and clubs are full of new men and women, who seem yet noisier, drunker and more confident: Maclaren-Ross; Tambimuttu, Colquhoun, MacBryde, Dylan Thomas, Nina Hamnett. The old gang have vanished very nearly without trace. I run into Paul Nash and David Gascoyne occasionally. I spotted one of Jenny Bodkin's toys in a shop window a couple of weeks ago. It was the teddy bear with the hammer, who growls 'Put me down' when he is picked up. At least I know about Ned Shillings. He is dead, as he promised he would be. Herbert Read and I still correspond, though with increasing acrimony. I read everything that Oliver Sorge has published in *Horizon* and elsewhere, but I have no idea where he lives and letters sent to Cyril Connolly for forwarding go unanswered. Cyril himself swears he does not know where Oliver lives now.

Oliver Sorge, Paul Nash, Jorge Arguelles, Herbert Read. Now it occurs to me that all these names and indeed my own name may give rise in the reader to false expectations as to what this book is *about*. This is not a history of the Serapion Brotherhood. Nor is it in any sense an autobiography, for I loathe being bored to death with the details of an autobiographer's parents, grandparents and great-grandparents, and then by an account of his (probably unhappy) days at school, to be followed by a lyrical evocation of spreading wings at university and so on, and so on. All that I hate. I have kept no diaries which might serve as the basis for an autobiography, but only a noctuary in which I record the little which has happened to me while I am asleep. If you are curious about my parentage, know then that Lautréamont was my father and Alice in Wonderland my mother. As for my infancy, I am still in it. In my studies <u>the whisky bottle has served me as a microscope</u> <u>and the brothel has been my laboratory.</u>

Neither is this book an artistic memoire. It is not more than incidentally concerned with my part in the organisation of the First Surrealist Exhibition in London, nor with my quarrel with André Breton and my expulsion from his movement. I am not planning to say anything very much about my career as a war artist nor about the court case brought against me by my psychoanalyst. The book is not really about me at all. Not only is this book not about me, it is also not written for you — unless your name is Caroline. What you hold in your hands is not literature, but a magical trap. Its sole purpose is to seek out Caroline. I have to publish the book of course and I imagine so many copies of *Exquisite Corpse* floating in so many stoppered bottles on strange and distant seas. The paradox is that publication on as wide a scale as possible is essential to my purpose, but really the book that is published is a private thing and destined for one reader only. If nevertheless you will persist in reading on, you will soon become aware of my literary failings. Oliver and Mackellar were the writers in the group and I, a painter, am working now in a medium that is quite foreign to me. Indeed, I tend to think of myself as writing a painting. I dab at the words and beneath all my dabbings and pentimenti lies a dark ground of melancholy and self-pity. I believe that the book will turn out like one of those murky canvases by the Genoese painter, Alessandro Magnasco — a sombre landscape of late evening in which we see with difficulty a rocky crevasse or broad swamp and where, in such a desolate landscape, half concealed by foliage and rocks, the emaciated and posturing anchorites or mountebanks can just be glimpsed, the highlights of their tortured figures being lit up as if in a flash of lightning.

After I had written these words, the longest stretch of words I have written since I ran away from school, I went for a walk along the South Bank. The Festival of Britain was in full swing and I had to walk past those cutely twee little jokey machines of Emmet, John Piper's so very English plasterboard follies, the dismal Skylon and the not very exciting display of G-Plan furniture. Here and there I saw were sad signs of the domestication of Surrealism. One now sees a lot of paintings of high-horizoned landscapes which are empty of all but a few mysteriously disposed objects and the advertising hoardings are crowded with images of disembodied hands and eyes. Surrealism has lost its claim to shock. Even its power to charm is now questionable. Some Festival!

We were more truly festive during the War. As I strode through the crowds I felt myself burning with an hideous intensity, so that I could fancy that if any one of these people touched me they would instantly catch alight and crumble to ashes, consumed by my psychic fire.

When I came back, I opened another bottle of whisky and stared at the wall. It hardly matters which wall I stare at, for, in a brief fit of enthusiasm for trompe d'oeil, I have painted false windows on three of the walls, so that these walls exactly resemble the fourth wall, which really does have a window which looks out on a railway siding. The door into the room is almost invisible, for it has been painted into the wallpaper. With my art I have created my prison.

Though I paint in this room, it would not suit many artists. The real window faces south, and all my colleagues, rivals rather, swear by a northern light. However, the problem with the light does not trouble me, for I no longer paint from life and I actually prefer the yellowy glow shed by the naked light bulb over my garish colours. I paint from within the head. I have only to close my eyes and the hypnagogic images appear unbidden. I see in silent turmoil shapes of men, beasts, buildings, symbols and landscapes. They ceaselessly chase one another across my eyelids before disappearing into the unilluminated area of my head. When I asked Dr Wilson, my psychoanalyst, about these images, he assured me that hypnagogic imagery was quite common and had something to do with misfirings or discharges from the retinal rods. (Or was it cones? I forget what exactly.)

When I consulted a dictionary, I found 'hypnagogic' defined as 'sleep-bringing, ushering in sleep'. Something is not right here, for I am never more awake than when I am watching these shapes dancing and twisting, covering my field of vision and dissolving into one another. A recumbent dog becomes a fruit bowl, its brown rump metamorphosed into the curving outline of a pear, and a narcissistic youth contemplating his image in a pool of water becomes, with just a tiny shift of focus, a skeletal hand holding an egg — even as my old friend (and by this I mean ex-friend) Salvador Dali has so successfully demonstrated with his paranoiac-critical method. As Dali puts it, we are working with 'a spontaneous method of irrational knowledge based upon the interpretive-critical association of delirious phenomena'. This is in full accord with the Surrealist Manifesto, for we follow Breton's prescription when we seek to take down 'thought's dictation in the absence of all control exercised by reason and outside all moral or aesthetic prejudice'.

Anyway I do not believe that hypnagogic imagery has anything to do with sleep, for I have hardly slept at all since Caroline vanished. Sometimes I lie on the floor with my eyes closed and passively let the images flow over me — ziggurats transformed into bonfires whose flames become tendrils in a great vineyard at the end of which is a wall with a door, but, as I approach the door, it transforms itself into a pool on which floats a duck which turns into an upturned foot and so on with unflagging energy — a plotless, scriptless, pointless cinema.

At other times however I am not so passive, for it is possible to force and shape what I see and I have a repertoire of concentration-building exercises. I make all the letters of the alphabet parade themselves before me. One by one they flicker uncertainly on my eyelids, longing to be something else. Then I relax my control and they dissolve and recompose themselves thankfully into ostriches, or windows, or banjos, whatever they have chosen. Or I may summon up the image of Hitler and make him swagger and salute, then run, then stand on his head and I may inflate his head to three times its size. However, the strain involved in this sort of visual drill is considerable. In particular, it is curiously difficult to summon up likenesses of individual men and women at will.

In general, hypnagogic forms are labile and pass swiftly out of my control. When I summon up images of nude or half-dressed women, these women frantically writhe and twist and recombine with each other and with the landscape. The women are desperate to escape my godlike clutches and eager to preserve their modesty by transforming themselves into myrtle bushes or cows or whatever. On occasions when I am able to freeze one of these images I may behold a woman caught midway in such a transformation with her arms beginning to grow leaves, her nose beginning to reshape itself into a stork's beak, her shapely legs fading into tendrils of smoke. It is impossible when contemplating such an image not to think of the 'exquisite corpse', one of those composite figures we used to produce during our Surrealist games of consequences. One artist would draw the head, then fold the paper and pass it to his neighbour who would sketch in the torso before folding the paper again and so on, until some marvellous hybrid emerged from the unfolded paper.

Novelists make use of exquisite corpses as a matter of course. I remember Oliver making this point quite forcibly. In *The Vampire of Surrealism*, the book for which he is best known the woman Stella is a kind of exquisite corpse, for while the brilliant white face and raven hair belonged to Felix originally, the wit, the bum and the thighs were taken from Monica and the breasts came from a woman glimpsed walking down the King's Road. So Oliver told me.

Naturally, I have tried to summon up an hypnagogic image of Caroline, but I was fearful and conscious that I was attempting something that was somehow blasphemous,

13

and it was perhaps because of these misgivings of mine that she did not appear — and has never appeared. So, if that form of conjuration failed, will this new attempt be any more successful? Will the magical letters on the page summon her presently to me? If I call, will she come? Perhaps. But suppose she is dead. Suppose that one evening, as I sit writing this in the upstairs room of this house in the backstreets behind Waterloo Station, I might hear a muffled but insistent thumping and I will go downstairs and open the door and a thing will stumble out of the smog into my arms. I will find myself embracing something putrescent and caked with earth. The blue dress will be stained and partly rotted away. The teeth that press against my lips will be yellow and loose. Yet I would embrace the thing willingly. The horror of that would be less than what I suffer now. It is certainly possible that she is dead. It is even possible that I killed her.

Chapter Two

1936

'Will any kind friend inform a poor blind man, who has lost the precious sight of his eyes in the gracious defence of his native country, England, and God bless King George! where and in what part of this country he may now be!' I was noisy and I am sure many people turned to look at me.

Mackellar, however, kept his voice low.

'We are coming up into the centre of Hampstead now. In a minute or two we will pass by Flask Walk. There's a bishop approaching in the opposite direction. Raise your hat to him and wish him a good afternoon. On your left there is a wine-merchant. If only you could see, you would behold a fine window-display of imported sherrys . . .'

MacKellar carried on, conscientiously describing shop after shop, but I was hardly listening, as I carried on with my Blind Pew act, tapping the ground ahead of me with an Indian sword-stick. The sword-stick had been provided by Oliver for the day. My hat (very like the one worn by Valentino in *The Four Horsemen of the Apocalypse*) had been lent to me by Apache Jorge. The coat I was wearing had been absent-mindedly left by Ned in my rooms a few days ago. The sleepmask over my eyes was, however, my own. While MacKellar struggled with words to create his version of London, I was seeing quite a different city laid out upon my eyelids, so that I appeared to advance through great chasms and pass by oriental temples. I saw nuns and priests shepherd crocodiles down otherwise deserted streets. I entered houses at random and walked through crowded drawing rooms in which all the conversations were animated but silent. Out of doors again, I confronted huge mobs and, though I could distinguish every feature of

15

every face in the mob with minute particularity, I noted without surprise that I had never seen any of these people before. So wonder after wonder unfolded itself on my eyelids as I walked blindfold through London.

> 'Fourmillante cité pleine des rêves
> Ou le spectre en plein jour raccroche le passant
> Les mystères partout comme des sèves
> Dans les canaux étroits du colosse puissant'

MacKellar shook me out of my Baudelairean reverie,

'We are passing a duchess. Raise your hat. Now we are passing a cheese-monger's. Magnificent cheeses! Smell them!'

I sniffed. The smoggy air was damp and heavy with coal dust. No cheese. The other reason for not listening to MacKellar was that he was lying. We had left my place in Cuba Street early in the morning and, after walking out of the Docks area, we had taken a tram. Lunch was in an eel-and-pie shop, probably the one in Whitechapel Road. MacKellar had helped me to feed myself, explaining to our fellow customers how I had been blinded in the service of Surrealism. Since then we had been walking a long time and I guessed that we were on the edge not of Hampstead but of Soho. However, MacKellar always lied whenever he could. It was more or less a matter of principle with him – essential training for a writer of fiction. He even pretended to be an admirer of Dr Josef Goebbels and would quote appreciatively, 'The bigger the lie, the more beautiful!' and MacKellar would add that lying was like lipstick, in that it did indeed make the world more beautiful and more interesting.

In the East End we had had some trouble. MacKellar had got into a fight with a crippled beggar who had thought that I was going to poach on his territory. A little later I heard a posh voice saying that I should be horsewhipped to get the nonsense beaten out of me. But since then there had been no excitements.

'I'm tired and bored,' I announced loudly. 'I want to be taken to a brothel – a really good brothel!'

'Hush man. I'm taking you to one. We are almost there. It is the best brothel in Hampstead.'

And in a few minutes we pushed through some swing-doors.

'Is this the brothel?'

'Aye, this is the brothel. But not so loud or you will scare the ladies.'

'Are the ladies beautiful?'

'Aye.'

'Describe them to me.'

'I will, but first I will get the madame to provide us with some drinks.'

MacKellar forced me down on to a hard wooden chair and I was left alone in what was evidently a crowded room. I could smell beer. I remember that I wondered why I was doing this. Defamiliarising the world might have its uses as an exercise in the cleansing of perceptions and it was true that there were the visions. Even so I was restless. I was waiting for something really exciting to happen – something that would change my life forever. When I had set out this morning my hopes had been high. I had been expecting the unexpected and I had visualised myself as a sort of goat tethered to a hunter's tree as bait to trap the marvellous.

MacKellar returned and pressed a pint of beer into my hand.

'For God's sake man, what do you see? What manner of people are these?' I cried.

'This is one of London's most exclusive brothels,' he assured me. 'Apart from us, all the men here are in white tie and tails, but the madame is a particular friend of mine and she let us in as an exception.'

I nodded patiently. I was fairly sure that this was one of two public houses in Greek Street. Probably it was The Eagle. I had visited the pub when I was researching my illustrations to De Quincey's *Confessions of an English Opium Eater*. (De Quincey met the prostitute Anne in this street.)

'By contrast, all the women are nude,' MacKellar continued. 'They are lying or sitting on red velvet sofas at the far end of the room. Some of them are looking at you curiously. They must be wondering what it would be like to make love to a blind man. Any moment now one of them will come over.'

'Are any of them beautiful?'

'I have told you, they are all beautiful.'

Until then all I had been able to smell was beer and Guinness, but then suddenly I caught a faint and bitter hint of a woman's perfume and from close by I heard a woman's voice asking softly,

'Why is he like that?'

'Ah, love is blind,' replied MacKellar.

Then he went silent. I fancied I could hear the scratch of his pen. That day and for that matter every day MacKellar carried a notebook in which he jotted down his impressions of the world. His constant fear was that he might experience an epiphany without having on him the means to record it. I sat and drank, thinking of MacKellar's many problems. Suddenly, and it was a little like missing a step when descending a staircase in the dark, I had the sensation that he was no longer with me.

'MacKellar? MacKellar?'

A young woman's voice, perhaps the same voice as before, answered me.

'Was that the name of your friend?'

I nodded.

'Well, he's gone out just now, but he wrote a message which he pressed into my hand.'

She read it out. It was plain from her reading that she was amused.

'Dear Miss _____,

You have a kindly face. I beg you, take care of this tragically afflicted young man. God help me. It has all become too much for me. Thank you and God bless!

His despairing father,

M.'

'MacKellar,' I sighed.

She giggled and then,

'You are coming with me.'

Her voice, though pleasant, brooked no contradiction. It was not a cockney voice, but then again it was not a Mayfair voice. I guessed that it was a voice from Metroland. Then, as I continued to listen to it, I thought that I could detect an exaggerated clarity of diction which reminded me of certain screen actresses. It was even possible, I concluded, that this young woman might have gone to elocution classes – not the voice of a debutante, but the voice of someone who wished she had been. There was a kind of constraint in it that I found erotic. It sounded as if all her vowels were bound in consonantal corsets.

She took my hand and led me out of the pub. I felt like a trusting child in an infant school crocodile. (That was the sweetest thing ever, her hand nestling in mine like a tiny bird.) It was indeed the first time I had held hands with anyone since infant school. The sun at last had beaten its way through the haze and I felt its faint heat on my face. At first I said nothing for I was concentrating, trying to visualise what sort of body would go with that sort of voice. Surely it is true that certain kinds of body go with certain kinds of voice. Hence opera singers. The voice that was now guiding me, I was sure, issued from a body shaped like a violin. Only a woman with a narrow waist and swelling hips could give birth to such a voice – so I hoped.

I was listening to the pleasant click of her heels upon the pavement when she spoke again.

'What do you do – for work I mean?'

If it had been MacKellar, he would have spun her some yarn about being a professional mah-jong player or a zoo keeper, but I spoke the truth,

'I am an artist – a painter.'

'An artist! How fascinating!'

I winced and I wanted to say 'No. No. It is not fascinating at all. It is solitary and boring. Most of it is technique and preparation for the application of technique – stretching the canvas, mixing pigments, diluting them with oil – all very boring'. Whenever I talked with Felix, it was always about where to buy certain oils, how to clean brushes and dealers' commissions. We enjoyed such talk, but nobody else could possibly enjoy it. Whenever I put a painting aside as 'finished', I still have the feeling that I could have spent yet more time on what I have been working on and have done it better. However, I was certain that this was not what she wanted to hear, so I gave her an uplifting version of my current work – a commission from a publisher to illustrate MacKellar's *The Girlhood of Gagool*.

On the previous day I had started work on a lithograph showing the young and beautiful Gagool triumphing over the corpse of Prince Ndomba and looked on by the respectful Kukwana guards. Gagool, dancing on the corpse of the prince, demands to know 'What is the lot of man born of a woman?' and the Kukwanas chorus 'Death!' Here and throughout his absurdist novel MacKellar, aiming at parody, had modelled his prose on that of the *Chums Annual*, but I was unwilling to follow the same juvenile model. In the book, Gagool represented the force of liberation arising in the heart of Africa, which was going to free us all from the forces of Western scientism and rationalism. I had shown the Kukwana warriors, leaning on their assegais, to be almost as stiff as the dead prince. Gagool, by contrast, all flashing eyes and floating hair, frozen in her spider-like dance, appeared to incarnate the force of life. It is one of the key moments in the book and the trick for the illustrator is to spot such moments.

So then she wanted to know about MacKellar and, after him, the rest of my friends. Were they all like that, writers, painters and philosophers and all a bit mad? Then she wanted to know my name. I told her it was Caspar.

'Caspar!'

I hastened to assure her that Caspar was not my real name.

'Nothing about you is quite real.'

I heard an undercurrent of wistfulness in her voice. I became defensive. Why should we let past generations impose their names upon us? As for surnames, they were labels devised for the convenience of the authorities, so that they could survey, tax and conscript us more easily.

By now we were walking on grass. It must have been St James's Park. I felt the sun intermittently, but it was obvious that the shadows were lengthening.

I took over the questioning.

Her name was Caroline. She was a typist and she worked for a fur importer with an office at the bottom of Soho. After work, if she went anywhere other than back to her room in her parents' house in Putney, then it was to the ABC cafe on the corner of Piccadilly with a friend from the office. ('She's awfully nice, but ever so boring!') This was the first time she had ever ventured alone into a pub after work. So this was her adventure as well as mine. When she had tremulously pushed open the door of the Eagle, she was entering a world which hitherto had existed only in her fantasy. Since she had never been in a Soho pub before, she had had little idea of the sort of people she would encounter in such a place, but she had vaguely imagined herself getting into conversation with some sort of louche, Bohemian artist. And then she had fallen into conversation with me. Life can be so predictable at times . . .

At work Caroline typed invoices and letters for the fur company. There were five of them in the office. It was all so normal and yet so strange to me that I was entranced. Office work! Regular hours! Office intrigues! Office jokes! To me it was a fantasy world in miniature, a modern Lilliput, endearing in the pettiness of its concerns. She told me how hard she had to work to satisfy Mr Maitland's high standards; how careful they all had to be in economising on typewriter ribbons and carbon paper; how Jim, the office-boy, teased her; how they quarrelled about what sort of tea to buy; how she dreamt of something vaguely different and better, but it was so vague that she could not

21

quite find the words for it. Suddenly I found myself longing to become part of this Lilliputian fantasy world.

'I should like to become an office-boy,' I announced. 'How does one set about it?'

'You are too old to be an office-boy.'

Her voice reproved me. She probably suspected me, quite unfairly, of teasing her. Too old at twenty-five to become an office-boy! Already one career closed against me before I was even really aware that it existed! I fell despondently silent. I should have liked to have found work as an office-boy in the same office as Caroline. I would take messages, make tea, put stamps on envelopes and tease Caroline. It would all be very easy at first, but slowly I would work my way up and take on more responsible tasks. And in the evenings Caroline and I would go out. Sometimes we would go to the pictures, but on other evenings we would walk together, window-shopping in Oxford Street, dreaming of how we would furnish a place of our own once we were married. Having become Mr Maitland's assistant, I then replaced him. Caroline and I married and moved out into a place of our own in Barnes. I learn how to smoke a pipe, fill in tax forms, plant vegetables, play canasta and wear carpet slippers. Such skills cannot be impossibly difficult. I have read about people mastering them. I am perfectly willing to learn. Anyway in this new life in Barnes occasionally I will switch on the radio and quite by chance catch a snatch of a talk about Surrealism, and I will think to myself what a lot of pretentious and boring rubbish! What was that all about? Of course in the life I am envisaging for us there will be boredom too, as I have to discuss international fur prices in the office and the pattern of curtains in the home. But that would be precisely the beauty of this amazing and strangely contrived way of life. It would all be quite beautifully boring. It would be a way of containing the commingled mysteries of sex and happiness. That is the whole point of the bourgeois way of life – putting sex and happiness at the centre of existence and making their achievement easy. It was evident to me as I contemplated the bungalow in Barnes, the predestined theatre of our thoroughly domesticated passion, that it was far more beautiful than any painting either I or Salvador Dali was ever likely to paint.

Caroline was impatient with my silence. She wanted to know what I had been doing sitting in a pub with a sleep-mask over my eyes? I tried to explain about the Serapion Brotherhood and its quest for convulsive beauty. It was important to train oneself to sense auras. It was necessary to disorder the senses, or even to switch them off altogether for a time, in order to become sensitive to the auras. My temporary adoption of blindness was a form of cognitive estrangement. It was a way of letting the darkness of the night and its dreams invade the daylight hours. With MacKellar's help, I had been sniffing blindly and casting about in the streets of London, hunting for the dream-woman – the woman who so far had existed only in the Brotherhood's dreams. I quoted Paul Eluard's verse in 'La Revolution surréaliste':

> 'Une femme est plus belle que le monde ou je vis
> Et je ferme les yeux.'

'A woman is more beautiful than the world in which I live, And I close my eyes.'

I was not making much sense even to myself. I took another deep breath, but she silenced me with a finger to my lips. I kissed the finger. I was aware that she was no longer beside me but in front of me.

'Well I think it is very silly,' she pronounced with mock solemnity. 'But it's quite nice.'

And we kissed mouth to mouth. I had no precise idea where we were and, for all I knew, there were a ring of thirty or forty people around us intently watching us kiss. I let the sword-stick drop to the ground and my fingers ran everywhere over her face. I was trying to use them as eyes. My hands caressed the hair which fell in waves down to the shoulders. Then my hands dropped to brush against the firmness of the breasts under the heavy fabric of her dress. My hands continued to explore lower down, passing the line of her girdle. Would she be violin-shaped like her voice?

Would she be wearing silk stockings? Might she not have only one leg? I would not have put it past MacKellar to have lined me up with a one-legged woman. However, she firmly prevented me from discovering how many legs she had and she pulled me down to sit beside her on the grass.

'So now, am I – what was it you said? – your convulsively beautiful, utterly mysterious woman?' The voice was teasing.

'I should like to paint you, Caroline. Come to my place – 41 Cuba Street in the West India Docks – and I'll paint your portrait. Come this weekend. My fingertips tell me that you will make a good portrait. Your skin texture is excellent.'

'Hmmm.' I could practically hear the sceptically raised eyebrow.

'I'd paint you with your clothes on.'

Silence.

I was trying to work out how to explain to her that my offer to do her portrait would not be the prelude to my seducing her, but this was difficult, since that was indeed my intention.

'I'm not sure,' she said. 'Let me think about it.' She removed her hand from mine. 'I'm going to get us some ice-cream.'

She left me sitting there. As I sat alone in the dark, listening to the ducks and the distant murmur of conversations, I could feel that the sun had finally sunk behind the trees and, though my skin was still warm, I shivered. She did not return. I was such a fool that I sat there for the greater part of an hour, but she did not come back to me. Finally I removed the sleep-mask. The park at dusk was still crowded and in every direction I looked I could see young women – blondes, brunettes and redheads. None of them appeared to pay me any special attention.

24

Chapter Three

The next morning I awoke screaming, but once awake I continued to lie with my eyes tightly closed. Soon work would begin in the ship-breakers' yards and the dry docks, but in the early morning all the sounds I heard were soothing: the chug-chug of barges proceeding up the Thames, the slop of water against the piers, the occasional boom of a foghorn, and the crunch of footsteps on the gravel path that ran behind the house on Cuba Street. The house I was renting in 1936 has since been destroyed by one of the big raids on the Docks in 1941. It was an oddity, a survival from the eighteenth century, sandwiched between and overshadowed by two enormous nineteenth-century warehouses. Apart from warehouses, the street boasted a stable for dray-horses, a hostel for seamen, a Chinese grocer and a public house (the Lonsdale Arms).

I lay there listening to the docks coming to life and thought of Caroline. Was she real? Perhaps not. The more I continued to think about it, the more likely it seemed that MacKellar had put some actress friend of his up to impersonating a fur-merchant's typist. My breakfast was a cigarette and a cup of coffee. My day was and is measured out in cigarettes. Then I had to bribe myself with another cigarette to get myself to the easel. I worked on a sketch in pastels of my image of Caroline. I portrayed her with a body shaped like a violin, but with no legs. It had occurred to me that Caroline might be black, so she appeared as a legless negress, hovering over the houses on the other side of the river, like the tutelary deity of Rotherhithe, and, above her head, I drew a blind, weeping eye.

Soon though I left the sketch and I turned to my work on *The Girlhood of Gagool*. But I could not concentrate on that either. I went out and took a tram into the West End and I walked up and down the streets of Soho. I failed to identify the offices of any furriers, but then she had never told me the name of the company she worked for. I went to the pub in Greek Street and sat there drinking and listening, but I never heard her voice. I lunched alone at the ABC cafe in Piccadilly and then paced about for a while in St James' Park.

Feeling faintly ridiculous, I returned home. I had thought I might go back to the pub later, but towards the end of the afternoon MacKellar turned up, anxious to see how my illustrations to his book were going – and a little curious too about how I had fared with the young woman after he had left me.

'For Christ's sake, MacKellar, what did she look like?'

'Look like? Oh, quite pleasant I thought. Er – brown hair and brown eyes, I think.'

'How many legs did she have?'

'Two, I think, but I couldn't swear to that mind.'

I continued to press MacKellar, but this was all I could get from him. Such vagueness was exasperating. He had no visual sense. And that was also evident in his comments on what I had done so far for his book. He found my illustrations 'too arty'. We were still bickering when Oliver walked in. He had come with a summons from Ned. There was to be a crisis meeting of the Serapion Brotherhood that night. (I suppose I should note here that the Serapion Brotherhood took its name from a visionary monk in a story collection by the nineteenth-century German writer, Hoffmann. Like our identically named brethren in Russia, with whom we corresponded, we were dedicated to the proposition that the imagination has the power to conquer time and space.) Now Ned had learnt that André Breton had written to the hanging committee at the New Burlington Galleries denouncing the Brotherhood and demanding the exclusion of works by its members. My presence at the emergency meeting was of course required and that of Manasseh. Manasseh lived not far away in Shadwell. As we walked towards Shadwell, Mac-

Kellar described to Oliver the previous day's experiment with the sleep-mask and the typist.

Oliver was contemptuous.

'The girl was right. The whole thing was just silly. But do keep away from typists, Caspar. Office workers are objectively a counter-revolutionary phenomenon. Besides, you'd only be allowed to get your hands in her knickers after she'd got you to promise to marry her.'

Oliver said this lightly enough, but I sensed an undercurrent of more serious annoyance. He resented the fact that I had spent the previous day together with MacKellar and with a dreary typist, rather than with him. Oliver turned to describing his lunch with a certain *contessa*. I am pretty sure that the *contessa* never existed. Oliver was always talking about his women friends, but I never met any of these women.

We collected Manasseh from his rented room. Manasseh's paintings really owed more to Jewish folklore than anything that could be described as Surrealist, but he seemed happy enough to be associated with our group. What is more, a painting by him plus some small steel engravings and a painting by me had been selected by the Burlington hanging committee — also something between a sculpture and an *objet trouvé* by Jorge. So we were directly threatened by this new Parisian *démarche*. However, the fact that all of Felix's submissions had already been rejected made for a tense atmosphere in the group's meeting that night.

Immediately we arrived, Ned launched into a tirade against André Breton.

'– the Black Pope of Surrealism. It is Breton, not us, who should be expelled from the ranks of the Surrealist movement. We must seek solidarity with other worker-artists in Moscow and Mexico City.'

While Ned ranted on from the only armchair in the room, Felix propped herself against his legs and rubbed herself up against him like a cat. In the end, it was agreed that Manasseh, Jorge and I would go round in deputation

27

to the Galleries the following morning to protest and to threaten a demonstration on the day of the private view. Then there was talk of other things – the Rhineland, Abyssinia, pierced ears and the death of G.K. Chesterton. I was inattentive. I kept thinking of Caroline. Talk moved on to the pressing need to invent new vices. After all, when was it that the last vice was invented?

Oliver suggested cigarette smoking as the most recently invented vice. Adrian snorted, but, even under such provocation, he said nothing. Adrian was very peculiar, I think. Adrian was always there. He features in every photograph I have preserved of the group, but he hardly ever said anything and we all wondered why he was with us. He had written some poetry, so he said, but he never showed any of it to us. He was a classicist and was known to be working on a book, provisionally entitled *Did the Ancient Greeks Smoke Cigarettes?* I do not know where Adrian is now and certainly his book has not been published, but I gathered from certain mumbled remarks that Adrian let drop that the planned book was going to demonstrate that there was indeed nothing new under the sun, that the ancient Greeks were great cigarette smokers and that there were lots of references to smoking in the *Iliad*, if only one translated certain words correctly. This, however, was practically all I, or anyone else, ever got out of Adrian.

However, I digress. Somebody else in the group proposed rubber fetishism as the most recent vice. Then Oliver suggested drilling more holes in people's bodies, so that there would be more orifices for sexual pleasure. The ideal lover would look like Emmenthal cheese. Eventually talk came round to my blindfold exploration of London and my encounter with the typist. Oliver was dismissive, arguing that quests for the Mysterious Woman were a waste of time and he declared provocatively that women had no souls.

Ned cut him short angrily. It was time for the Surrealist sermon. Ned told us how the Marvellous was out there in the streets of London trying to signal to us. It was only

28

necessary to be alert to the possibility of its presence and to seek out chance encounters and coincidences. He quoted Baudelaire on the ragpicker. 'Everything that the big city threw away, everything that it lost, everything it despised, everything it crushed underfoot, he catalogues and collects.' Women were channels through which the Marvellous manifested itself. According to Ned, a woman could be materialised by the insemination of chance by desire. Then the appearance of these women would in turn lead to the transformation of the world into the domain of the perfectly Marvellous.

'Things are not created by factories. That is a bourgeois lie. Things are created by our desires. If we truly desire a thing, but do not have it, it is only necessary to increase our desire in order to have it. I brought Felix into existence simply by desiring her,' Ned concluded grandly.

Felix's slitted eyes opened just a fraction and she muttered something. I am not sure, but I think it was 'Kiss my cunt'. In the awkward silence which followed, Jorge produced a planchette. No meeting of the Serapion Brotherhood could conclude without the playing of some game or the carrying out of a group experiment.

With the aid of the planchette, we set out to interrogate the spirit of the Absurd. We all gathered round the table to place our hands on the board which rolled on smooth castors. Only Monica sat outside the ring, acting as the stenographer and recording the answers of the spirit of the Absurd. The pencil attached to the board moved slowly and uncertainly.

Question. What is a dream?

Answer. A wingless barrt.

Q. What is art?

A. A displaced lecture.

Q. Who will win the war in Abyssinia?

A. Paradogs.

Until towards the end of the seance MacKellar wanted to know who was Caroline?

A. Deliriam of grief.

29

Then MacKellar asked 'Who are you? What is the name of the spirit who has been communicating with us?'

A. Stella.

Oliver stroked his nose thoughtfully.

'It is Stella we should be hunting for,' he said. Then he asked, 'Stella, old girl, where we can find you?'

The board began to move rapidly – too rapidly. The planchette now appeared to be out of our control and in the possession of a frenzied spirit. It lifted off the table and flew across the room.

Ned brought the seance to an end.

'I think we should be wary of this Stella. I think she may be something that bastard, Breton, has sent our way.'

As I walked back from the tram-stop that night. I chanted 'I'm mad, I'm mad, I'm completely mad'. People turned to give me funny looks and I scowled back at them. I wanted nothing to do with them. I was concentrated, alert to any possibilities chance might put my way in these shabby streets. Somewhere, sometime, soon I would have a conversation with an organ grinder, or a hand would beckon me into a pawnbroker's shop. Perhaps I would hear a passing undertaker utter something curious, or maybe I would hear screaming in a darkened alley. Anyway, something would happen that would change my life forever. Perhaps it was already happening, even though I was not aware of it. The streets I walked down seemed to vibrate and waver, as if they were on the verge of dissolving before the force of my expectations. In those days I thought that there were infinite possibilities ahead of me and I could see the clouds rolling across the ink-blue night sky stretching on forever.

In bed at night I cling to my hypnagogic imagery for as long as possible, seeking to delay the onset of sleep and dreams. I do not know why, but I usually have very boring dreams. They usually concern work schedules, shopping and waiting for buses. Such dreams are perhaps useful as training for waking life as a *petit bourgeois*. 'See!' my dreams tell me. 'This is how one purchases a pound of

sausages! And this is how one hails an approaching bus!'
But such perverse dreams are useless as a source of inspiration for art.

The following morning, Saturday, we – Manasseh, Jorge and I – went round to the New Burlington Galleries. Although it was the weekend, Penrose and Mesens were there, planning the layout of the exhibition. They were astonished to see us. They had heard nothing from André Breton, nor had they received any representations protesting at the showing of works by members of the Serapion Brotherhood. Penrose told us that he looked forward to seeing us at the private view and we shuffled apologetically out of the Gallery. Once again we had fallen victims to Ned's raging paranoia.

Angry at the time wasted, I returned to Cuba Street and did some preparatory sketches of angry lions for *Gagool* – the sort of lions to whom one could feed Shillings or Breton. Then, almost as dissatisfied with my lions as I was angry with Ned Shillings, I stretched myself out on the floor and closed my eyes to enter an hypnagogic trance. I decided that I would conjure up a vision of a woman. Streams of lava coursed over my eyelids, but I was not in the mood for volcanoes and I set myself to concentrate and to superimpose the image of a woman on this red-hot molten stuff. I had something half like a woman, half like a flame wavering in my vision, when I heard a voice say,

'What a spiffing place!'

According to the literature on the subject, hypnagogic voices are not unknown and, for an instant, I fancied that the voice had been conjured up together with the image of the flaming female. But I opened my eyes and, though I had never seen her before, I recognised that it was Caroline. The young woman discovered by my desire, perhaps even invented by my desire, was standing in the doorway.

'I'm sorry. We did knock, but you obviously didn't hear and, since the door was not properly closed, we pushed it open and jolly well came up anyway. Are you all right?'

I continued to lie on the floor, gazing up at her and not

saying anything. Caroline did have brown hair and brown eyes and two rather shapely legs. She wore a blue dress and blue gloves that came up almost to her elbows and she carried an umbrella and a handbag. Her face . . . and here, in this anti-memoire, I find myself in real difficulties. The pitiful truth is I no longer remember quite what her face was like. Not a day, not a waking hour, has passed since she vanished that I have not thought of Caroline and how she looked. I remember that she was beautiful and that it was a very English sort of beauty, with just a faint trace of puppy fat about it. But really memory has worn thin. I remember not exactly Caroline's face, but rather the memory of an earlier memory of a memory of Caroline's face and this *ersatz* sort of memory relies heavily on assistance from the portraits that I painted of her and which I have kept. So I am at the mercy of the images I have made of her and it is no longer possible for me to walk behind those canvases and to check their likenesses against that of the sitter.

'This is Brenda,' Caroline introduced her companion. Brenda, a rather ordinary looking young woman, stood a little behind Caroline and stared curiously down at me.

'What a spiffing place!' Caroline said again. And she started to pace about the room, inspecting it and picking things up. She tried on the gaucho's hat. She stabbed a finger at the botched version of a perpetual motion machine, cast in brass, that I had on the table, setting its complicated array of pendulums going. She sniffed suspiciously at the opium pipe. She also briefly inspected the ox skull, the Klein flask, the carefully selected pile of driftwood, the portrait of Mussolini mounted as a darts board, the statuette of Isis, the phrenological bust, the huge Tibetan abacus, the ivory sculpture of the Virgin Mary crucified upon the Cross, the great pile of picture books about Africa and of course my paintings and drawings scattered everywhere about the room. Her eyes were wide with delight. As she walked about, she kept talking.

'I've come to apologise. It was unforgivably rude of me.

I'm sorry I left you in the park, really sorry. I can't explain. I just had a feeling – I get them sometimes – but it was silly. I can't explain it. I just sort of panicked.' She looked quizzically at me, seeking absolution. 'Anyway, I have come to see if you were serious about painting me. Brenda is my friend from the office, whom I was telling you about. You can paint her too if you want.'

Brenda, evidently Caroline's chaperone, continued to stare nervously down at me. Finally she summoned up the courage to ask me what I was doing on the floor.

I told her that I had been attacked by boredom and that it had overcome me. Then I recited the following lines,

> 'Rien n'égale en longeur les boiteuses journées,
> Quand sous les lourds flocons des neigeuses années
> L'Ennui, fruit de la morne incuriosité,
> Prends les proportions de l'immortalité.'

Caroline was enchanted.

'That's French!' she said. 'I got a distinction in my school certificate.'

'That was Baudelaire.'

'Was it? Well, we didn't do him at my school.'

I motioned languidly for them both to join me on the floor, so that they could join me in contemplating how the play of sunlight upon the river was reflected in a dancing golden skein on the ceiling of my studio. However, though they may have been briefly tempted, they decided that my floor was far too dirty for their dresses and, telling me not to be so lazy, Caroline set to pulling me to my feet. Brenda helped and in a matter of minutes Caroline had got me organised to make tea for them.

She was perfectly ignorant about painting and I think she expected me to start work on a portrait in oils immediately. However, I had no canvas primed and, even if I had had one ready, it is my invariable practice to start with some preliminary sketches. So I took my drawing board and, since it was a sunny day, we went out on to the quayside. I had Caroline pose uncomfortably on a bollard and I set to work. Brenda looked enviously on and in time she was joined by a circle of sailors and dockers, who made flattering remarks about Caroline's looks and less flattering ones about my sketches. I like to get my sitters to talk while I work on their portraits. I have to know who they are and talking gives their faces animation. Caroline's face was almost bovine in repose, but, as she talked and a crowd of admirers gathered, she began to glow with life.

I said as little as possible, needing to concentrate on my drawings, but I fired off quick questions whenever necessary, in order to keep her talking. It was she who had to do the work, for it was she and not I who was going to have impose her personality on her portrait. The previous portrait I had done had been of Oliver. Oliver had claimed that he found the whole business of sitting, posing and being made to talk quite ridiculous. But then, since he liked ridiculous things, he announced that he was going to invite people round to his flat where he would get them to 'sit' for his novels and short stories. He particularly hoped that Monica would come round and pose, so that he could find the right words to describe her bum.

But I digress. Hitherto the only women I had known at all well were society hostesses, nightclub singers, artists and prostitutes. Caroline came from another world. Her happy childhood and home life, the schoolgirl japes, the minutiae of office life, her love of cats and dogs and of dancing and amateur theatricals, her collection of coffee mugs, her struggles to master dress-making, all that seemed quite natural to her, but I was baffled and fascinated. Did this way of living work? If so, why should I not take up dancing and amateur theatricals too? What was there to stop me?

With surprising suddenness the sky clouded over and a cold wind started to blow from the East. I took a few hasty photographs. The purpose of the photographs has invariably been misunderstood by my sitters. It is not that I intend with my paint-brush to mimic the likeness produced by my Brownie box camera. Rather, I take photographs of likenesses only in order to go beyond them. Once one has seen what is visible, it becomes easier to paint the invisible.

Caroline kept talking. She wanted to travel the world and have adventures. Her eyes were alive with excitement. This was her first spiffing adventure – having her portrait painted by a Surrealist artist. We hurried in out of the cold and I served them whisky. Caroline was amused by my picture of the legless negress of Rotherhithe. She said it was 'super', but Brenda was shocked. Caroline promised to return the following Saturday. I told her to be sure to wear the same blue dress. She turned her cheek to me to be kissed. Then Brenda and I shook hands.

The next Saturday she arrived early and alone and I set to work straightaway. Although I have a certain swift facility as a book illustrator, I am a slow worker in oils. I work with ox-hair brushes, making minute strokes that are so closely worked as to be effectively invisible. Every area of the canvas is treated in the same detailed manner and all of it is equally brilliantly lit. Despite the modernity of my subject matter, my technique, as several critics have noted, is modelled on that of the Flemish Primitives, especially the Van Eyck brothers.

I wanted to catch in two dimensions Caroline's solidity, the volumes of her flesh, the degree to which she was fully in the world. My first thought had been that she was a creature from another planet, but, of course it was the reverse which was true. It was I who came from another planet and observed the goings-on on Earth with an alien's vision – never quite part of them and baffled by the most commonplace things. Since I wished to reproduce the heaviness of her flesh, I asked if she would agree to being painted in the nude. She refused and, indeed I think I would have been disappointed if she had agreed. I loved her *pudeur*. Even so, I set to work on a painting strategy that would effectively sidestep her refusal to undress.

This time I painted indoors, for it would have been too

much of a performance to lug paints, easels and chairs down to the quayside. However, it was hot in the room and Caroline's face grew sweaty and we kept having to break off while she powdered her nose. Even when she was posing, her eyes roved restlessly over my cluttered studio and it was impossible to get her to keep her head still for a moment.

She talked about children, how she would like to have lots of children and how she would mother them. I kept her going, feeding her questions, while all the time my mind was on something else. The painting of this portrait was a magico-erotic act, a form of mutual seduction, in which I, by trapping her image in paint, would in turn find my image trapped in hers. It seemed to me like one of those processes portrayed in old alchemical manuscripts, in which the Red King lies with the White Queen in a glass retort and the fruit of their coupling is the fantastic parti-coloured hermaphrodite.

I did not want to express myself in the portrait. I did not want to possess but to be possessed. At the end of it all, I wanted to be able to declare, 'I **is** the Other!'. So I plunged deeper and deeper into self-abnegatory investigations. Alas! After barely two hours' work, the sitting (or seance might be a better word) was broken by the unexpected arrival of Oliver.

The pretext was that he had come to collect the sword-stick that he had lent me. He was startled by the presence of a woman in the room and not at all pleased when I introduced Caroline. However, Oliver always had perfect manners.

'So you are the beautiful but invisible typist! I am Oliver Sorge, the writer.' And when she did not respond, he added, 'Although, I am not well-known yet, I plan to be. I don't suppose you know anyone called Stella by any chance?'

She shook her head.

'Such a pity . . . Are you sure now that you don't have any sisters called Stella? I have decided to start a new affair,

I don't care who with, except that she simply must be called Stella.'

And Oliver rattled away about how he had fallen in love with the mysterious Stella over the planchette and then about how he had been out of town, staying in a large country house, whose *chatelaine* simply adored him, and he of course adored her, but they really were impossible for each other. Caroline must know how such things were?

He offered her a cigarette from a gold cigarette case, a gift from Emerald Cunard, he said. Caroline did not smoke. Oliver said that Caroline and Emerald should meet. Oliver looked modestly down at his hands while he was talking, but he was wasting his time with this gambit. Caroline simply did not know who Emerald Cunard was. Nevertheless, after her initial alarm, Caroline was charmed by Oliver. He had the looks of a matinee idol and she could not see how he was patronising her and, for much of the time, talking over her shoulder at me. There was always a faintly anguished look in his eyes when he talked to women and he would resort to the extremes of courtesy and flattery to protect himself from any aggression on their part.

That day, I remember, before coming round to Cuba Street, Oliver had gone to an early performance at the cinema to see Chaplin's latest film, *Modern Times* – his first with sound. Chaplin, is a saint in the hagiology of Surrealism, canonised both for his bizarre comedy and for his devotion to cunnilingus. Oliver went along with the orthodoxy and he quoted Louis Aragon's pamphlet *Hands off Love!* in praise of 'the little man'. However, I have always loathed 'little men' and their tawdry version of humour and we got into a fierce argument, during which Caroline sat silent and uncomfortable.

Discussion of the scene with the robotic men in the factory led on to a discussion of the future. What would the world be like in 1950? And what would be our part in that world? (This used to be a frequent topic of conversation in the group, though it was only desultorily pursued.

None of us expected to live beyond our thirties and Ned, I remember, declared that he would die at the age of thirty-three, the age of the good revolutionaries, Jesus Christ and St. Just.) However, that afternoon in May 1936 the three of us conjured up a world of metropolises composed of skyscrapers and ziggurats encircled by great spiral ramps. The air would be crowded with tiny little airships cruising from tower to tower. Britain in 1950 would be a republic run by Controllers, who would preside over great technico-economic corporations. Oliver would betray his vocation by writing propaganda and speeches for the Controllers, while I would betray mine by becoming (oh, the shame!) a Fellow of the Republican Academy. When Oliver asked Caroline where she would fit in the technocratic world of the future, she replied unhappily that she did not know. All she wanted was to live in a cottage with honeysuckle growing round the door.

Soon after that she said she had to be going. I saw her downstairs. She promised to return on Sunday and again she offered her cheek to be kissed.

Once she had gone, Oliver relaxed.

'So that's your *objet trouvé – femme trouvée*, I should say. Nice bodywork. A shapely looking bit of driftwood, I think one must concede that, but in the long run you must let her drift on. She's not for you.'

I kept my voice noncommittal.

'How not for me?'

'Oh, debauch her by all means. She looks as though she could do with a good debauching. But, if one is serious about one's art, one must be serious about the life that is going to go into one's art. Everything that will be of any real importance to a writer or an artist happens to him between the ages of sixteen and twenty-five. Everything! After that it's just elaborations, variations, footnotes, and recollecting things in tranquillity. So it is vital to lead as interesting, as intense and as bizarre a life as possible while one is still young. I'm afraid that an affair with little Miss Typist just isn't the ticket.'

Oliver was watching me very intently as he said all this. Then, after a few minutes of uneasy silence, he walked over to examine the canvas I had been working on. Since I had not let Caroline see how I was handling her portrait, Oliver was the first to look on what I had done.

'Even so, it must be admitted that your portrait of her is already quite brilliant. O bravo!'

'Striptease' is perhaps the best known of all my paintings. Though I have always refused to sell it, it has gone on show many times. In 'Striptease' I have painted Caroline's head, upper arms and legs blue and additionally I have taken pains to mimic the texture of cotton in those areas. Her dress and gloves on the other hand I have painted in flesh tones, so that it is evident that she wears a dress of human skin. People tell me that they find the effect disturbing.

Caroline, true to her word, returned the following day. She had never heard people argue about films the way Oliver and I had done. She wanted to know more about his affair with the lady in the large country house, but I decided that I was not prepared to be a party to Oliver's imposture.

'There is no lady in a big house and no affair. I'm sure of it. It is all Lombard Street to a china orange that Oliver is homosexual.'

Her eyes widened.

'I've never met a homosexual before – not knowingly at least.' (Another spiffing adventure!) 'He was quite nice, I thought, but are all your friends like him, so strange and talking all the time in that way?'

My 'no' was pretty sincere, for, when I thought about it, I realised that Oliver was one of the more normal of my friends. It would probably be a good idea, I decided, to keep Caroline away from the Serapion Brotherhood. Anyway, then I started asking her things about amateur theatricals and I got down to some serious work on the portrait. This time, as she was leaving, I told her that I should need to get to know her better, if my portrait was going to work. She smiled and agreed to meet me on Wednesday when she got off early.

Chapter Four

We met at the ABC restaurant. Caroline was cheerful. Mr Maitland had commended her for her swift and tidy typing. Since she wanted to do some shopping, we took a bus to Gamages. It was raining when we got off at High Holborn and we walked pressed together under her umbrella. I smelt her perfume and, smelling her perfume, thought nothing. As so often, Baudelaire did my thinking for me.

> '*Et des habits, mousseline ou velours,*
> *Tout impregnés de sa jeunesse pure,*
> *Se dégageait un parfum de fourrure.*'

Gamages, the heart of the Empire! – the Empire of Women, I mean. Once inside, I saw very few men. I was excited. I could not remember ever in my life having been in a department store before and yet I recognised the place as the theatre of so many of my night journeys – those cavernous halls sealed off from natural light and those long passageways that ran between counters piled high with objects, stretching seemingly to eternity and patrolled by sonambulistic floorwalkers – this, night after night, had been the stuff of my dreams. The shop was a Broceliande, an enchanted place, in which all sorts of adventures were to be had amidst the forest of its columns. Caroline took me by the hand and, starting with haberdashery, I think we covered very nearly the whole shop. It was impossible not to be amazed by the collections of *objets trouvés* piled high on counters and divested of their domestic contexts. I was particularly struck by the hundreds of hats without wearers, assembled like so many lobsters stranded on a beach.

Yet, though hats, teapots, ribbons, ashtrays and shoes seemed stranded in this Museum of Everyday Life that was

Gamages, I knew with another part of my brain that every object there was destined to be found – just like the lost orphan in a snowstorm in so many old and sentimental silent films. I noted moreover that there was an unmistakably erotic flavour to the practice of finding and paying for the objects of desire. The very draperies were stiff with sex. I stopped to watch a fat woman stroking the sides of a lampshade, until it had seduced her into buying it.

Caroline wanted another coffee mug for her collection. I looked over the hundreds of coffee mugs spread before us. There in the crockery department, I found a disordered reverie of life, for in the course of one's life, over the days and years, one will encounter a thousand coffee mugs, but in Gamages one could encounter them all at once. Caroline offered me a penny for my thoughts and I told her some of this and, even while I was talking, I was regretting it, for I was terrified that she would think me mad. When I had finished, she did indeed look thoughtful.

'You are very mysterious, you know. You are just like the Count of Monte Cristo.' (That was what was on her school's syllabus, instead of Baudelaire.)

Then she went back to appraising coffee mugs. The shop had just taken delivery of Edward VIII coronation mugs and in the end Caroline bought one of those. Next door, in kitchenware, I too made a purchase. Resting forlornly among an assemblage of whisks and graters, was a tin cube, open at its top and its bottom and with a twisted metal blade somewhat like a ship's propeller running from one of its sides to the other. When I asked the assistant at the counter what it was for, she confessed that she had no idea. She offered to go and find her supervisor, but I paid up gleefully. The thing's tenuous grip on reality and its tawdry mystery appealed to me. Ninepence had secured my *objet trouvé*.

Upstairs in Women's Clothing, where the garments either have acquired or will acquire an erotic sacredness through being placed next to the skin of a woman, I found that I had an erection. Caroline did not have enough money to buy a new dress, but she still wanted to try some on and she kept disappearing behind those mysterious curtains, like a conjuror's assistant going into a vanishing cabinet, before she emerged to parade herself before me, time and again.

'I need your artist's eye,' she said.

'You should be clothed in mystery,' I said.

She kept trying on dresses and I stood there holding her umbrella and handbag. I was thinking of the Veil which protected the Holy of Holies in the ancient Temple of Jerusalem, when I heard a voice calling.

'Caspar! Well, this is a coincidence! Caspar, over here!'

I turned and saw that it was Monica, calling to me from next door in hosiery. Swivel-hipped and vampish as ever, Monica came over and, when Caroline next came out from behind the curtain, I introduced them to each other. Monica and Caroline chatted a bit about dresses and stockings, but, every now and then, Monica would give me a funny look. I thought then that it was merely that she was surprised to find me in a department store, or perhaps it was that she was overwhelmed by the sheer coincidence of our meeting. However, I now know that Monica was surprised to find me with a woman, for she had decided some time previously that Oliver and I were lovers.

Monica was a freelance journalist, who also dabbled in collages. But the thing that really marked her out in the group was her card-index. She kept an index about everyone she had ever met, plus dated records of the conversations she had had with them, as well as notes on the people they said they knew. She once gave a lecture to the Brotherhood on the scientific importance of her card-index (which already filled several large flood and fire-proof steel cabinets). In the long run, Monica claimed, careful collation and analysis of such meticulously kept records would enable a scientific researcher to demonstrate how it was that objective chance, the external expression of our desires, actually operated in the world. Coincidences, those little peaks of the iceberg sticking up above the surface of the waters of consciousness, could be used as mapping points in the delineation of the submerged depths of the marvellous. Monica had smiled all the time she talked and none of those who listened to her lecture could decide if it was quite serious.

'You must bring Caroline along to the next meeting of the Brotherhood,' said Monica, at last turning to me.

I grunted a yes, but meant no. It was not just that Caroline would be out of her depth in the Brotherhood and that they would patronise her. I feared for her should she ever encounter Ned Shillings. Women (and men too) found the power of Ned's mind quite mesmerising and Ned's intellectual ascendancy had given him a kind of *droit de seigneur* over the women in the group. Monica herself had only recently been cast aside in favour of Felix.

Monica bade us farewell and walked away looking preoccupied. Doubtless she was memorising the conversation she had just had for entry in her card-index. Caroline thought that Monica was 'nice'.

'Are all your friends nice?'

Again, I grunted. The truth was that I did not think that any of us were at all nice, myself included. However, if being 'nice' qualified me to kiss Caroline, then I was prepared to go along with the imposture, but the truth was that I had only been standing there, holding her umbrella and handbag, as part of a long-term strategy to fuck her senseless.

We took the escalator down from Women's Clothing. By now my erection was quite painful. Caroline paused to buy a birthday present for her father, a pipe rack. It looked almost as bizarrely pointless as my kitchen utensil. I told her that I would like to meet her parents. She was surprised and then evasive.

'They are just ordinary,' she said.

I took her to a pub I know in Red Lion Street and introduced her to the Penny Man. He was to be found there most evenings, sitting in a corner. You gave him some pennies and he swallowed them, allowing you to put your ear to his stomach and hear them clink as they hit the bottom. On a good night he could make three or four shillings – more than enough to pay for the following evening's beer. He's gone now. I think he must have been killed in one of the German raids.

Outside in the rain again, we pressed close to one another under the umbrella and this time Caroline allowed me to kiss her on the mouth. 'Every kiss is a conquest of repulsion,' as Larry Durrell remarked to me some years later, when we were relating to each other our unhappy dealings with women. Back then in 1936, all of a sudden I experienced a sort of anti-epiphany. Suddenly, while kissing Caroline under the umbrella, my vision was out of focus. Her eyes were like a pair of jellyfish surrounded by thin black tendrils, and between the jellyfish there was a kind of hump, or perhaps it was a beak, and, below the beak, a voraciously mobile red orifice. An instant later I was seeing correctly again and she was the most beautiful thing in the world. Such disturbances in my field of vision were not new to me. Kenneth Clark has taught us to see the human nude as the most godlike of forms, but there have been moments, when I have been having one of my turns, and I have been unable to see the human nude, stripped of clothes and culture, as anything other than a forked mandrake root, something which screams when it is pulled out of the filthy earth.

Caroline said nothing about my erection, though she must have been able to feel it pressed hard against her. At length she pulled away.

'When can I see you again?' I wanted to know.

'I'll come for another sitting on Saturday, darling,' she replied.

Darling! No one had ever called me that before. The word made me think of a family closely clustered by the fireside, listening to the wireless and drinking Ovaltine. There was a kind of *frisson* to the word 'darling'. I hugged this word to myself as I walked back to Cuba Street.

However, the desire that raged between my legs made every step agony.

The next member of the Brotherhood she was to meet was MacKellar – no, come to think of it, he had been the first person she met, even before me. Anyway, that following Saturday, I was wondering how to handle the highlights on Caroline's skin-coloured shoes and Caroline was talking about her cat, when the door burst open and MacKellar came dancing in, carrying a Gladstone bag in one hand and a bundle of *Wide World* magazines in the other. He was delighted to see Caroline.

'Why, it's the young lady from the brothel – er, I mean pub!'

He dropped the magazines and the bag and started whirling round the studio, chanting,

'Now you have taken over, I'm set free! I'm free! I thank you from the bottom of my heart.'

Then, out of breath, he stopped and stood looking at us and stroking his moustache with pleasure.

'I have taught young Caspar here always to be respectful to women. I trust you have no complaints on that score?'

Caroline shook her head. Whereas Oliver at first had made her nervous, I could see that she was already amused and charmed by MacKellar.

'Who are you? You aren't really Caspar's father, are you?'

'I am MacKellar,' and then in an eerie half-echo of Oliver Sorge the week before, 'You won't have heard of me. I'm struggling to remain unknown.'

'Like Oliver?'

'Oh, you have met Oliver then! No, no, I'm not like Oliver. I could never be as good as him. He's so clever and poetic. I know quite a lot of his stuff by heart.' MacKellar closed his eyes and started to declaim, 'The fluting of the blue-nosed mandrills suits the curates who daily press their suits into the shapes of hearts, clubs, spades and trowels, wishing thereby to show their contempt for the directors of large railway families and their bulimic offspring. O

Mardi Gras! O Pentonville! O Maria! What has become of the steel-tipped leopard, who, with feet of fire, patrols the concourses and the swimming baths and douses the bathers with the rainbow colours of his breath . . .'

It was all drivel of course and MacKellar was lying as usual. Oliver and MacKellar were reluctant literary allies against the rest of the world, but they actually despised each other's work. At this time, in the spring of 1936, Oliver was experimenting with automatic writing. Writing simultaneously with his left and right hands, he was trying to tap and use the unconscious as a source of inspiration, writing without thinking and relying on free association to produce vivid imagery. Actually I don't think that MacKellar's impromptu parodies of Oliver's work were any worse than the stuff itself. Oliver, for his part, characterised MacKellar's novels as mere schoolboy japes. I find it odd that MacKellar's novels are indeed now quite forgotten, while Oliver still has a definite reputation, if only in the world of literary coteries and small magazines.

Once embarked on his parody of Oliver's stuff, MacKellar was all but unstoppable and Caroline had to tie her scarf across his mouth to bring the performance to an end.

'A tragedy that such a brilliantly gifted writer, one of the foremost geniuses of our age, should have to scrape a living by performing conjuring tricks in nightclubs!'

'Is he really a conjuror?'

MacKellar assured her that this was true — and so it was. The lie here was MacKellar pretending that he thought this was a tragedy. People meeting Oliver and reading the (carefully planted) details of his dress and manner invariably deduced that he had something like a large flat in Kensington and that a private income probably dispensed him from any need to earn his living. In fact, he lived in lodgings just off Tottenham Court Road and though he had managed to acquire a tailcoat, he was too poor to buy most of the conjuring equipment he needed and too poor also to hire an assistant.

The sitting was now suspended and MacKellar was

showing Caroline the *Wide World* magazines he had brought along with him, full of pictures of Zulus and pygmies, and he was telling her the plot of *The Girlhood of Gagool*. Caroline was baffled by MacKellar's account.

'I don't understand. What are you getting at? Why have you written it?'

'It is simultaneously a blow struck in defense of African womanhood and a pataphysical denunciation of European imperialism,' he declared grandly.

'Whataphysical?'

'Pataphysical. Pataphysics is the science of imaginary solutions.'

Marching up and down the room, MacKellar favoured Caroline with his pataphysical impressions of Africa. He had never been to that continent and when he set out to write the novel, he conscientiously did no research for it whatsoever. It was a continent of dark fantasy, in which the poet, Rimbaud, and his gang of slavers and ivory hunters, drifted like ghosts through elephants' graveyards and down long highways flanked by mysterious stone colossi, in search of the legendary sexual treasures of a woman called Gagool.

Then MacKellar wanted to see my latest lithograph for the book. I had just completed the scene in the Halls of the White Dead, where Da Silvestra, the sinister Portuguese, tempts Gagool to have sex with him by offering her his umbrella. While we were poring over this exciting image, Caroline tiptoed over to look at my portrait of her. Hitherto I had adamantly refused to let her see what I was doing.

'Oh! It's horrible! Oh, Caspar, how could you?'

I had never seen her angry and upset before and I found it painfully affecting.

'It is as though you had undressed me,' she continued. 'Is that really how you see me? And what's the point of it all, doing something so weird and horrible like that?'

I could not think what to say. Indeed, my sort of paintings had no point at all in her world. But in my world they were gateways into another reality. Weirdness is beauty, beauty weirdness. But she was in pain and I felt her pain as my own. I had not wanted to hurt her, yet I could not have prevented myself. I had painted the only sort of painting I knew how to do.

She continued to gaze at me reproachfully. Her eyes were moist. She was waiting for an answer. MacKellar had not noticed her distress – or perhaps he had.

'Oh, that is just Surrealist painting for you. There is nothing bad or frightening in it. It is a beautiful joke. Surrealism is full of jokes. Surrealism is like Shakespeare's enchanted isle, "full of noises, sounds and sweet airs, that give delight and hurt not".'

(Another of MacKellar's lies. At the dark heart of Surrealism is ugliness and terror. Surrealism was to destroy Ned. I wished to God it had taken me when it took him.)

MacKellar continued,

'Let me tell you about the Surrealist–Pataphysical novel I am currently working on.'

And with a flourish he threw open his Gladstone bag and produced a skull and a dentist's hand-drill. He didn't so much tell her about *Dentist of the Old West* as act it out. It was the exciting yarn of Doc Milligan, Dead Rock's only dentist and a keen Roman Catholic. Indeed Doc Milligan wants to become Pope, but the Jesuits, who are strong in Chicago, hire Billy the Kid to deal with him. MacKellar did an imitation of Billy the Kid's toothless mumble after Milligan had finished with him. Then he rushed on to the penultimate scene in the book, the Crazy G Saloon, where Milligan, surrounded by a ring of cowpokes with guns trained upon him, still succeeds in killing Cardinal Vito Borgia by filling his teeth with poisoned amalgam.

MacKellar *had* been doing research for this book and seizing the skull, he started drilling one of its molars, all the while improvising the showdown dialogue between Vito Borgia (rather strangulated because of the number of instruments in his mouth) and Milligan (silkily triumphant).

49

MacKellar drew Caroline in to act as his ravishingly pretty assistant – hitherto a goodtime girl and torch singer in the Crazy G Saloon, she has decided, under Milligan's inspiring example, to go East and study to get dental qualifications. MacKellar got us both to join him in singing 'Home on the Range' at the tops of our voices, while he drilled away, the idea being to drown out the screaming of the doomed cardinal. Then having inspected the hole with a little silver mirror, he showed us how to fill the hole with a special sort of cement which he also produced from the bag.

Finally, he displayed himself to us as Pope Milligan, sitting on his throne in Rome and displaying the head of his arch-enemy on his knees. Only when we had knelt to kiss his papal ring was the performance over, and then MacKellar went rushing off downstairs to find one of my bottles of whisky.

Caroline would have liked to have been still angry with me, but, of course, it is not possible to sustain a fury against someone with whom one has just been singing 'Home on the Range'. I agreed to put 'Striptease' aside (it was far enough advanced anyway for me to finish it without any further sittings) and I promised to do a nice normal portrait of her, starting next Saturday.

Caroline sat on the sunny window-sill and looked down on the river behind her. MacKellar reappeared with the whisky and proposed a toast to the *objet trouvé* from Gamages. As we drank, he started talking about the cinema. There was to be a Serapion Brotherhood outing to the cinema that coming Friday to see *Mystery of the Wax Museum*. He urged Caroline to come too. Evidently it was not going to be possible to keep the group away from Caroline. I passed MacKellar a cigarette and wound up the gramophone and the strains of 'Who's wonderful? Who's Marvellous? Little Miss Annabel Lee' filled the room.

Chapter Five

I spent the day working on the scene where Rimbaud and Gagool walk through a herd of hungry wildebeests, while he explains to her the principles of Symbolist poetry. Then, towards evening, I headed towards Piccadilly to meet Caroline. The group was congregated outside the Vitagraph. (Appearance at these group outings was more or less compulsory and only Manasseh consistently refused to go to the movies.) MacKellar was in high spirits, for he had discovered that Zane Grey, the author of *Riders of the Purple Sage* and scores of other westerns, had started life as a dentist. So MacKellar had just sent off a long letter to him with a list of technical questions about dentistry. I introduced Caroline to Jenny Bodkin, the toymaker. Oliver came up, looking resplendent in what was admittedly a rather frayed tailcoat. After the film was over, he would be going on to perform at the Dead Rat Club. He clicked his heels in the manner of a Prussian aristocrat and bent to raise Caroline's hand to his lips, but, as he kissed it, he shot me a curious sideways glance. Then – it could be delayed no longer – Ned and Felix came over to us on the corner of the pavement. Felix matched her step so closely to Ned's that she appeared to be strapped like a knife to his waist.

'Hullo Caspar. Still doing those Gollywog's Girlhood pictures?' Felix enquired. Then she looked up with a brilliant smile.

'And you must be the Caroline we've all heard about. It's lovely to meet you. And it's lovely that Caspar's got a normal woman at last. I was getting fed up with all those tarts of his. I'm Felix by the way. We must have a long chat some time.'

Caroline, though she towered over Felix, looked stricken and vulnerable, but there was nothing I could do to protect her at that moment. Ned, who now had a hand squeezed tight on Felix's shoulder, introduced himself and then added affably,

'Felix is a bit mad.'

'Well, as to that dear, we're all a bit mad,' said Felix and she continued confidentially, 'Ned likes to flog his woman – flog her until he draws blood – before he can ever start any creative work. Mind you, when he's finished he's terribly apologetic and I make him kiss and lick me all over. But really I shouldn't be saying all these things. Tell me about yourself, Caroline. You don't mind me asking do you? I do like to get my nose in every crevice. What do you do? Dance? Paint? Write?'

Caroline, whose eyes were a little moist, said nothing and I replied for her.

'She's a secretary, Felix.'

'A secretary!' she exclaimed in tones of exaggerated disappointment. Then she added, 'I don't see how one can be a Surrealist secretary.'

'That's because you don't think, Felix,' said Ned (who was unable to take his eyes off Caroline). 'Either the Surrealist revolution is for everyone, or it is for no one. When the Serapion Brotherhood takes over the country, we will need Surrealist taxi drivers to take us to mysterious destinations, we will need Surrealist sewer workers to investigate the depths of the Unconscious and we will need Surrealist secretaries to take down the dictates of the Marvellous at 120 words per minute.'

Caroline said she thought that she could only manage a hundred words per minute, but Ned assured her that her speed would get better under Surrealism and at this point MacKellar confirmed that his typing had improved no end since he became a Surrealist.

The Brotherhood always made a point of sitting together in the front row, so that we could be in the closest possible communion with the flickering dreams on the screen in front of us.

As we were making our way down the dark aisle to the

front of the cinema, Caroline sniffed and then turned to whisper noisily in my ear,

'Being licked all over by one's lover is no substitute for a proper wash. I think that woman should use soap and water occasionally.'

Felix, who had overhead, looked up delighted,

'And I think you should try being licked all over by Caspar,' she said.

Oliver was in earshot during this exchange and, though I could not see his face, I could imagine his expression.

Ned wanted Caroline and me to sit next to him and Felix, but Caroline paused, allowing Oliver to come between them and us. Behind Caroline's back, Felix winked at me and I winked back.

After a newsreel featuring Italians marching though Addis Ababa, the main film began. *Mystery of the Wax Museum* starred Lionel Atwill and Glenda Farrell, plus Fay Wray in a supporting role. However, it was Fay Wray (she of *King Kong* fame) that the Serapion Brotherhood had turned out to pay homage to. Ned and Felix had seen the film twice already and they chorused the dialogue in time with the actors on the screen. Whenever the villainous Ivan Igor came out with lines like, 'If you will forgive this poor crippled stump, my dear, I am happy to know you', a cheer went up from our group, but there were others in the cinema who took the film more seriously and halfway through the manager came down to remonstrate with us, threatening that he might have to ask us to leave.

In the film Fay Wray was abducted by Igor, because he wanted to coat her in wax and display her as Marie Antoinette in his necrophiliac waxworks, but I thought that Caroline was more beautiful than Fay Wray and therefore I paid little attention to what was happening on the screen. When Igor crept into the Bellevue Morgue and bent, gurgling and retching, over the darkened silhouette of a young woman's corpse, Caroline shrank against me and allowed me to put an arm around her. I slid that arm round further to gently fondle her right breast, while with my other hand I stroked one of her knees. I suppose Caroline's knee was not very different from anyone else's. The knee is such an ordinary thing, yet sitting under the luridly coloured flickering light coming from the screen and stroking Caroline's silken, rounded knee I felt intensely happy. The knee is a transitional zone between the functional calf and the erotic thigh. A woman's knees are clashing rocks between which man's frail craft must venture to find the warmer waters that lie beyond. Not that I was thinking all these thoughts at the time. I would have to have been mad, madder than I actually was, to have done so, but I have often returned in memory and reflection to that evening with Caroline in the cinema.

Caroline's knee poking out from beneath the skirt seemed touchingly, touchably vulnerable. Surely it was an absurd thing to be doing, sitting there, paying homage to someone's knee, but then I have dedicated my life to the absurd, and, besides Caroline suffered me to stroke her knee. She accepted it placidly, in much the same way that a horse accepts being patted and stroked. I almost hated her for making me want her so much and yet I was so happy that I remember thinking that no matter what happened to me thereafter, no matter what eternity of hells might be my destiny, these minutes spent stroking Caroline's knee made everything worthwhile. In the light of what I have suffered since, I find it interesting to recall that moment and that thought. This fondling was the lightest and most refined of pleasures, and so when *Mystery of the Wax Museum* moved towards its climax and we closed for a kiss I was sad to do so.

As the credits began to roll down the screen the Serapion Brotherhood made a rush for the exit, for it was a matter of principle with us never to stand for the National Anthem. We moved on to the Duke of York. Caroline took out a little mirror and remade her mouth. Jorge went off to buy a round of drinks. Jenny Bodkin started talking about Hans Bellmer's sinister Surrealist dolls, some of

which were going to be exhibited at the New Bur
Galleries the following week, but Ned cut across
wanted to know what Caroline had made of the filr

Caroline smiled,

'I suppose it was a bit silly. Even so, I found it quite frightening.'

'That's exactly right,' replied Ned. 'Though I would prefer to say that it partook of the Absurd. And for me then the question is "What are the sources of the fear evoked by this film?". It is a fair bet that those sources are both sexual and unconscious in their nature. Any convincing analysis of the psychosexual potency of *Mystery of the Wax Museum* will have to be made at several levels. Essentially what we are confronted with on the screen is a psychodrama in which unacknowledged desires are made visible in disguised forms. What after all are waxworks? Essentially they perform the same symbolic function as automata, mannequins and dolls. They are markers on a dangerous borderland between life and death. The wax figures have the appearance of life, but it is the appearance only. At the same time the waxworks' functional relationship to the dolls of childhood games signals that in this film we are regressing back to a world of infantile desires and fears. It's not merely, of course, that all small children desire to have their toys come alive and they pretend that they have actually done so. It's more than that. Ivan Igor, the monster who runs the wax museum, stands here for the father figure – superficially benign but actually a threat to his children. Fay Wray and Glenda Farrell in the film are subconsciously Igor's daughters and like all daughters they desire to sleep with their father.'

Caroline looked doubtful and I could see that she was considering the idea of sleeping with her father (who I gathered was a rather elderly man who worked for the railways and smelled of pipe tobacco), before she put the idea swiftly out of her mind. I was unimpressed by Ned's harangue, for I had heard him deliver an almost identical analysis of *Gold Diggers of 1933* only a few weeks previously. Ned always talked in paragraphs, without any ums or ers. His performances had a snakelike, hypnotic effect and, beyond our circle, other drinkers in the pub had turned to watch and listen.

'And of course, it will not have escaped your attention that there is a family resemblance between Igor and the women he traps and kills. Igor, after his accident in the fire at the beginning of the film, is a mutilated monster, and women, as we all know are also monsters in that, in a certain sense, they must be seen as castrated, i.e. mutilated men. This takes us on to another level of analysis of this profoundly interesting film and that is the sense in which the unfolding of events represents a threat to the primal patriarchy, for clearly what we are seeing is the –'

'Hold on a minute, Ned,' Jenny Bodkin interrupted. 'Would it not make more sense to see man as a sort of monstrous woman? Take the Hunchback of Notre Dame. Is it not obvious that the hump of the Hunchback is in symbolic terms a displaced penis, that is to say something that is perceived as a deformed addition to the perfect female body? And in *Mystery of the Wax Museum*, it is hard to see Fay Wray as anything other than the mother figure whom Igor perceives as threatening his doubtful virility. Surely, Ned, you can see that?'

Jenny smiled triumphantly, but Ned, having waited until she had finished speaking, resumed his own discourse as if she had not spoken.

'Clearly, what we are seeing is a symbolic representation of man's fear of female sexuality. Igor is a kind of Bluebeard figure who can only neutralise female sexuality by coating his female victims in wax. Moving on to something much more obvious –'

'Hey stop it a minute Ned! What about what Jenny was saying about man being a deformed woman?' Felix was determined to stop Ned's flow.

'If you stop to think about it, you will see that Jenny and I are saying the same thing,' replied Ned blandly. 'Now to continue with something much more obvious, it is striking is it not that when Igor kills Fay Wray he then transforms her body into a waxwork of Marie Antoinette, a woman who is centuries older than he is, i.e. his mother? But this is only half the story. Indeed, if you press me, I should have to say that though male fears of –'

'Stop, Ned! Stop! You and Jenny are not saying the same thing. You were saying that a woman is a deformed man, but she was saying exactly the opposite.'

'You are being tiresome, Felix,' Ned replied, still without taking his eyes off Caroline. 'As I was saying, although male fears of female sexuality are explored in the basement of the Wax Museum, in the end I should say, if you pressed me, that ultimately this is a film about woman's fear of her own sexuality. This is what gives it its profound and universal appeal. It's the Beauty and the Beast complex. Woman's sexuality seems both frightening and absurd to her. I have to say that a surprisingly large proportion of the young women I have taken to bed were afraid to acknowledge their own sexual needs.'

Ned looked hard into Caroline's eyes. She sat bolt upright over her glass of shandy and gazed fearlessly back.

'The only thing women who sleep with Ned should be afraid of is the likelihood of getting the clap,' said Felix loudly.

'Anyway, that is how I see the main areas of tension in the film,' concluded Ned imperturbably. 'Though of course one can also see *Mystery of the Wax Museum* as a parable about voyeurism and the dangers of treating women as sexual objects. In the end however, the film's infinite ambiguities defeat any conclusive analysis.'

There was a silence, then Oliver said that he saw the film in pretty much the same way too. Jenny started talking again about Bellmer's dolls. Bellmer and Dali would both have waxworks in the Burlington exhibition.

'You must come to the private view, Caroline. You will bring her, won't you Caspar?'

Felix said that she needed another bloody drink after

listening to all Ned's fucking rubbish, but Oliver said that they ought to be moving on, as he was due on stage quite shortly. Most of the group were going on there anyway as drinking-up time approached. Oliver invited Caroline and me to come too, but she refused, saying that Mummy and Daddy would be waiting up for her. I wanted to see her home but she only allowed me to walk her to the bus-stop, insisting that I should then go on to the club. As we waited at the bus-stop she asked me what Felix had meant by 'all those tarts'.

'They were just what Felix said – "tarts".'

'Tell me about them.'

'I will sometime. Meanwhile would you like to come to the private view that Jenny was talking about? It should be quite an event.'

She nodded thoughtfully,

'That would be nice.'

I think she would have returned to the subject of the tarts, but at that moment the bus came along. If she had persisted, then she might have forced her way into a sort of Bluebeard's chamber of past sexual encounters. I had lost my virginity at the age of fifteen in Istanbul. There was (and, I suppose, still is) a street of brothels in Pera, not far from the waterfront and the Galata Bridge. The Turkish men walked up and down looking at the half-naked women displayed in the windows and doorways and I and my guardian walked with them until we had fixed on a woman whom we agreed was the prettiest. She was crop-headed and hard-faced and her breasts were like tennis balls. My guardian passed me some money which I paid to the cashier at the foot of the brothel's stairs. I pointed to the crop-headed woman and she led me upstairs. She threw herself onto the bed and, not suffering herself to be kissed or stroked, she parted her legs and hurried me on, though this was hardly necessary as I came very quickly. She then promptly rolled off the bed and hurried to the bidet. A few minutes later, my guardian decided that he would try her too.

Later I had had more satisfying though also more expensive experiences with Janine in Paris and one memorable night with Kiki de Montparnasse and a whole string of women in London whose love I paid for, including a prostitute of mature years who was particularly attached to me and whom the group dubbed Old Mortality. These women had in a sense been my mothers. But now I hoped to be rescued from them and their kind.

I hurried away from the bus-stop to the Dead Rat Club. Pamela and Oliver had agreed to a double act. Pamela sang first 'Ou Sont Tous Mes Amants' and then the 'Chanson du Rat Mort' in that dark, fumy voice of hers. Meanwhile Oliver, under the stage-name of Mandryka, in perfect silence performed feats of legerdemain with a double pack of cards, creating waterfalls, fans and other exhibitions. He made the cards run up and down his arms and then he had them float in the air between his hands. Make-up accentuated his saturnine melancholy and under the heat of the spotlight sweat coursed down his face and mingled with the mascara, so that he looked like a Pierrot weeping black tears.

I made my way to the Brotherhood's table where a drink was awaiting me. I sat there drinking and reflecting on my evil nature. I was like Igor, I thought, a monster who preyed on innocent and unsuspecting women. But (and it was a crucial difference), I wished to be redeemed. I wished to be able to say 'I is the Other'. What was I doing in the club? If it had not been for the excruciating dullness of my dreams, I would have preferred to have been asleep – much preferred it to all this smoke, noise and tawdriness. None of us looked cheerful that evening. Felix's face, in particular, looked puffy and it was evident that she and Ned had been quarrelling again.

Ned was talking about how marriage was disgusting. Basically, it was a disguised form of commercial transaction, in which the woman sold sex in exchange for goods and services provided by the husband.

'Sex should be a free and communal activity entered

into by equals without any obligations,' he said. Then a thought struck him.

'We should have an orgy – I mean the group should. It will help bring the Brotherhood closer together and give it more cohesion. Why, we could hold it right here in this club! We'll need more women though, so most of the men should try to bring along a woman.'

MacKellar was enthusiastic,

'The wife was complaining only a few days ago how she never gets invited to the group's activities.'

However he was the only one to be so enthusiastic. The rest of us stared gloomily back at Ned.

Just then Pamela's and Oliver's act finished and, relinquishing the stage to a comedian, they came over to our table.

'Hello, Caspar,' Pamela greeted me fondly.

'He's got a new girl!' the rest of the group chorused up at her.

She made a little *moue*. I shrugged apologetically and begged for one of her shoes. Then, snatching a bottle from Jorge, I filled the shoe with champagne and drank to Pamela's beauty. Effectively immobilised, she subsided on to my knees and, after she had taken a sip from it, her shoe circulated among the rest of the group. We all agreed that the club's champagne tasted better out of a shoe.

MacKellar was especially appreciative,

'It's like red wine with cheese isn't it?'

In fact he was so keen that he took off one of his own shoes and filled it with champagne as well. Pamela on my knee was quietly crooning the lines of 'Ou sont tous mes amants?'.

Meanwhile Ned, ever obstinate, had reverted to the subject of the orgy.

'We'll have everyone enter the room blindfolded and on all fours. Caspar, where did you get that sleep-mask of yours?'

'I bought it in a shop off Wigmore Street. It sold medical things – prosthetic limbs and things like that.'

'Excellent. Get twenty or thirty sleep-masks then – and a few false legs. They should be good for the orgy too. They ought to help blur the frontier between reality and unreality. Jorge will give you the money for the legs.'

Jorge nodded sombrely.

Oliver lit up a cigarette from his Emerald Cunard case and blew a smoke ring, before drawling,

'Aren't orgies rather *vieux jeu*?'

Ned looked irritated,

'I'm not talking about a bourgeois orgy, which is just a party with no clothes on. I am talking about a total immersion in polymorphous perversity and the systematic derangement of the senses. Blindfolds will facilitate the workings of chance and objective desire and we will create an human carpet of interlocked limbs, tongues and sexual organs, rippling and throbbing in a single mysterious rhythm. Sex has to be liberated from marriage and reproduction. What's more, we men need to lose our fear of each other's physicality. Nothing should be forbidden as we move beyond the conventions of good and evil.'

Turning to Oliver, he said,

'You can bring your *contessa*.'

And to me,

'You can bring Caroline.'

Then he continued,

'The great thing about an orgy is that in Surrealism there should be no discrimination between the beautiful and the ugly and blindfolded –'

But Ned never finished the sentence, for, while he had been talking, Felix had unsteadily stood up on her chair and now she screamed down at him,

'It's just because he's bored with me. Well, it's not half as fucking much as I'm bored with him!'

And then she poured half a bottle of champagne over Ned's head. Norman, the club's manager, hurried over to ask if she wanted another bottle, but she gestured him impatiently away. Then she attempted to kick Ned in the face, but, in doing so, she lost her balance and fell, concussing herself lightly on the edge of the next table. Ned plunged to join her on the floor and she slowly recovered consciousness in his embrace. When she started to cry, Ned set to licking her eyeballs. Jorge passed glasses of champagne down to them.

Then we started drinking seriously. I do not remember much about the rest of the evening. I remember Ned saying that detailed organisation of the orgy would be sorted out at the next meeting. I also remember him saying to me apparently *à propos* of nothing in particular,

'That Caroline, she's very intelligent. You know that, don't you, Caspar?'

I was unable to conceal my surprise and Ned, seeing this, continued,

'Her face is intelligent. The eyebrows especially. Faces can be read. You as a portraitist should know that. As people pass out of childhood they begin to lose the face they were born with and they acquire the face they have worked for. If you look at me, you will see that I have acquired a lion's face. It is the sort of face I need, if I am to lead the Brotherhood. Then look at your own face with its lack of laughter and sorrow lines and you will see that you have grown yourself a mask, but it is a mask which conceals nothing, for by now your mask and your face are identical. But Caroline's face is a fine, intelligent face.'

I was drunkenly trying to pull myself together and remember where the door was which led out of the club, but Ned held me by the sleeve and what he said next surprised me even more,

'Besides, as a general rule of thumb, people who lead regular lives and engage in the difficulty and discipline of ordinary work are more intelligent than the artists, writers, singers and whatnot that modern mythology has made out to be some sort of elite. Look down the table, Caspar. Look at them. What do you see? Admit to yourself, what you have secretly always known, that the Serapion Brotherhood mostly consists of the walking wounded, pitiful figures on crutches, helpless without drinks, drugs and lots and lots of attention. Caroline, however, is not like them and she will take exactly what she wants from life.'

'That's very interesting, Ned,' I said and I broke away from his grip. But, before I could find the way out, I got caught up in a great conga, which swaying and sweating, wound its way round the tables of the club and in my fancy I can see that conga going on and on, snaking along a path that was to peter out in the battlefields of the Second World War.

Chapter Six

The First International Surrealist Exhibition opened to the public on Saturday, June 11, 1936. The private view was on Friday afternoon. I had arranged to meet Caroline from work. Although we could have walked to the exhibition, as a surprise for her, I had arranged for Jorge to pick her up in his car. As we rolled up, she was standing on the corner outside the fur importer's office studying a copy of *Les Fleurs du Mal*. This she stuffed into her handbag before being ushered into Jorge's car and waving back up to Brenda and Jim who gazed down enviously upon us from a high window. Caroline was wearing an elegant, long, white dress which clung to her hips before flaring out at the calves. I was astonished to hear that she had made the dress herself. A broad-brimmed black hat trimmed with pink wax stems was set at an angle on her head.

'What a pretty car!'

'I am so pleased that we have the opportunity of meeting again.'

All the emptiness of the pampas was in Jorge's slow and formal diction. Out of consideration for Caroline's hat, lest it blow away, Jorge drove slowly, so slowly that we were even overtaken by a horse-drawn hearse. New Bond Street had seized up with traffic heading for the view and we had to park some distance away. We found ourselves walking in behind the Sitwell trio and the Movietone cameras swivelled away from them to follow our advance into the exhibition. Just as we passed through the doors Caroline, suddenly timid, looked to me for reassurance. I squeezed her hand and we shouldered our way in.

We arrived just as Herbert Read, standing uneasily on a rather springy sofa, began his speech of introduction for André Breton.

'Do not judge this movement too kindly. It is not just

another amusing stunt. It is defiant – the desperate act of men too profoundly convinced of the rottenness of our civilization to want to save a shred of its respectability . . .'

It was horribly hot and crowded and people were looking impatiently at the drinks laid out on the trestle-tables behind Read and he kept having to raise his voice to get it to carry over the steady murmur of conversation. Caroline was getting me to point out to her people that I recognised. She was excited, a little nervous certainly, but also a little confident, for I think that she was aware that she already knew and understood more about Surrealism than many of the drones and liggers at this private view. Besides her dress was spectacular and, as Emerson remarks somewhere, 'the sense of being well-dressed gives a feeling of inward tranquillity which religion is powerless to bestow'. She was smiling. Smiles came so easily to her then. I just wanted to stand close to her and steal some of her happiness.

Together we identified those we could. André Breton and Ned Shillings faced one another like heraldic lions and they exchanged frigid formalities. Oliver was being charming to Baroness D'Erlanger and Lord Berners. MacKellar in cowboy gear was talking vigorously to Constant Lambert and he later told me that he was proposing that they do an opera about cowboys together. MacKellar wanted to call it 'The Rio Grande'. Close to where we were I could see Henry Moore with Salvador Dali and it looked very much as though the former was getting a lecture from the latter on how to wax moustaches.

This particular private view had turned out to be the unscheduled event of the season and *le tout Londres et Paris* was there in the room that day – painters, poets, patrons, critics. The paintings and sculpture furnished the formal pretext of our assembly, but really it was the women who were on display. I became aware of this from listening to Caroline. Her reading of the fashion magazines had made her an expert in this matter and she whispered to me the names of the designers of the women's dresses – Meinbocher, Steibel, Schiaparelli, and others. I marvelled at the triumph of the mysterious Spirit of Fashion. The women in the gallery, driven by instinct and desire had moved together as a herd – wild and indisciplined, but still a herd. Individuals might stray a little away from the herd – a dip in the neckline, the adoption of a new sort of hat pin, an almost imperceptible adjustment of the hemline, a deeper shade of the prevailing colour – little shifts, but in the long run the direction of the great herd was precisely dictated by those countless little shifts that the fashion-conscious individual women composing the herd had made in their tentative attempts to stray away from it.

Hunting round the Gallery, I located my own works. My 'Second-hand Bookshop no. 1' hung between paintings by Max Ernst and André Masson. My experimental steel engravings to *Confessions of an English Opium Eater* were in a glass case which also contained Tenniel's illustrations to *Alice in Wonderland* and Picasso's design for a cover of *Minotaure*.

As soon as Read's speech finished, there was a surge towards the drinks. Once we had secured our glasses, Caroline wanted to make a careful study of 'Second-Hand Bookshop no. 1', so I left her and started to push my way around the edges of the gallery. Felix was doing the same, stabbing her finger at one picture after another, hissing noisily 'Shit! Shit! Shit! That's shit!' Lady Winbourne went over to complain to one of the keepers and after only a few minutes, Felix was escorted out of the Gallery.

Then MacKellar accosted me, clutching a sheaf of paper pinned to a clip-board. He had taken it upon himself to organise Ned's orgy for him. Would we like to put our names down near the head of the list? Thirty or forty would be needed to make the party go with a swing. I hastily declined on behalf of Caroline and myself, but suggested that Edith Sitwell was a likely prospect and MacKellar hurried away.

My own responses to what the gallery displayed were slower than Felix's, but eventually I came to roughly the same conclusion. The trouble was that the British Surrealists were so drab and anaemic, childishly obsessed with circuses and seasides, and desperately concerned to be polite and charming. Every Mayfair smartie and dealer was there looking at this stuff. I stood surrounded by people whose mouths were full of cheap wine and 'isms' – Impressionism, Post-Impressionism, Neo-Romanticism, Dadaism, Fascism, Anarchism, Communism, Freudianism. Surrealism was just another 'ism' on the same level as the rest. I heard some voices proclaiming their outrage and others declaring that they had seen it all before. Surrealism was supposed to be about a revolution in our perceptions, but this was just wine-and-cheese chat about some belated specimens of fantastic art. But I knew that Surrealism was not an 'ism', and neither did it have any relation whatsoever with neo-romantic ideas about fantastic art. Surrealism was and is a science dedicated to the revelation of the Marvellous in everyday reality.

I stood there drinking and thinking furiously, then I came to my decision. My work was not going to be part of this Movietone-Sitwell-Schiaparelli jamboree. I found a chair and lugged it through the crowd to 'Second-Hand Bookshop no. 1'. Standing on the chair, I got my picture down. Mesens and Penrose came over to expostulate.

'Caspar, what's got into you? You can't do that!'

'But I have done it.'

'You are under contract to the Gallery,' Penrose pointed out.

I laughed,

'What has the Surrealist revolution to do with contracts?'

Mesens chipped in,

'Isn't this rather arrogant, Caspar? Do you think that your work is too good to hang beside Picasso, Nash and Dali? Aren't you being a little immature?'

Caroline, who had been talking to some people whom I did not recognise, came over to find out what was going on.

I swept my arm round to encompass the drunken, chattering throng in the Gallery.

'These are grown-ups? God save me from maturity!'

Mesens shrugged and smiled. Looking back on that confrontation, I now think that he was not at all displeased by my gesture. I think that he thought that the private view was going too smoothly. He actually wanted outrage and scandal, the more the better.

I was about to lay into the Mayfair smarties and dealers who had turned up for the event, but at that point Caroline intervened,

'Leave your painting where it is, Caspar. You are making yourself look silly.'

And before I could make some protest about artistic integrity or whatever, she was close by me and her breath hot in my ear,

'I want your work to be a success. Do this for me, Caspar. Do it for me, my love.'

And then with no more thought about artistic integrity, I rehung my painting and backed apologetically away from Mesens and Penrose.

'And now I want you to meet these nice people I've just been talking to,' said Caroline, taking me by the hand.

The 'nice people' she introduced me to were Paul and Nusch Eluard and Gala Dali. Paul Eluard, a serious and gentle looking man, offered me his hand. His hand had a pronounced nervous tremor, as did mine, so that our handshake was like the momentary intertwining of tendrils of seaweed in an ocean swell.

Then Paul turned towards Caroline and recited the opening lines of a poem of his;

'Une femme est plus belle que le monde ou je vis
Et je ferme les yeux'.

A dizziness seized me. The couplet that I had quoted to Caroline during my first blind encounter with her was now being quoted to me by their author, to whom I had just been introduced by Caroline. I had a brief, almost instantaneous glimpse of the real way the world worked and of tunnels criss-crossing under the universe and a sense of infinitely deep abysses folding in upon themselves. I felt my glass slip from my hand, though I no longer quite knew what a glass or a hand were. I could see nothing – rather I saw a lattice-work of silvery metallic threads crossing over and under, over and under one another and filling my whole field of vision. I swayed on my feet, but somebody, probably Paul, caught me by the shoulder. Then the centre of the metallic lattice-work started to thin and break apart and I thought that I glimpsed tall black shapes wavering in a submarine cavern. But this soon resolved itself into a large room filled with pictures and people, although I recognised nobody and nothing. Then I recognised some of the people, but I did not know what they were doing in that place. Finally, I came fully to myself. I was facing Paul and Caroline and I felt as though my brain had just been opened and given a good scrubbing with a wire brush before being closed up again.

Caroline was wide-eyed with alarm,

'Caspar! What is it?'

'Too much to drink,' suggested Oliver who was standing with a neighbouring group of people.

'I have just seen that there is a logic to the universe, but it is a logic that does not quite make sense.' My voice was slurred but emphatic. 'Surrealism is really true though.'

While this exchange was going on, Paul had rescued my glass, which had been rolling about under our feet. This he now presented to me. I accepted it. Then I lit a cigarette and stared at him suspiciously, for it seemed possible to me that this earnest French poet with a receding hairline and a shaky handshake might not be what he seemed at all. This thing in a tweed jacket and flannel trousers might in fact be an ingeniously disguised gateway into another universe. He, for his part was regarding me with equal suspicion.

MacKellar reappeared,

'Edith said no. I think that she might have agreed, if it wasn't for those two brothers of hers.'

He looked down at his shirt front which was stained with red.

'After a while,' he continued, 'I found that I was concentrating my enquiries among those drinking white wine. Monica said no. Gascoyne said that he was going to be out of the country. A Welsh poet – I can't remember his name – said yes, but only after he was cured of the current dose of clap. A man from the BBC said he might if we were serious. Penrose was very rude. Some people just pretended not to know what I was talking about'.

The Eluards could not decide what to make of MacKellar. Caroline and Nusch turned to discussing 'Secondhand Bookshop no. 1'. I remember noticing that Caroline's French was surprisingly good. Oliver Sorge and David Gascoyne now joined our group and Paul and David started canvassing Oliver and me about the Serapion Brotherhood's views about the need to harness the Surrealist movement of liberation to a broader movement of political revolution. Oliver gave them the Serapion line, as preached by Ned; politics does not really exist. Politics is a fantasy, a sort of group psychosis. It is an after-the-event explanation for why things really happen. Both Capitalism and Communism are powerless before the omnipotence of Desire. Eluard, who had never heard of the Serapion Brotherhood before, was baffled and disturbed by what Oliver was telling him.

Then the women interrupted, wanting to know what I meant by my painting. It showed the interior of an antiquarian bookshop lined wall to wall with dusty leatherbound volumes, but in front of the shelves of books and partially obscuring them one saw a great heap of naked and emaciated corpses.

'What are the corpses doing there?' the women wanted to know.

'It is rather a question of what are the books doing there?' I replied, laughing and drinking madly. A silly answer, of course, but what answer could I give that would not diminish my painting? If I had thought that

'Secondhand Bookshop no. 1' could have benefited from an explanation, I would have written one out and attached it to the frame. Even more crucially, what answer could I give that would not allow Caroline some access to the monstrous horrors within me?

'Well, why the books then?' Caroline persisted.

That was easier to deal with,

'You are looking at a shop which deals in unwanted and useless knowledge. Secondhand bookshops, full as they are of discarded and rejected knowledge, leatherbound outcasts and losers, corporately constitute the unconscious mind of bourgeois society.'

But Nusch's mind was still on the corpses. Giving her husband's arm an affectionate squeeze, she declared that it was curious that, while Paul's poetry was full of images of beauty, delicacy and love, what she had seen of the exhibition did not appear to match the poetry at all. As it happened, our group had moved on and we were now standing in front of Marcel Jean's painting, entitled *'Rue coupée en deux'* in which a legless and armless woman was displayed upon a pedestal with a sheet trailing out of her shattered womb. And Nusch pointed across the gallery to Hans Bellmer's *La Poupée*, a doll whose limbs were grotesquely splayed in such a manner as to suggest that this was a girl who had just been raped.

'Surrealism has to make a shock assault on the senses,' said Oliver. 'It is precisely the nobility and the vulnerability of women that gives these images the power to shock'.

Nusch was unpersuaded by Oliver's words and I was about to argue against him – something on the lines that the women in these Surrealist paintings were images of irrationality and that they were displayed as worshipful icons of unreason. I thought the women in the paintings were symbols of a necessary opposition to masculine rationality. However, my thoughts were vague and I never managed to articulate quite what I meant, before Jorge came over with something that proved to be Sheila Legge. I write 'something that proved to be Sheila Legge', for

71

what Jorge introduced us to was described by him as the Phantom of Sex Appeal and what we saw was a figure in a long white satin gown and black leather gloves, topped not by a human head, but by a thick cluster of roses. Sheila Legge was indeed clothed in mystery. Jorge and Sheila had decided that it was time for this particular Surrealist manifestation to be given a more public airing, so Sheila was going to walk over to Trafalgar Square to be photographed by the press. Jorge urged us to come too. Although I had hopefully kept my empty glass in my pocket, the wine had in fact run out some time ago. We all agreed that the walk and some air would be a good idea.

Nusch had to get her coat. While I was waiting with the rest, standing slumped against the wall, Caroline turned on me and put her hands over my shoulders pinioning me with her body against the wall. She looked searchingly into my eyes before announcing,

'I love you.'

I shrugged and smiled carelessly.

By now Ned was nowhere to be seen. Presumably he had gone off to comfort Felix. The members of the organising committee had also vanished. Nevertheless a great gaggle of Surrealists and members of the Serapion Brotherhood set off following the Phantom of Sex Appeal on her Surrealist pilgrimage to Trafalgar Square. Outside the gallery a couple of barrow boys in cloth caps whistled at the Phantom. We made a bizarre procession through the shabby London streets. I remember that Caroline and I were walking next to Max Ernst and that Max, whom I already knew well, was talking to us about Lop Lop, the giant bird that was simultaneously his muse and his persecutor. Max and Caroline wanted to know if I had a similar muse.

And here that memory of the procession down Piccadilly in June 1936 comes stumbling to an abrupt an ignominious halt. I have checked and double-checked. I have looked at old newspapers, consulted books on art history and even asked Roland Penrose about it. There can be no doubt about the matter. Our conversation with Max Ernst never took place, for he was never in England that year. He was in France all through June. And yet I think that I remember him so clearly – his high-domed, white-haired head, his sharp nose and his strangely poetic pronouncements about painting and what Lop Lop did for his painting – and all that set against the backdrop of some dreary High Commission in Pall Mall belonging to Canada or Australia. My memory of Ernst that day is a false memory and doubtless it is only one among many, but it is rare that I have the opportunity of checking my memories against recorded history.

Now why did I think that Caroline and I walked alongside Max Ernst, sharing confidences with him? What real memory does the false memory mask and who did we walk and talk with that day? It is impossible for me to say. If only Caroline were with me now, so that we might compare our recollections of that day, but when she vanished she took a large part of my past with her. She has stolen my memories and I blame her for that.

I have a similar but different problem with the lecture, entitled 'Paranoia, the Pre-Raphaelites, Harpo Marx and Phantoms', which Salvador Dali gave in the Conway Hall some ten days later. He attempted to give his lecture on the paranoiac-critical consciousness dressed in a deep-sea diver's suit, from which heavily muffled and totally incomprehensible sounds emerged. His arms waved wildly and after a while it became evident that he was suffocating in the suit. Gala Dali followed by the organisers rushed on stage and set to banging at the rivets which held the helmet clamped down onto the rest of the suit. Everyone in the audience was laughing, but it proved to be a close-run thing and Gala told me afterwards that Salvador had nearly died. The event was filmed, photographed and reported. Every account of the First International Surrealist Exhibition mentions this attempt of Dali's to plumb the depths of the unconscious. My problem is that I cannot now remember whether I attended the lecture or not. I might have, but then again it seems possible that what I am remembering is a compilation made from the reminiscences and camera-work of others.

Anyway as we walked down Pall Mall I am sure that I remember Caroline proprietorially taking my arm, but perhaps that too is false. In Trafalgar Square the Phantom Sheila was surrounded by photographers and pigeons. These pigeons clustered on the shoulders of the Phantom, heightening the strangeness of the apparition. Passers-by stopped to gawp. One of them, an apprentice city gent by the look of him, turned appealingly to Caroline, who by now had let go of my arm and had purchased a bag of crumbs which she was feeding to the pigeons. Perhaps she looked the most normal and approachable in our group.

'What's going on? What is it for? Is this some student rag?'

'That is the Phantom of Sex Appeal,' Caroline said confidently. 'She is a Surrealist manifestation of the unconscious,' she added a little less confidently.

'I'm sorry, you must think me an awful duffer – my name's Clive Jerkin by the way – that doesn't mean anything to me. What is Surrealism? Is it some kind of political party?'

Despite his admission of howling ignorance, I thought the man looked intelligent. His pixy-like face and his bright sparrow-like eyes suggested a perpetual state of intense alertness.

Caroline was patient with him.

'Surrealism is a movement which tries to liberate people from their ordinary ideas and prejudices and – er – it wants to show them things they were not aware of before. It goes beyond all reason.'

'Gosh! It sounds jolly strange, but rather fascinating. You wouldn't let me buy you a drink in exchange for explaining it a bit more would you?'

Caroline, suddenly seized with shyness, shook her head vigorously and moved back to my side, taking hold of my arm once more. The city gent tipped his hat and walked on. Then Jorge came over. It was all arranged, he said. The Eluards were finding it too disgustingly hot in London, so tomorrow we – Jorge, Paul, Nusch, Caroline and I were going down to Brighton for the day.

Chapter Seven

Since Gala Dali and Oliver wanted to come too, we needed two cars for the journey to Brighton. Monica was persuaded to take some of our party in her Model T Ford in exchange for an interview with Paul Eluard. So on the Saturday, Jorge, Oliver and I set off early to collect Caroline from her home in Putney, leaving Monica to pick up the Eluards and Gala from their hotel. (Salvador Dali had said that he would have liked to come too, only he had a meeting with Edward James that day to advise on the decor of the millionaire's new flat in Wimpole Street. In retrospect, though, I am sure that Gala had told Salvador that she did not want him to come.) Caroline was waiting for us on the pavement outside her house. I opened the car's door to let Caroline climb in beside me and as she did so, I noticed her mother, dressed in a flowery housecoat, leaning out of an upstairs window and looking down on us thoughtfully.

Caroline leant forwards to tap Jorge on the shoulder.

'Jorge, I've got to ask you something. My friend Brenda came round last night and she wanted to know what sort of car it was that we went to the gallery in yesterday. I said it was a blue car, but she got jolly annoyed with me. She wanted to know the make and I'm hopeless at cars and things like that. What is it?'

'It's a Hispano-Suiza' said Jorge tonelessly.

'Hispano-Suiza, Hispano-Suiza. I'd better write it down or I'll forget it,' she said. Then, 'Isn't it a super day!'

Unsmiling Jorge made no reply as the Hispano-Suiza rolled silently off. For Jorge, the Serapion Brotherhood was a kind of long-running party which he gatecrashed repeatedly and to which he kept bringing bottles but at which he was never fully at ease. On occasions when he did try to participate in conversations his contributions tended to bring discussions to an end.

Very soon the car's acceleration made conversation impossible as the wind stripped all our words away. Caroline leant heavily against me and kept her scarf tight around her face.

We motored down through deepest England, bowling along between high hedges, overtaking cyclists, haywains and ramblers. I looked out on it all quite baffled. I was supposed to be an Englishman, but the truth was and is that the country I have grown up in is quite foreign to me. Trees crossed branches over the roads and I did not know the names of the trees. The hedgerows were bright with things that I knew were called flowers, but I could not have been more specific than that. I saw men toiling on farmlands and could not guess at what they toiled. Ramblers would wave to us as we passed and I wondered what devil it was that possessed them and drove them to plod through the countryside.

We rendezvoused with Monica's party on the front at Brighton. Despite our early start from London it was already hot on the sea-front. We hired a bathing-hut and the women changed first and then the men. I emerged in time to see Caroline and Nusch run down to the sea together. As they neared the water's edge they each instinctively pulled at the edges of their costumes to cover their bottoms more completely.

Paul, Jorge and I followed them in. It is hard for anyone who has read Freud intensively (as all of us in the Brotherhood had done) to plunge into water of any sort and not to experience himself or herself as metaphorically diving into the depths of the unconscious. My plunge into the dark green murk rendered me chilled and sightless. I resurfaced swiftly and, as I did so, Caroline came swimming towards me. Her long dark hair hung in an eerie veil across her face, but she pushed it aside and we managed a briny kiss. Jorge produced a beachball and Caroline and I splashed about with it like little children under his gloomy supervision. Oliver and Gala did not swim. It was fairly obvious that Gala did not like the seaside and I think that she had only come with us to Brighton in order to be close to Paul. I was unable to decide whether Paul and she were still lovers or not. She sat on the shingle looking out disapprovingly on us with those unforgettably dark and deep-set eyes that her husband's paintings have made so familiar to everybody since. Oliver sat beside her and after a while Gala produced a pack of tarot cards from her handbag and set to telling his fortune. We watched her muttering and throwing up her hands in gipsy-like gestures and once or twice she pointed to us in the water, but we were too far out to hear what she was saying and I was never to discover what Oliver's fortune was.

Monica was another non-swimmer. Instead she had brought a great pile of newspapers down from London and these she spread out on the beach. There were reviews of the Surrealist exhibition in almost all of them and, while we were drying ourselves Monica and Oliver read out choice passages. According to J.B. Priestley, Surrealists 'stand for violence and neurotic unreason. They are truly decadent. You catch a glimpse behind them of the deepening twilight of barbarism that will soon blot out the sky, until at last humanity finds itself in another long dark night'. He went on to suggest that we were all sensation seekers and sexual perverts. I remember remarking that hearing all this seemed particularly unfair after we had just had a bracing dip and an energetic game of beachball. Had Priestley done anything half so healthy that morning? He was probably still scraping the dottle out of that disgusting pipe of his.

Oliver felt the same way,

'We should hold a Surrealist sportsday and invite jolly Jack Priestley to participate. *Kraft durch Unheimlichkeit*, Strength through Weirdness, should be our winning motto.'

And Paul was puzzled by Priestley's description of the Surrealists as 'sensation seekers'.

'Surely it is good to seek sensations?' he mused. 'That is what poets are for.'

This last remark provided the opening for Monica's interview with him. Eluard spoke fluently if somewhat delphically, a natural oracle. Eavesdropping on the interview, I gathered that in his vision of life poetry was a force for political change and that the poet's place was on the barricades. The poet was not so much one who was inspired as the one who inspired. The inspirational teachings of the poet would restore to the proletariat the natural poetry that had been stolen from them by the capitalists. He quoted Lautréamont; 'Poetry must be made by all. Not by one.'

As Eluard moved on to discuss the misfortunes of the Popular Front in France, Oliver, who hated politics, grew bored and rolled over towards Caroline.

'And what about you? I'm sure that you've found better things to do than read poetry.'

'Oh, but I love poetry! I've just been reading Baudelaire's *Les Fleurs du mal*. Have you read it?'

She had him on the defensive, for he had not. Turning to me, she continued,

'Baudelaire's jolly gloomy isn't he? I can't see how he managed to keep writing all the time, if he really was as sad as all that. And doesn't he make being beautiful sound really sinister? Still he did like cats and that's good. And he did love the sea.'

Then suddenly she sat up and, looking across the water, declaimed in a high clear voice,

> '*Homme libre, toujours tu chériras la mer!*
> *La mer est ton miroir; tu contemples ton âme*
> *Dans le déroulement infini de sa lame . . .*'

By the time she had finished reciting all four verses of *L'Homme et la Mer*, Eluard had stopped pronouncing on the poet in politics and was gazing curiously at her, while Oliver was quite slack-jawed. 'Little Miss Typist' had at last succeeded in impressing him.

'Clever old you,' he said weakly.

Caroline smiled and lay back to cuddle against me on the hot shingle. She hissed in my ear,

'Would you like me to be a Baudelairean woman, debauched and deliciously impure, with a cruel soul and sharp teeth? Then we could live together in jewelled squalor. The squalor wouldn't be too bad, as long as we had all the jewels.'

We closed for another kiss. She was so soft and wet, it was like drowning in another sea.

'You know, you're very bad for me − like chocolate cake,' she whispered. 'That kiss in the park was the first time I ever kissed a man. Your being blindfold made it seem safer somehow.'

Then as I still said nothing, she continued,

'I feel like I have been brought up in a goldfish bowl which you were sent to smash. Mummy and Daddy spend all their time protecting me, trying to save me for Mr Right. And now you come along and I've just realised what your secret surname must be − Mr Wrong, Caspar Wrong!'

We lay entwined for a while until Nusch, Gala and Oliver bullied us into accompanying them on a beach-combing walk, looking for interestingly shaped pebbles and pieces of driftwood. We walked for a long time, until we were out of sight of the pier. Before turning back to rejoin the others, we sat and rested. Oliver was at his most charming. He talked about his forthcoming examination by the membership committee of the Magic Circle and did a few tricks with Gala's tarot pack. Then he started to conjure pebbles out of the women's ears. Laughing crazily, he informed Nusch:

'As you see I have no sleeves to hide things in today. However, there are concealed pockets everywhere in the universe where one can hide anything. It is merely a matter of distracting the audience's attention while one fumbles for the pocket.'

It turned out that Nusch was somewhat vague about the

difference between conjuring and sorcery. I assured her that the two things were quite distinct and that Oliver had no belief whatsoever in the latter. But at this point Oliver stopped smiling and interrupted me. He was looking at me very strangely, almost as if he feared me.

'Up to a few days ago I could have agreed with Caspar and let that pass. Now though, I am not so sure. No . . . rather it is that I am sure, but I am not sure about what . . .'

He hesitated, evidently undecided what, if anything, he should say now. Then, to my amazement Oliver told the women about the seance that the Serapion Brotherhood had held a few weeks previously and about how it had been concluded by the spirit 'Stella' signing herself off in vigorous fashion.

'For some reason the name intrigued me,' he continued. 'It seemed significant, though I had no idea why. So I put the matter aside and I decided to concentrate on rehearsing the repertoire which I was going to present to the Magic Circle. But no sooner had I decided to stop grappling with the problem of the significance of 'Stella' than it came to me where I had seen the name before.'

Oliver paused dramatically. He really looked very striking. I think that the reason he had not swum that day was that he had not wanted to spoil his mascara.

'You know that the Serapion Brotherhood is named after a fictional hermit who tells stories and who believes in the unlimited powers of the imagination. He is a character in a collection of stories by E.T.A. Hoffmann, a tormented nineteenth-century German musician and short-story writer. Well, quite by chance, I had recently purchased a second-hand copy of Henry Clute's life of Hoffmann and in this book I had read about the writer's difficult and impoverished life, and about the weird sources of his weird stories, his terrible illnesses and his ever-present fear of going mad. I read also of his ill-fated love for a certain young girl he glimpsed across a crowded ballroom in Berlin. In the very instant of that vision in the ballroom

81

he knew – he thought he knew – that elective affinity had brought them together and that she was his love predestined from all eternity. But Hoffmann was deceived in his certainty. Though his health was indeed poor and the girl, so gay and sparkling in her pretty ballgown, had seemed the very picture of health, in truth her condition was more parlous than his. Stella – that was her name – was to die of consumption, before Hoffmann had ever summoned up the courage to approach her and declare his love for her.

'Now we in the Serapion Brotherhood, Hoffmann's children if you like, have trained ourselves always to be alert, so that we are in a position to recognise and fully respond to those curious epiphanies known to the rest of the world as "coincidences". But I did not regard the manifestation of Stella's name at the seance as any sort of coincidence. I recognised it for what it was, a sign sent to me from across the centuries, like light from a distant star. The name Stella – it means star, of course – possessed me. I thought about it constantly, so that the name in my head pulsated in time to the beating of my heart. At length I had to acknowledge that I had fallen in love with a girl simply by hearing her name. I was possessed. I still am. *Amour fou*, mad love, is the name for my condition.

'So then, how does one go about courting a ghost? I had no idea, but I did the best I could. I tidied up my sordid digs off Tottenham Court Road and on an appointed evening I served up a dinner for two on a candle-lit table covered by flowers. I did not wait for my unseen companion, but, as I ate, I spoke to the darkness beyond the reach of the candles' flames. I began by invoking her name. "Stella, Stella, Štella, Stella, Stella," I cried again and again. All my will, all my concentration was focussed on imagining the reality that might lie beyond that name. "Stella, I love you. Stella, I would serve you and worship you all my days. Stella, I am poor, but I can make myself rich, if riches would make you happy. Although I am poor, I have talent . . . No, let me be honest. I have genius, both as a writer and as a conjuror. I am certain that I do not deceive myself in this, for I see my faults as clearly as my abilities. My faults . . . I will not, must not conceal my faults. Stella. You shall know me as I truly am. So then, you should know that I am vain and easily made jealous. I have to excel and praising others comes hard to me. I need affection, but never dare ask for it. I particularly crave the affection of men and I am terrified of women. Only now for the first time do I feel that it might be possible to love a woman.'

By now it was my turn to listen slack-jawed. I was astounded. I had never heard Oliver talk in this way before, nor had I guessed that he was capable of such self-awareness. At first as I listened I toyed with the idea that Oliver was using us, fooling about and merely rehearsing a short story in the manner of Sheridan Le Fanu or indeed of Hoffmann. Perhaps then we would soon see it in printed form in, say, *Blackwood's Magazine*. But no, this was not Oliver's usual experimental style and, besides, this was all far too serious and self-revelatory.

'Am I not one of the Brothers of Serapion?' Oliver's address to Stella continued. 'It is only necessary for me to train the will in order to use it to conquer time and space. My will which is limitless is the source of my genius. Either one is serious about this or one is not. I am absolute and my love for you, Stella, in whatsoever incarnation you may appear is also absolute. Come what may, I shall succeed in life, but my success will come more easily and taste the sweeter if you are with me and my pen shall make you famous. Stella, Stella, Stella. Come to me, I implore you. I am not weak and unhealthy as poor Hoffmann was. I am strong, young and determined. Also, at the risk of pointing out the obvious, I am alive, whereas by now even Hoffmann's bones have turned to dust.'

Oliver's eyes glittered as he spoke. The verb is not used lightly. His eyeballs shone as if there was independent life in them. His jaw was tense and he seemed to find difficulty in continuing to speak.

'All that evening I continued to address what was to all

intents and purposes an empty room. After I had finished eating I still continued to talk to the emptiness, but I also started to perform card tricks, hoping to entertain the spirit in that manner. At length – it was a little after midnight I think – I felt, there was no mistaking it, something cool brush lightly and briefly against the back of my neck. It was the kiss of the virgin.'

The sun still scorched down from a flawlessly blue sky. As Oliver had talked, my eyes had been resting on children building castles out of heaped pebbles and old men paddling with their trousers rolled up. It seemed so incongruous to be listening to all this on Brighton beach and I shuddered. It was not that I believed for a moment in Stella, the ghost or vampire, but I shuddered because I believed that my friend must be going mad.

Oliver was smiling tensely and for a time he seemed to be gazing on nothingness. Then he turned to Caroline and me.

'It was a kiss of absolution perhaps. Or perhaps a pledge of future love. At all events it was the first time I had ever been kissed by a woman. So what now? I really am not sure. I have no map of the way forward. But, just as I am certain of the holiness of my passionate devotion to this woman, so also I am certain that one day, in one way or another, she will be made flesh and on that day we shall consummate our love. You know, I feel that I can hypnotise reality and make it do what I want.'

He paused and looked down on the sand debating within himself. Then he continued in a more matter-of-fact vein,

'To that end and in readiness for the day of consummation I am going to buy a settee or divan – a divan I think and it should be covered in red velvet and on this Stella and I shall make love. I have pawned what's left of the Sorge family jewels to raise the money. Even so it will have to be second-hand. I thought I might try the Fulham Road. The trouble is, though, I have never bought furniture before. You wouldn't like to come and help me choose one would you?'

Caroline shook her head decisively. She was terrified, I think, of this new and strangely serious Oliver. Nusch looked equally nervous, while Gala just sat grinning up at the sun, as if she had not heard a word of what he had been saying. He shrugged and let the matter of Stella drop and a few minutes later we stood up and started walking back towards the others. Nusch, who had once worked as a mannequin, was a slender, sweet-faced young woman. As we walked together, she told me about her girlhood in Germany and about her dreams and how she produced collages based on her dreams.

After Caroline's recitation of Baudelaire and Oliver's even more out-of-character declaration of ghostly passion, I half expected when we got back to find Nusch's husband displaying an equally unexpected talent for tap-dancing and playing the ukelele. But no. He and Monica sat quietly talking and I think that Monica was trying to explain to him what the Serapion Brotherhood stood for.

So the rest of the day passed. We swam again and tossed the beachball about. Paul talked earnestly to Caroline about which French poets she should read next. He and Nusch pressed us to come and stay with them in Paris. There should be closer contacts between the British and French Surrealists, and Caroline, who had never been abroad, would enjoy Paris so much. They made her promise that she would come with me and Paul pressed a signed copy of his own poems upon her. I sketched first Caroline and then Paul with Gala. Paul and Gala kissed occasionally, but Nusch seemed not to mind. Monica scribbled furiously in her notebook, Jorge slept and Oliver sat a little apart, brooding and watching us all. Then I remember talking to Caroline about how I could easily increase my income by doing posters for the railways or for Shell Petrol.

I often think about that day. If I truly were possessed of Serapion's powers then I think that I would choose to spend the rest of my life imprisoned in that day, forever playing beachball with Caroline and listening to Paul discoursing on the poetry of love. However, the curious thing is that I also have a sense, very vague admittedly, that it was on that day that I failed some sort of exam – an exam I did not even realise that I was taking.

We left the beach reluctantly. Caroline had lost one of her shoes somewhere on the beach. So I carried her back to Jorge's car. I loved even her heaviness. Jorge drove Oliver, Caroline and me back to London, but he refused to take Caroline back to her house, insisting that she must come and see his place first. After that she could take a taxi which he would be happy to pay for. Jorge's home was indeed one of the marvels of London and a sort of substitute for the man's uninteresting personality. He lived in a huge custom-built caravan, which he called his 'Chariot' and which at that time was parked just off Park Lane. He claimed that one of these days he was going to drive it to China, where he would introduce the benighted warlords to Surrealism and where he would of course smoke lots of opium.

Although there were tiny dormitory rooms for a butler and maidservant in the caravan, in fact Jorge had staff from one of the big Mayfair hotels come in daily to attend to his needs. As for Jorge's own quarters, the walls of the red leather interior were broken only by mahogany doors. Caroline, who had been preoccupied with her own thoughts during the drive back to London, came to life again. She was enchanted and her reactions were like those when she first visited my studio in Cuba Street. She skipped around, opening cupboards and pressing buttons. If one stood at the control panel in the living room and cranked one of the handles, a pair of heavy leather armchairs swung out from the walls and unfolded themselves and, if one turned another handle then a card-table was hydraulically thrust up from the floor – all this under a ceiling studded with artificial eyes.

Jorge watched the excited Caroline benignly. I think it is

true to say that for him the display of his wealth was more pleasurable than sex.

'It's the simplicity of the raggle-taggle gipsy life that I'm after,' he said wryly.

'It's spiffing!' said Caroline. 'You are lucky Jorge!'

'Well, yes. I suppose so. But I find that money doesn't make one happy. But then again, who gives a damn about happiness?'

Chapter Eight

We went to Paris in November. I was pleased to be out of England. Ned had been lecturing the Brotherhood almost every week on the liberation that came from separating sexual delight from procreation and he was increasingly pressing about holding an orgy, in order to break down 'bourgeois and pseudo-familial bonds'. As for Oliver, since he had been accepted into the Magic Circle, his vanity knew no bounds and he seemed to regard himself as a latter-day Cagliostro or Rasputin, rather than what I think he was, an entertainer with a skill at palming cards. His obsession with the long-dead girlfriend of Hoffmann showed no sign of abating and apparently he had actually bought a red divan, in the hope of one day consummating his necrophiliac fantasy upon it. MacKellar, when we told him about Stella, thought the whole thing hilarious and took to staging mock seances with the declared aim of raising Gagool.

'Gagool! Gagool! Come out, you naughty black thing you. I know you are hiding in the shadows somewhere. I conjure you. You are black but comely! Just wait till I get that loincloth off!'

However, since the illustrations to *The Girlhood of Gagool* had been completed, I was seeing less of him.

Caroline had told her parents that she was going on holiday with Brenda. I was surprised by her determination to go to Paris and by her readiness to lie to her parents.

We made our way from the Gare du Nord to the *pied à terre* which Jorge had lent us for the week. It was a steep climb up into Montmartre to his place, which was a step away from the Place Pigalle. Since Jorge rarely spent the night away from his magnificent 'Chariot', it was a mystery what he needed this tiny flat for. However a clue of sorts was provided by the masses of vellum and Moroccanbound pornography shelved in an alcove above the bed-head. Some of it was Surrealist – images by Man Ray and Bellmer and prose by Dali – but most of Jorge's collection consisted of anonymous or pseudonymous nineteenth-century works. In the evening when we staggered back breathless from our random peregrinations through the streets of Paris, we would fall upon the stuff, reading out snatches of lascivious but unintentionally comic dialogue to one another and we puzzled over the pictures.

One image, a steel engraving in a book called, I think, *Sombres dimanches*, particularly haunted me. During the whole of that week we were in Paris the cryptic tableau that I had discovered while flicking through pages of *Sombres dimanches* was rarely out of my mind. I can still summon up every detail of it even today.

A young woman in a high-necked dress of black satin knelt at a *prie-dieu*. The carved side of the *prie-dieu* was covered with a gothic tracery, making it resemble a choir stall. The woman's knees rested on a densely patterned carpet, while her head and prominent bosom were pressed upon the pages of a large book that lay open upon the desk. Caught in profile, the woman's face had a look of gentle resignation. Her fair hair was pinned up under a large, flower-laden hat of the sort fashionable in the 1890s. The walls of the room were covered with a mottled wallpaper on which a floral pattern could just be discerned. Behind the woman was a bed half concealed by white drapery which cascaded from an unseen point above. Over the lady's head was a mirror in an ornate oval frame. The kneeling woman had drawn up her heavy skirt and petticoats to reveal a perfectly white bottom. Behind her stood a mustachioed gentleman in evening dress and he appeared to contemplate that almost luminous twin-mooned apparition. As he did so, he also brandished a lady's looking-glass with a coralline frame. The angle he held the mirror at suggested that he intended to spank the lady with it. The man's face could only fully be seen in the mirror above the lady's head. His expression seemed to be one of anxious enquiry. The looking-glass that he carried displayed a reflection of the lady's bottom. Yet the respective positions of his face, her bottom and the mirrors were such that these reflections should have been impossible. It may simply have been a matter of artistic incompetence, but I doubted it. More disturbing yet was the general mood of the image and the quaintly frozen postures of the lady and the gentleman. I had the impression that I was spying upon something which regularly took place, a ritual that was only tangentially concerned with sex. Everything was pressed into the corner of the room and one could not see the rest of it, yet I had the impression that it was very small and that beyond that room there were only more rooms, each one very like the one I was looking at. The air seemed somehow frowsty and I had the feeling that whatever was taking place was taking place towards the end of a wet afternoon in mid-winter. It filled me with foreboding.

Having stumbled on this image, I closed the book hastily and hid it under the bed. I did not want Caroline to see this picture and be affected by it as I was. But in the days that followed, when Caroline was shopping or getting some food ready, I furtively returned to the picture again and again. I was possessed by the ridiculous notion that if only I studied the picture with sufficient attention to its details, then it would yield up its secrets – secrets that were perhaps concealed in the fall of shadow, or in the pattern of the carpet, or in the arch of the lady's single visible eyebrow.

By now it was a little like that with my portraits of Caroline. Time and again I would commence with a rough likeness, which I would correct or refine and then after more study I would make yet further adjustments. Yet all I succeeded in producing were approximations of Caroline's likeness. I hoped through intensive study of her face – that face which was simultaneously so wonderful and so ordinary – to mimic it exactly on canvas and thus my brush moved in minute strokes across my image of her face like a laboriously travailing insect. Yet with each portrait I completed of Caroline I was being forced to the conclusion that she was coming to seem more, not less mysterious. She was holding something back from me. I was sure of it. And she was changing. Perhaps it was something to do with the process of being painted. Sometimes during our sittings I caught a look of apprehension pass over her face like a cloud across the moon. I began to think that it was possible that I would never really know her until I had known her in the Biblical sense and penetrated her. By the time we set out for Paris it was obvious to me that the paintbrush had proved inadequate as an instrument of investigation, but I still had hopes for my penis.

I also had high hopes for that first night in Jorge's flat. I was in a fever of impatience that was difficult to conceal. Indeed I do not think I was successful and I think that Caroline must have noticed my tormented restlessness. Whether she had or had not, she heedlessly lounged on the bed leafing through Jorge's amazing collection of erotica for almost two hours, before announcing that she supposed that it was time that we went to bed. While she went to the lavatory, I stripped and leapt under the sheets. She re-entered the room and began to undress in that lovely sequence of movements peculiar to women; bending to unfasten suspenders and roll down stockings, pulling the dress over the head, and arching and stretching to unhook the brassiere. Caroline kept her girdle and panties on. She came to the end of the bed and paused. She seemed to be admiring her half-naked body in the mirror of my eyes.

Then she said,

'Darling, we are going to sleep together, but that is all. Like brother and sister, I mean. I don't think that we are ready for anything more.'

I started to protest, but she cut me short.

'Caspar, don't! It's just that we don't know one another well enough yet. I need time, that is all. And we have all the time in the world. Just be patient and don't spoil things.'

'Why should sex spoil anything?'

'Oh dear! I was afraid of this. Caspar, I'm sorry. When I said that I was going to come to Paris with you, I did mean to sleep with you. I admit it. And you have paid and everything . . . I'm sorry I'm being such a weed. It just doesn't feel right now, that's all.'

'What doesn't feel right?'

'I don't know. I'm in a muddle. I can't say.'

'Well come to bed anyway and stop shivering. And don't start crying. I'm not going to rape you or beat you up.'

She looked at me dubiously, before getting into bed on the far side. I rolled over to her side.

'Look but don't touch,' she said.

Despite what she had just said, it was still possible that her 'no' meant yes. Perhaps she did want to be forced. Perhaps this was a token refusal, something to satisfy her conscience, or something to provoke me into asserting a dominant role? Whatever the truth of the matter, the strength of my desire made me weak.

'Caroline, I would do anything for you.'

She looked at me solemnly.

'Really?'

'If you asked me now, this minute, to cut off my right hand, I would do it this instant without thinking.'

'Really? Well, all I want you to do is not to rush me into sex tonight. That's not such a big thing to ask is it? I certainly don't want you to cut off your right hand. It's a very nice right hand.'

And she kissed it. Then after gazing into my eyes for several minutes, she said,

'But if you mean what you say, I would like you to do to me what Ned does to Felix. I want to be licked all over. Lick me – if you'd like to, that is.'

I moved to the bottom of the bed and set to licking her feet. Then, as she rolled over onto her stomach, my tongue began to work up her leg. I am not sure what game she was playing that night, but it was certainly some sort of game. At the same time that she played with my desire, I think she was testing the strength of her determination to resist it. While I worked on her feet, she turned the pages of Jorge's copy of *The Lustful Turk*.

'Super,' she murmured drowsily as my tongue moved up to her thigh, but then as it reached the lacy edge of her panties and I slid my hands up to pull them down, she turned over and sat up.

'Now you are being naughty,' she said. And then, 'But you may cuddle me until I fall asleep.'

Sleepless I held her and watched sleep steal her away from me.

That first morning in Paris I awoke screaming. I had forgotten to warn Caroline that this was likely to happen and she threw herself upon me in a frenzy of alarm, but, once I had reassured her, she rested comfortably on me and picked at and teased the hairs on my chest. We were loath to leave our bed, for the weather that day was not welcoming. From the gable window of Jorge's flat we looked out over oilcloth roofs, leaded windows, shadowed courtyards and pigeons – all grey in the pearly dull light. The clouds were low over the houses and I quoted one of Malcolm de Chazal's aphorisms to Caroline, 'Without the shadows, light could not ride the objects, and the sun would go everywhere on foot'.

However, we did have to venture out, for we were expected later that day by the Eluards. Caroline's mood that morning was strange. Though she did not seem to share my sense of oppression, I got the feeling that she was somehow on the run as she clattered down the steps and took a zigzag course through the streets of the unknown city. But was she escaping with me or from me?'

It was a long walk to the Eluards and we almost had to run the last part to arrive before lunch. Paul served us pastis and plunged immediately into a disquisition on the war in Spain. Since Ned did not believe in politics, we in the Serapion Brotherhood had paid little or no attention to the progress of the Civil War. In Paris, however, people found it difficult to talk about anything else. Franco had been stopped south of Madrid, but everyone was aware that the reprieve was temporary and the Republican government itself had just moved to Valencia. Eluard was asking himself what were the duties of a writer or an artist in this perilous situation? What could he do in order to help the forces of liberty and progress? But over lunch talk turned to less portentous matters and Nusch wanted to know how we had first met. Having heard our story, which was not exactly a story of love at first sight, Paul gravely suggested that going blindfold was probably also the best way to see Paris. Before we left the Eluards, we arranged to meet again. Moreover, since I had business to transact with André Breton (not otherwise relevant to this anti-memoire, so I will not trouble you with the details), Paul, even though he was no longer on intimate terms with the Surrealist leader, agreed to effect an introduction.

In the days that followed we explored Paris in the approved Surrealist fashion. We did not visit the Louvre (a cemetery for dead art). We did not see the Arc de Triomphe (a celebration of militarism). We did not go near the Eiffel Tower (a monstrously vulgar piece of ironmongery). Instead we walked hand in hand through places which were nowhere, quiet shops and unfashionable *arrondissements*. We never passed an *impasse* without walking to its end and back again and we never passed a flight of steps without either ascending or descending. If a statue seemed to be pointing in a particular direction then we followed its direction.

Whenever we passed a second-hand bookshop, we paused and I would make a sketch of its exterior. For her part, Caroline wanted to stop at the rag-trade sweatshops where dresses were made. She wished to learn as much as she could about Paris's fashion industry and sometimes she would succeed in striking up conversations with the *arpètes* and their supervisors. She would point to dresses walking ahead of us in the street and identify them as a Schiaparelli, a Vionnet, or whatever.

She had hitherto vaguely thought of French as a complicated system of cunning tests devised by English school-boards. It was hard for her to get over her amazement at discovering it to be a living language, fashioned for use and spoken by real working people. Her French was good, if a little formal. Mine was, by contrast, rather slangy, most of it having been picked up during the six months I had spent in a Marseilles jail.

All that week in Paris the air was heavy and moist. The sky was like a muddy river flowing over the city and I imagined etherial fish swimming in its murk. Drops of water would collect on the edges of awnings and on the leaves of bushes before heavily plashing down into puddles. Walking beside Caroline, I tried to see the city through her eyes and, following the directions of her eyes, I found myself looking into puddles, shop-windows and the faces of other men. It was slowly borne in upon me that it was not exactly water, glass or faces that she was studying, but rather herself, finding herself reflected in every part of Paris. I was happy to follow her in this.

The city in the damp autumn seemed to be rotting away. Everywhere one saw leprous stretches of peeling paint and rusted and leaking guttering. The smarter residential areas were, I remember, especially sombre – appropriately oppressive stage sets for my unconsummated passion. The *portes-cochères* were always locked. Dark trees and shrubs set the great houses at a distance from the roads and the green shutters on the windows of the houses were, like the *portes-cochères*, closed. We speculated what went on behind those shutters and I thought again of the mustachioed gentleman and the lady caught between the two mirrors. (It only now occurs to me that the couple in the picture may have been about to carry out an experiment in the erotics of catoptrics, making use of the reflection of reflections to multiply the appearances of the lady's bottom to infinity and in so doing to similarly multiply the delight that came from contemplating her bottom also to infinity.) Anyway, on only one occasion, when evening was coming on, did we walk past one of these windows which had carelessly been left unshuttered and then we saw a naked woman dancing with her back to us on a red settee. We stood and watched for a while and then walked on in silence. The curious tableau made me think of Oliver and his bizarrely useless red divan.

We went nowhere special and we were nobody special. It is hard to imagine anything more banal than a pair of lovers walking through the streets of Paris. (Since I do have a strong imagination I can imagine things that are even more banal, but I will not trouble you with them here.) Occasionally we would find ourselves walking behind another pair of lovers also arm in arm and I would find myself almost unable to walk, practically swooning, overcome by the ordinariness of my love and theirs.

We used to rise late and walk late into the night. In the night the rain gave a silvery gleam to the buildings and the sphinxes, gargoyles and obelisks with which Paris is so richly blessed. Then, after walking, we would drink brandy in some zinc bar before returning to study more pornography in Jorge's flat.

After the first night she trusted me enough to stop wearing her uncomfortable girdle in bed. Each night I requested permission to lick her and this was always smilingly granted. I stopped her taking baths, for I preferred her sweaty. I also kept a glass of Pernod on the floor beside the bed to refresh my tongue. This substitute for real sex was just barely tolerable, since it was innocent enough for her ('I feel like a kitten being washed!') and perverse enough for me (I felt like a sex slave). I could even persuade myself that there was something Surrealist in our nocturnal ritual, for Caroline's way of dealing with my desire reminded me a little bit of Salvador Dali's much underrated novel *Hidden Faces* in which he introduces the world to what he claims is a new perversion, cledalism, *amour-voyance* or orgy-incontinence. In cledalism things are taken to such an extreme that lovers attain orgasm without touching one another at all, by purely mental means. The only sex I had in Paris that week was mental. I tried to tell

96

myself that this was what I needed or wanted, but I knew that this was not so. I had had bizarre sex with Kiki de Montparnasse and others. Now I wanted normal sex and I wanted Caroline to bear my children. Not because I gave a damn about children. I did not. But because childbearing would bind Caroline more closely to me in a traditional little bourgeois family circle. That was my fantasy.

Anyway after most of her body had been licked (she would not allow me between her thighs), Caroline would sleep and for hours I watched her sleeping. She slept like a seal, turning in the bed as if in water. My own sleep was more fitful. Even so, early one morning I awoke with a start to find that she was no longer beside me in the bed. Rolling over, I discovered that she had left a note on the pillow.

'Darling,

This morning I suddenly feel the need to be alone for a little bit, so I thought that I would let you sleep on and I have gone off on a purposeless little walk on my own. Meet you at the Cafe de Dome at one sharp.

Love and kisses,

XXXXXXXXXXX'

I stumbled over to the window and, gazing dopily down, I glimpsed Caroline walking smartly down the Rue de Clignancourt. I did not pause to think. I did not even pause to put on any shoes. I hurled myself into trousers and shirt, and, having leapt down the flights of stairs from Jorge's flat, I started running down the Rue de Clignancourt. It and its continuation, the Rue de Rochechouart, proceed directly for a long way into the heart of Paris. So it was that I was successful in spotting her ahead of me. She was walking briskly down the road, looking neither to the left nor the right. Although she was walking fast, I could have overtaken her, had I continued to run. However, I did not. Instead I shadowed her from a safe distance and I moved from tree to *urinoir* to doorway in the somewhat stagily secretive manner that I had seen this done in the movies. I think that half of me was playing and enjoying the pretence of being a red indian or a private detective, but the other half of me was sick with a kind of dread. I could not, however, identify the source of my dread.

At the end of the Rue de Rochechouart Caroline produced a map from her handbag (I did not know that she had this map) and thereafter she kept consulting it as she pursued a twisting course into the crowded centre of the city. We walked quite a way and it was not long before one of my feet was bleeding. From time to time I glanced back at the gory spoor that my foot was leaving on the pavement.

At length she arrived at the building which proved to be her destination and, after paying for her ticket at the *caisse*, she went in. I limped across the street to stand in front of the building's entrance, even though I had already recognised the goal of Caroline's journey as the Musée Grevin in the Boulevard Montmartre. Above the entrance, beneath the images of two somnolent women, I read the legend *Cabinet Fantastique. Palais des MIRAGES*. However, I dared not enter the waxworks and I would not confront her. Instead I concealed myself in the doorway of an office on the other side of the Boulevard and I waited. Almost two hours had passed before it occurred to me that the waxworks might have an exit that was separate from its entrance. I crossed the street once again and discovered that this was so. The Musée Grevin had an exit in the Passage Jouffroy, the covered arcade that ran along the side of the building. It was most probably that Caroline had already left and I was now in danger of being late for our rendezvous at the Cafe du Dome.

I took a taxi and hobbled out of it into the cafe. Caroline arrived about ten minutes after me. She was looking preoccupied and perhaps even afraid, but that may have been only my imagination. I was ready to imagine anything.

'Sorry I'm late. I was ambling about without thinking. Darling! What have you done to your feet?'

Looking down at my feet I simulated vagueness.

'My shoes? Oh, I must have forgotten to put them on.'

'Oh Caspar, you are hopeless. Are you expecting me to carry you home?'

I smiled at Caroline. Then, snapping my fingers I summoned over a shoeshine boy and got him to blacken and polish the tops of my feet. As the boy worked away, we chatted about what we had been doing that morning and she proved to be as vague as I was on that subject. Then she turned the conversation round to a proposed expedition to a fashion showroom on the Place Vendome. I hardly listened to what she was saying, for I was reproaching myself for having shadowed and spied on her. I told myself that this action was typical of my mistrustful, creepy nature – that this was exactly me, a pale creature who lurked in the shadows of dark doorways or behind *urinoirs*. I disgusted myself.

Finally we did set off for the Place Vendome. As chance would have it, there were wax mannequins in the window of the showroom, dressed in Schiaparelli's latest creations, bizarre evening-gowns with designs by Salvador Dali. Caroline studied the window display earnestly and I studied her, unable to decide whether it was the evening-gowns or the wax figures which so held her attention.

That evening, while she was washing and binding my feet, she told me that I was crazy and mysterious and that she did not think that she would ever succeed in discovering the real me.

The following day, our last full day in Paris, was also the day of our meeting with André Breton at the Cafe Flore. We found him and Jacqueline playing cards with the Eluards on a table outside. Paul acknowledged our arrival, but signalled that the game was reaching a crucial stage and must not be interrupted. André dealt out two cards to Paul, five cards to Jacqueline, four to Nusch and three to himself. The rest of the pack he divided into three dummies. Paul turned over the top card on the first of the dummies and whistled through his teeth before rejecting it. Jacqueline turned over the top card of the second dummy. It turned out to be a two of clubs and Jacqueline, showing the Queen of Spades from her hand, scooped the rest of the dummy. Nusch did not turn a card over, but she exchanged three out of the four cards in her hand with cards from the third dummy and then laid out two court cards from the hearts suit on the table. And so play continued in this perplexing manner for another fifteen minutes or so. From time to time a player might announce a 'grand slam', declare that jokers were trumps or demand a reshuffle of one of the two remaining dummy packs.

Finally, this somewhat random game, whose rules only came into existence as players thought of them, broke up in roars of laughter and at that point Paul rose and with solemn courtesy introduced us to André and his wife. I went into a close huddle with André for a while, talking business and then, once the business was concluded, I found myself having to field questions about Ned and the Serapion Brotherhood. André did not regard Ned as serious and he wanted me to ditch him and come over to the Paris Surrealists. Meanwhile I think Jacqueline was telling Caroline about her former career as a professional swimmer.

Then talk became more general. André produced a letter from Benjamin Péret. Péret was fighting in the Durrutti column of anarchists helping to defend Madrid against the Fascists. Saragossa had fallen to the Fascists only a few days previously. Liberty and democracy were under siege. A great war could not long be avoided. I was unused to such talk, for as I have already remarked, Ned had no belief in politics. (According to Ned, politics was just like astrology, a totally spurious system for explaining why things happened and democracy had no more real existence than the Fairy Commonwealth.)

Then André talked about plans to hold the next great Surrealist exhibition in Paris in the coming year. He hoped that I would exhibit and perhaps Jenny Bodkin too.

'Recently Salvador Dali has been producing interesting work using mannequins and wax-figures. And Bellmer too,' said André.

100

'Yes, Jenny has been doing the same,' I replied, raising my voice as I did so. 'She finds wax a stimulating medium to work in'.

As I replied, I watched Caroline out of the corner of my eye. However, there was no sign that she was listening to our talk and she seemed wholly concentrated on feeding crumbs to a dog under the table.

Only when she had finished feeding and teasing the dog did Caroline rejoin the conversation. She talked to Paul about his collection of poems, *Les Yeux Fertiles*, and about what poets she should read next. Then she turned to André and asked him what novels she should read.

André exploded,

'What novels, Mademoiselle? No novels! Never again read novels! And try to forget those novels you have already read! The novel is an outdated art form and useful for nothing. The reading and writing of novels cramps and constrains the imagination. Novels delude us into thinking that time and space are fixed things in which we are trapped. Novels teach slavery to life. They present people's characters as fixed and that is a lie. Novelists are tyrants.'

André had started out so angrily on this tirade that Caroline cringed back into her seat, but as he continued to talk it became clear that André was only now really seeing her for the first time and his tone softened.

'Read only poetry, Mademoiselle, for only poetry is a suitable vehicle for the celebration of the mysteries of love and womanhood.' And then, quoting himself, 'The problem of woman is the most marvellous and disturbing problem there is in the world'.

Caroline looked a little doubtful. It may have been that she did not like to think of herself as a problem, whether marvellous or not.

Jacqueline wanted to know how we had met and once again Caroline described finding me blindfolded in Soho and again Paul urged us to explore Paris in the same fashion. So Caroline tied her scarf tight round my eyes. Our audience with André Breton was over and blindfolded

101

I made my formal farewells, shaking hands and kissing cheeks.

I do not know where she led me on that last day in Paris. I was thinking about other things. Why on the previous day did I not follow Caroline into the Musée Grevin and confront her? Or why did I not ask her later what she had been doing in the waxworks? Well, nothing is simple. Everything is absurd. In part I think I was paralysed by my shame at having followed her. What could I say? How could I explain myself? But there was more. Somehow I had the sense of an interdiction, some sort of prohibition. I played with the fantasy that if now, while she was leading me blindfold through the city, I asked her directly about her dealings with the wax figures, then she would show me the truth and it would be a truth that I would rather not have seen. In my absurd fantasy she would lead me by the hand into the Musée Grevin and then, when she had taken my blindfold off, I would behold the bloody corpses of other foolish young men, so foolish as to ask the same question that I had just asked, and they would all be hanging on meat-hooks in a chilling chamber, prior to their being embalmed in wax.

Well, it was absurd and it was impossible to think of Caroline doing anything really naughty, never mind seriously evil. She was an old-fashioned English girl, kittenishly, teasingly affectionate on that last day in Paris.

Suddenly my mind was made up. I tugged her to a halt and kissed her. Then,

'Caroline, will you marry me?'

There was a long silence. My heart was beating so furiously that I thought I might die.

'I don't know. Let me think about it.'

There was another long silence and I suddenly became possessed by the notion that there was someone standing close by and listening to all that we said. I stripped the scarf away from my eyes. We were standing alone beside the Seine. There was no one anywhere near us, but now I could see that she was silently crying.

'It's not that I'm unhappy,' she explained. 'I'm crying for happiness.'

'Caroline, I need your love.'

'But darling you have my love.'

'No. I need your passion, not your affection.'

'No darling, just now you need my affection and you have it, all of it.' And she continued. 'But you don't know me. You keep watching me as if I was something you were just about to eat, but you don't know me at all.'

Chapter Nine

That winter things fell apart. One Sunday in early December, after several cancelled dates, she came to the studio in Cuba Street for what proved to be her last sitting. I had been studying the Hilliard miniatures in the Victoria and Albert Museum and I was trying my hand at a portrait of Caroline which would be small enough to fit into a locket.

When I sensed that we were getting near the end of the sitting, I proposed that she came again the next Saturday afternoon. She shifted uneasily in her seat.

'I can't come so often for a bit. Mummy and Daddy have been complaining that they don't see enough of me these days, and – I've been meaning to tell you – I've got a part in the *Vortex* by Noel Coward. It's being put on by the Putney and Barnes Thespians, and I've been given the part of Bunty Mainwaring, you know, the girl who is engaged to Nicky the drug addict. It's the best part I've ever been offered. Anyway the rehearsals are going to take up a lot of the weekends'. She looked apologetic. 'The opening night is towards the end of January. Come and see it if you like.'

I was angry and I allowed my anger to show. Didn't she care about me? Did she think nothing of these fantastic portraits I had been doing of her? Was she just going to walk away and leave everything in mid-air? Was she going to let amateur theatricals get in the way of real art?

She was angry in response,

'I'm sorry darling,' she said.

(I had never heard 'darling' used as a term of hostility before.)

'I'm sorry, but you have a lot to learn about life. You can't always get your own way, and this will teach you more quickly than you think – if you let it.'

I was speechless, astounded to find myself being patronised by this girl, but she pushed a strand of hair away from her face and continued,

'You and your friends in the Brotherhood sit around talking about the Surrealist revolution and about doing all sorts of fantastic things, but where is the reality in all that? You must recognise yourself for what you really are and then act on it. For how long are you going to keep on doing these weird paintings? And how is the world going to benefit from them?'

She stood up to go and then looked serenely back at me.

'I've said everything I'm going to say now. If I were you, I'd say nothing in reply, in case you say something that you might regret.'

And with a final blown kiss she walked out of the room and out of the house.

Since Oliver had stopped coming to see me in Cuba Street, I went round to see him in his grimy rooms off the Tottenham Court Road. I found him in shirt sleeves, sitting at a table covered with brightly coloured cards. I had seen similar ones before in the hands of Gala Dali and recognised them as from the tarot pack. A pattern of ten cards was upturned on the table in front of Oliver, and he with difficulty raised his gaze from them.

'Good evening, Caspar.' Then peremptorily, 'Look at this would you? There are four cards from the Major Arcana in the hand I have just dealt myself – the Fool, the Magician, the Star and the Hanged Man. Can you see that one of the cards is special? Don't answer straight away, but think carefully.'

I looked, but could see nothing.

So Oliver picked up the Star. The card showed a star and under it a naked woman who knelt and poured water from two vessels onto land and into a stream.

'It's Arcana 17. It symbolises hope, a light to be guided by. Inspiration from above. The determination of the future. The transcendence of normal limitations. I dealt it and so this card has been directed to me. You haven't got it yet, Caspar? The Latin for Star is Stella.'

I was unable to stifle a groan. I had hoped that all this Stella nonsense might be fading by now. Alas, no.

'So according to the cards, what is your future?'

'What? Oh no. I don't believe in fortune-telling.' Oliver was seriously offended. 'That sort of occult rubbish is for illiterate gipsy women. No, no, what I've dealt here is part of the plot of my next novel. It's going to be called *The Vampire of Surrealism* and its plot is going to be based on random shuffles of the tarot pack. It's my new way of using chance to stimulate the sources of creativity in my unconsciousness. These ten cards I've just dealt myself will be the ten leading characters in my novel. Of course the most important one is Stella.'

I thought that this was all quite interesting and I was about to sit down on the red divan placed under the window and discuss the procedure more fully, when Oliver screamed,

'Don't sit there! Don't sit there! Don't touch it! That is reserved for Stella. It is where Stella and I make love. Here, have my chair. I don't mind standing for a bit.'

Oliver quickly calmed down, and once he had done so, he apologised. He had been preoccupied and a bit depressed, he said. Norman, the Manager of the Dead Rat Club, was now demanding that Oliver should tap dance while he did his card tricks.

'I can do it of course. I can do anything if I put my mind to it. But it's so . . . degrading.'

But then Oliver waved the problem away and asked me what had brought me round to see him.

I did not come to the point immediately. Instead I filled him in on some of what Caroline and I had been doing in Paris, though I held back from telling him about the evenings and nights in Jorge's flat and about Caroline's hurried visit to the Musée Grevin, and then I reported what Eluard and Breton had been saying about our duty to the people of Spain and how we were all under threat from Fascism and so on. However, there was a tightness about Oliver's jawline which suggested boredom. So reluctantly I came at last to the topic that I wanted to talk about and at the same time did not want to talk about.

'Caroline was with me this afternoon.'

'That's good, isn't it?' said Oliver deadpan.

'Yes, but she doesn't want us to see each other so often and she lectured me. She was saying that I and the rest of us were poseurs and that all our Surrealist activities were pointless. She also seemed to be suggesting that I was running away from myself.'

Oliver shrugged, but I continued,

'No, listen. The thing is that, while she was saying this, I thought that she actually despised me, and the strange thing is it was precisely at that moment that I desired her more than I had ever done before.'

Now Oliver exploded,

'For Christ's sake, Caspar! I did warn you that she wasn't for you. Can't you see how much you are making a fool of yourself running after her? People are laughing at you – no, not me, but others. Ditch the silly girl, as you should have done the first day you met her. She's just not your type.'

'That's it. It is just because she is not my type and she's wrong for me that I want her. I want to be loved by the sort of person who would not love a person like me.'

'Well,' Oliver said. 'If that is how it is, you are going to suffer. You won't believe how much you are going to suffer. Mind you, suffering is good for the artist,' he ended, somewhat piously I thought.

'But Oliver, you too are in pain. Would you prefer to have the pain which is supposed to be good for your art, or would you prefer to have Stella?'

He smiled bitterly,

'These days I have both.'

'Oliver?'

'Yes,' he looked irritated, wishing this conversation would end.

'I remember you talking, years ago, about the seances

and trances that André Breton, Robert Desnos and others were holding. Magnetic fields came into it somewhere.'

'The period of trances. Yes. They were hypnotising each other in order to extract things from the unconscious. In the end though they abandoned these experiments as too dangerous. One or two subjects were getting violent and they also experienced difficulties getting people out of the trance states. Yes, I remember reading about it and talking about it. What of it?'

'Oliver, I also remember that you went on to teach yourself mesmerism. Would you teach me?'

'What?' he said vaguely and then, once he had realised why it was that I wanted to learn mesmerism, 'Oh no! Oh no!' His voice was high pitched and sounded even a little crazy. 'You can't compel someone's love like that and, even if you could, it would be like making love to an automaton or a wax doll.'

'Please Oliver . . . you are my oldest friend. Teach me mesmerism.'

'No, no, no! And again no! It's dangerous and it's evil. Look at the Reichschancellor in Germany. Adolf Hitler. One can see that he has dabbled in mesmerism. And that fat man we sometimes see drinking in the Wheatsheaf . . . what's his name? . . . the one that smells . . . Aleister Crowley. You don't want to get mixed up with those sorts of people.'

'But from what you have been saying recently, it sounds as though you are trying to compel the love of this spirit, Stella.'

Oliver's laugh rang out noisily.

'But I know what I'm doing! And I am aware that what I am doing is terribly dangerous. It's all in the eyes. The power leaks out through the eyeballs. It doesn't do to meddle with the eyes. You, Caspar, you need your eyes to paint. The matter is closed.'

I rose somewhat huffily to go. Oliver put his arm about me and said,

'Please don't take offence and let's stay friends. As you

say, we have been friends a long time and I'm sure we'll continue to see one another, but please, I beg you, don't come here again. You are disturbing the psychic atmosphere and I need to concentrate. Stella might materialise at any moment. Only I know that she will not materialise while there is someone else in this room.'

Then he picked up the Hanged Man from the cards on the table and brandished it before me.

'My story demands that someone be sacrificed for the fellowship to be redeemed. There is no telling yet who it will be.'

Feeling thoroughly rejected by now, I walked aimlessly down the Charing Cross Road. I had a few drinks in the Green Man – no, damn it, a lot of drinks. Then I decided to go and see Ned. (This was after I had decided against going to visit MacKellar, in case I ran into that awful wife of his.)

Felix greeted me affectionately at the door.

'Poor Caspar,' she said, without me having said anything to her. Then she went out to do some shopping, leaving me alone with Ned.

I described Oliver's strangeness to him.

'Oliver's near the end of the path he's chosen and he's cracking up,' he said shrugging. 'Let's just hope that he doesn't decide to appoint himself as a Sacrifice for the Redemption of the Fellowship.'

'Ned, there's something else you should know. These last few months I have painted nothing that you could call Surrealist. Indeed, I can hardly hold the paintbrush at all in the state I'm in. So I'm thinking of leaving the Brotherhood and giving up Surrealism. I think that I can earn more as a commercial artist and a painter of posters.'

'It won't be as easy as you think to give Surrealism up; if it happens, it will be more a matter of it giving you up', Ned's tone was dispassionate. 'But this isn't about money is it?'

'No. I'm thinking about a total change in my life. I haven't decided yet. I definitely haven't made up my mind, but, if I do decide, then it will be a break with everything and then I will write to you and everyone else telling them that I don't want to see them again. There won't be anything personal in it, but I thought I should warn you. If I am to reconstruct myself as a totally different person then I shall need new and different friends.'

'Except Caroline. You aren't going to send Caroline a goodbye card,' said Ned looking at me keenly.

'Except Caroline,' I agreed. 'I am going to turn myself into the sort of person she wants me to be. I might even give up art altogether and go into business.'

Ned was silent for a while, except for the drumming of his fingers. Suddenly he came to a decision.

'It's a good idea,' he said. 'Get out while you can. Surrealism has just about had its moment. Every path has been explored and every path has turned out to be a dead end. It's become like a ghetto in an ancient walled city, full of dead ends and closed courtyards. If you follow Surrealism to the end, all you will find is madness and death. Besides, there is a great war coming in Europe and I cannot imagine that there will be any useful role for the Brotherhood in that war. I have to stay with the group for as long as I can because I have a responsibility to it, but it's different for you. Half of me will be sorry to see you go, of course, but it is good that you are thinking of it. You should follow your star. I reckon that what is important is not what happens in a man's life, but what he leaves behind him for eternity. There are only two ways for us to achieve an eternity of sorts: one is by works of art, through which one's ideas and reputation live on after one. The other is by having children. You've done enough painting anyway. I think that it makes more sense to have lots of children. Marry Caroline with my blessing. She's got good childbearing hips. It's a pity though . . . I was counting on you two for the orgy.'

After this we talked of indifferent matters, but I was glad that I had talked to Ned about what was in my mind, for earlier – and I feel ridiculous and childish confessing this – I had entertained a ludicrous, half-formulated fantasy that, if I announced that I was going to defect from the Brotherhood, then I would have been tipped the black spot and hunted down as a renegade. So I was relieved that Ned took things so calmly. Only a little later did it cross my mind that he might have been putting me off my guard and that even now he was instructing trusted stranglers from within the group on where to find me . . . But no, really these fantasies proved to be absurd.

I now took to drinking in the Wheatsheaf. It was on the seventh evening that I ran into Aleister Crowley. (I smelled him before I saw him.) Although I bought him several drinks, he was morose and not at all forthcoming. However, eventually he did suggest that I visited Watkins's occult bookshop in Cecil Court, off Charing Cross Road, where I might find, if I were lucky (or unlucky?) a copy of Dr Aczel's *Exercises in Practical Mesmerism*.

'Do let me know how you get on, dear boy,' he said as I thanked him and left.

I did find the book that he had recommended and I set to practising its regime of eye-exercises in front of a mirror. (The long-term effects of these exercises can be seen in some of the self-portraits I did later.)

On the Wednesday after my meeting with Crowley, Caroline agreed to meet me for drinks and a meal. She was bubbly and friendly and full of stories about the first read-through of *The Vortex* and about the rest of the cast. I offered to come down to Putney and take a part myself, but I was told that all the roles had now been allotted.

Relaxed and happy at the end of the meal, she smiled and said to me,

'Isn't this nice? We just have to take time to get to know one another better.'

'To that end, would you agree to be my partner at the Chelsea Arts Ball on New Year's Eve? It's fancy dress and this time the theme is the eighteenth century. Come on. You can't possibly have a rehearsal on New Year's Eve.'

111

She sat silent, obviously tempted. Then she said,

'All right darling, that would be utterly super.'

And then we settled down to discussing what sorts of costumes we might wear.

I persevered monotonously with my exercises in mesmerism. Dr Aczel was a great believer in training up the muscles in the eyeballs. However, he also said that the hypnotist had to win the trust of the person who was to be hypnotised, so that that person was ready to surrender up part of his or her consciousness to the guardianship of the hypnotist. Therefore there were evidently limits to how far I could proceed on my own.

One evening in the Dead Rat Club when Oliver was absent (I think he was performing at Maskeleyne's Theatre), I brought the topic up with the group and asked for volunteers. MacKellar was first to agree to be guinea pig, but he was hopeless. He just sat there with a fatuous grin on his face, saying things like,

'Has it started yet? When am I going to be under your influence?'

Then Monica offered herself. To my surprise, I found that after only a few passes of my hands I had led her into what seemed like a trance-like sonambulistic state, but others in the group were more sceptical. I got her to raise and lower her arms, but that was judged to be no real test. Then Ned suggested getting her to undress.

'You can't get a hypnotised subject to do anything unless he or she actually wants to,' objected Jorge.

'Tell her that she is in her bedroom and that it is time for her to go to bed,' suggested Ned.

I did as Ned proposed.

'You are in my power, Monica. You will do what I tell you until I release you. But for the moment you are alone in your bedroom and it is late. It is time for you to undress and go to bed.'

A faint sleepy smile spread across Monica's face. Her eyes were slits. Slowly but without hesitation she bent to unzip her skirt and step out of it. Although others in the club were clapping in time to some sort of striptease rhythm, she seemed unaware of it and those in the Brotherhood sat silently watching. Looking back on it, I am certain that there was more than pure science in their observation. For some of us at least, there was just a streak of pleasurable malice in watching Monica make an exhibition of herself, for there had been a certain amount of resentment at the way she always sat on the edge of the group from where she observed us and took notes on our conversations.

But when she finally stepped out of her panties and began to grope uncertainly for the whereabouts of her bed, Felix shrilled at me,

'Stop it, Caspar! Stop it! Bring her out of it! It's gone too far!'

Felix's sudden outburst of fear unsettled me and, flustered, I found that the passes that I had previously rehearsed did not suffice to rouse Monica from her trance and I kept having to retreat before her as she continued to grope blindly for the non-existent bed. Finally though I did succeed and, when she came to and saw her condition, she shrieked and, grabbing some of her clothes, ran off in the direction of the Ladies cloakroom.

Monica's breasts and hips had been wonderful to behold and the whole thing should have been good harmless fun, but I knew that it was not. I had the queasy feeling that a vessel of nastiness had been inadvertently unstoppered.

Anyway, thus it was that I was responsible for Monica's leaving the Serapion Brotherhood. We still saw her around occasionally, for she went off and attached herself to the other group of Surrealists, who were based mostly in Blackheath. She hung around with Charles Madge, Roland Penrose and Humphrey Jennings and we heard that she had become involved in the Mass Observation project. According to Jennings (who incidentally was the translator of Paul Eluard into English) Mass Observation was going to carry out 'a sounding of the English collective unconscious'. Participants in Mass Observation – and there were hundreds, if not thousands of them – were going to take notes and report on such things as 'the behaviour of people at war memorials, shouts and gestures of motorists, the aspidistra cult, the anthropology of football pools, bathroom behaviour', and so on and so on. In this manner the texture of English life would be caught in a way which owed nothing to the techniques of a literary elite. For the first time the working class would be presented with their own culture. Jennings believed with Lautréamont and Eluard that 'Poetry must be made by all, not by one'. Ned was very suspicious of Mass Observation at first, but . . . But I digress.

New Year's Eve approached and I could think of little else except the night I would spend with Caroline at the Ball. We met briefly from time to time. I always brought roses to these meetings. The reason it was always roses was that it was practically the only flower I knew the name of to ask for. We discussed, among other things, our costumes. I was going as Count Cagliostro and was hiring most of my costume from a theatrical suppliers, but Caroline, who had decided to go as Marie Antoinette, was making her own dress. As she described it, it was a spectacular feat of soft engineering – an elaborate creation of hoops, frills, furbelows and layered petticoats. What with her office work and her amateur dramatics, she ought to have been worn out, but she was full of energy and it was I who was often preoccupied and despondent.

The night of the Ball, the night when one bad year gave way to what proved to be a worse year, finally came. Before the War the Chelsea Arts Ball was the biggest party of the year. It may be still, for all I know. At the entrance, confronted by the Pathe and Movietone news teams and the flashing bulbs of the press, Caroline paused to slide her cloak off onto my arms and she spread her skirts before the cameras to reveal herself dressed in an astonishingly elaborate panniered confection of pink, blue and white. As we progressed into the Albert Hall, she instructed me on the distinctive functions of the skirt's countless furbelows, ribbons, puffs and bows. She had stuck buckles on her shoes to make them look more antique. She seemed feverishly excited, though this may only have been the effect of the patches of rouge she had pressed to her cheeks. In that antique make-up and with her powdered hair piled up in high tightly curled rolls she also looked much older. She might have been a seasoned courtesan – one with a long list of dangerous liaisons behind her. I still have the photograph taken of us by the Ball's official photographer and in it she looks almost sinister. Indeed, we both look a little strange. The floor of the Albert Hall was fringed with mock pavilions and pergolas and crowded with English, French, Russian and Venetian aristocrats in powdered wigs, as well as grenadiers, highwaymen and their molls, milkmaids, *banditti, sans cullottes* and figures from the *Commedia dell' Arte.* Many of the revellers wore domino masks and these had the effect of making the eyes seem brighter and the smiles sharper.

The music that night was provided first by Jack Hilton and then later by Ambrose and his Band. It was somewhat curious to behold the perruqued and silken-clad crowd dressed for the minuet but dancing to the strains of 'Night and Day' and 'Begin the Beguine'. Caroline seemed so softly yielding that, as she rested her head on my shoulder, I found my hands straying everywhere, down past the bodice and stomacher and hopelessly fumbling at her panniered skirt, but, after only a little while, she broke away.

We left the dance floor to sit out the next few dances in one of the many sitting-out rooms. When I was sure that she had recovered from her annoyance, I began,

'Caroline, there is something you should know.'

'Oh yes?'

'Caroline darling, I've been thinking about what you were saying about my weirdness and how my strange paintings didn't seem to have any point, and my not really living in reality and things like that and I have decided to give up Surrealism. I am going to get a job. I am certain I can get commercial work from the Post Office or the

Underground or something like that. So then I would be doing a regular job for steady money. What do you think?'

'You are doing this for me?'

'Yes, for you.'

'Oh Caspar! Can't you see how ridiculous you are being? I don't want you to give up anything for me. I only want you to be your real self.'

'The myself that I am just wants to be whatever you want me to be,' I replied.

But Caroline did not seem interested. Her eyes slid away as if she were thinking of something else – or someone else. With sick-making suddenness I was seized by the conviction that I knew what the matter was. When I next spoke to ask her to confirm my sudden insight I heard the tremor in my voice and I hated my voice as I heard myself speaking,

'Caroline, there's someone else isn't there?'

She nodded and kept her head low, ashamed to look at me any more.

'Who? Why? You must tell me.'

She sighed. Then,

'Clive.'

'Come again. Who?'

'Clive Jerkin. You must remember him. When we were walking round Trafalgar Square with Sheila Legge and the others, he came up to me and asked me to explain what it was all about and invited me for a drink, but I refused. Well anyway, I thought no more about him, but then a few weeks later I met him on the train into Waterloo from Putney and we got to talking about Surrealism and about my work and about us both living in Putney and what there was to do there in the evenings, and I mentioned the Putney and Barnes Thespians. Well, again I didn't think any more about it, but that was the next place I met him – at a meeting of the Thesps. You know that I got the part of Bunty Mainwaring in the play? Well Clive got to play opposite me as my fiancé, Nicky Lancaster. He's a good

116

actor. He's bought a car – it's an expensive one I think – and sometimes he drives me into work now, and once he's taken me boating in Henley.

'Clive Jerkin is a silly name.'

'Oh yes, Caspar?'

'What's he like – apart from being a good actor?'

This was hardly idle curiosity on my part, for I was madly thinking that if she loved Clive, then I would discover as precisely as possible what Clive was like and make myself exactly like him in all details, only better.'

Now that she was free to talk about this man, the man she loved, she felt able to look me full in the face again.

'He's very nice. You'd like him, I think.'

The Hell I would I thought. The only way I would like him is dead. But I kept my voice quite ordinary sounding,

'What does he do?'

'He's a business broker. I suppose he breaks up businesses or something,' she continued vaguely. 'Anyway he makes lots of money and he says he's going to be a millionaire before he's thirty. He's not just interested in making money though. Besides acting, he's a good musician. He plays the piano and the bassoon. He's good at sports too. He played county cricket for a while. His mother and his sisters practically worship him.'

She smiled. She was happy just thinking about him, I thought bitterly.

'The thing about Clive is that he really makes a woman feel appreciated when he talks to her.'

I sat with my head in my hands. It struck me as a little bizarre that I should be listening to all this while dressed as Count Cagliostro. I could see that my case was hopeless. I had done some remarkable things in my life, but I could not see how I could master business-broking, the bassoon, the piano, play-acting and county cricket – not quickly at least. And anyway how could I possibly manufacture an adoring family for myself?

She put a consoling arm around my shoulders.

'Oh darling, I can't bear to see you so sad. Listen. Clive

and I aren't having an affaire or anything. I don't think he's in love with me particularly. He has lots of girlfriends. I'm just very fond of him. I am very fond of you both. Come on. Don't let's spoil a perfect evening. I am ready to dance again now.'

Now the dancing was hideous. She was in my arms but her eyes were closed for much of the time and I supposed that she was imagining herself dancing with Clive. I moved through the garish revelry sick with misery. Almost literally so, for at any moment I thought that I might have to leave Caroline and throw up the entire contents of my stomach in some private place and every time I thought of Clive pawing her I felt my gorge rise. However, I did manage to keep on dancing. Midnight approached, the massed pipe band marched in, balloons descended from the dome, the heaving throng on the floor started singing 'Auld Lang Syne'.

Later that night, while the student floats of the Sun King and his Court, the Assizes of Judge Jeffries and the Marriage of Venice to the Sea were being rolled across the dance floor, we found ourselves once again in one of the sitting-out rooms. We had been bickering on and off through much of the night. Caroline was talking about how she was not going to marry anyone for quite a while yet. She said that she treasured my love, but that she wanted our love to be Platonic. I wondered what exactly Platonic love was but said nothing. I just kept passing my hand backwards and forwards across her satin bodice, murmuring as I did so,

'Caroline, Caroline, Caroline, Caroline . . .

But suddenly she pulled away and shrieked,

'The eyes! Your eyes! Stop looking at me like that! Caspar, what's wrong with your eyes?'

And she covered her own eyes with her hands. She was shaking and crying. Quite hysterical. A Chelsea Arts Club steward, passing by the door, stuck his head in and asked if she was all right. (I think that he suspected that I had been trying to rape her.) But she waved him away and commanded me to see her out to a taxi. I lowered my gaze and obeyed. The evening, in which I had invested so much hope in advance, was over.

All that winter and spring I was miserable, but I treasured the misery (and still do), for at least I continued to be allowed to see Caroline – on certain conditions. We met only in public places – cafes, restaurants and cinemas – and she persuaded me to wear dark glasses most of the time. I felt a bit ridiculous, but she insisted that seeing my eyes boring into her made her nervous. Sometimes she had only a little time for me and much of that time I had to spend listening to her talk about Clive, about how Clive didn't really love her, and about how I was the only person she could talk to about Clive, and stuff like that. *The Vortex* came and went, but she would not allow me to come to any of its performances in case I did something silly or was rude to Clive.

Only once during these meetings did I lose my temper and allow my feelings to show. Then I started shouting. Why should the Clives of this world get everything they wanted? Public school and Oxford was he not? In their blazers and flannels, spouting their special slang, the Clives rubbed each other up in private dining clubs and then with oily assurance the Clives took what they wanted as their right – jobs, money and women, above all the women. I hated the smart-suited, smooth-talking, easy-mannered, cherubic-faced creeps. If Caroline had any sense she would hate them and him as I did.

Caroline did not trouble to argue. She hinted that she did not think that I was feeling well that day. I did not know Clive and I did not know what I was talking about. And if I seriously thought that money had anything to do with it, then she was going home right now. Not only did she force me to apologise, she also made me promise that I would always speak of Clive with respect in future.

As I have already remarked, I usually brought roses to these meetings. On one occasion when she was in a hurry to leave, she left the roses I had brought for her lying on the table. I picked them up and ran after her. I turned one corner and then another, before I glimpsed her running cheerfully into the arms of Clive. They both looked so cheerful. I slunk away with the roses in my hands before they could have noticed me.

While all this was going on I was losing my friends. In February we saw Oliver off to the war in Spain. Everyone was flabbergasted. No one in the Serapion Brotherhood was very political and of all the members of the group Oliver had surely been the least political.

Almost the entire group assembled at Charing Cross Station to see him leave. Even Caroline pretended to her boss that she was ill so that she could get the day off. Oliver would be taking a boat from Dover to Calais and from there trains through France and down into Catalonia. Our leave-taking at the station was a somewhat furtive affair, for Chamberlain's government had banned people from volunteering to go off and fight in Spain. Indeed, when Oliver returned he might well find himself facing a two-year prison sentence. In Spain, Malaga had fallen to the Fascists and it did not look as though Madrid could hold out much longer. Most of the British volunteers were going off to join the International Brigade, but Oliver told us that he could not stomach the attacks on Surrealism that had been made by the Russian and French Communist parties, so he was going to enlist in the Trotskyist P.O.U.M. or the Anarchist F.A.I. – whichever one would have him.

'This is *par excellence* the intellectual's war,' said Oliver. 'All the people who matter are going to be in Spain this summer; Malraux, Hemmingway, Péret, Orwell . . . It's an opportunity I felt one just could not miss. And, of course, I shall be taking some packs of cards with me so that I can entertain the troops . . .'

I could make nothing of all this. Oliver had been my oldest and closest friend in the group. Only now it was as if our friendship had never been, for it was obvious that I had never really known this man at all. Oliver, seeing my distress, took me to one side and then walked arm in arm with me to the end of the platform and back.

'This is a bit of a farce, isn't it?' he said. 'I don't even know what the fuck the Popular Front is. Still, you can guess why I'm doing this, can't you?'

I shook my head and he looked surprised.

'Well, I'll tell you as much as I dare and maybe one day you will understand it all. It's Stella. Things have reached danger point between us. It's all too passionate and she's feeding on me. There have been mornings when I have been unable to get up, because she's drained so much from me. I need to escape. I doubt very much that she can follow me to Spain. Anyway, I'm sure they don't take women in the P.O.U.M.'

He laughed nervously and continued,

'I need to get away and breathe a different air. I don't know what it will be like out there, or if there will be any time to do any writing. Probably not. But my plan is to write this novel about Stella, *The Vampire of Surrealism.*'

And it was at this point that Oliver explained how Stella's appearance in the novel would be a sort of exquisite corpse, a composite thing, which made use of Felix's face, Monica's bum and the breasts of a woman whom Oliver had once glimpsed walking down the King's Road.

'Why don't you simply describe Stella as she actually is?' I asked.

Oliver shuddered,

'Stella would not let me use her that way in a novel. You don't know what you are asking. I simply dare not.'

After this curious little *tête-à-tête*, we rejoined the others and they each individually made their farewells.

'Look after yourself, Olly dear,' said Caroline and she kissed him full on the lips.

Oliver looked faintly horrified. A minute or two later the train began to pull away and his face vanished in its smoke. Those who were left adjourned to the newsreel cinema in the station and watched a dismal report of the fighting in Spain.

The next person to disappear was Manasseh. Jorge drove him down to Southampton and Ned and I came too. The boat was sailing to New York. While porters took his luggage up, Manasseh talked to us on the quayside. He was furious at what he considered to be our frivolous insouciance.

'There's a war coming,' he said. 'And the Nazis are going to win it and, when they do overrun this country of yours, they will come looking for people like me'.

Here he made a throat-slitting gesture with the blade of his hand, before continuing,

'England today is a fool's paradise. Well, I may be a fool, but I have had enough of living in a phoney paradise. It's all coming to an end – and not just for us Jews either. You are smiling as I talk, but what do you think will happen to you when the Nazis enter London? I'll tell you. It's no big secret. The Reichs Minister of Culture, Dr Josef Goebbels, has spelt it out. Surrealist artists have been deemed to be degenerates, and as degenerates you too will go to join the Jews, the gipsies, the homosexuals and the mental defectives in the camps. So you are honorary Jews already! But I don't want to learn of your deaths in the camps. Look, please, do what I am doing and take the next boat out to New York. Gentlemen, I beg you, wake up from the Surrealist dream!'

Caroline and I continued to see each other, even though our meetings were, at best, politely tense. Then, one ill-fated day – it was Sunday, April 27, 1937, quite unexpectedly she came to see me in Cuba Street. She stepped into the studio diffidently, as if she had never been there before. If I had been expecting her, I would not already have had so much to drink. I was delighted to see her and I poured her out a large tumbler of whisky. I had been planning to present her with the miniature locket-portrait, but now I could give it to her that evening. She had come round, she said, because she wanted to tell me something and to ask something of me. I knew that I did not want to hear what she had to say, but she pressed on anyway.

'Caspar, I think that it is better that we do not see one another for a while. It's not good for us, these meetings, with you looking at me like a hungry hyena. I'm sorry, but it is like that. I just need space to breathe. I'm only talking about a couple of months or so, then, after two or three months, we could see how things were and how we felt about one another. I don't want to lose you as a friend, Caspar dear. With things the way they are, I need all the friends I can find.'

I went on my knees before her and rested my head on her lap.

'I don't want to be your friend. If I am not your lover, then I am nothing,' I said.

Stroking my head absently, she replied,

'Can't you see that what you call your "love" is just making you intensely miserable?'

'I'd a thousand times rather be miserable with you than happy with anyone else. I don't want happiness. It doesn't interest me. I want you.'

'Well, what about me? Think about me for once. Do I have to share in your misery?'

'It is not me who is making you miserable. It is Clive. Don't deny it. You cry all the time. You didn't used to be like this.'

She sighed. She was full of sighs.

'You just don't understand. And you don't know me.'

'Sleep with me. If we slept together properly, then we might begin to feel that we were getting to know one another.'

She could not keep the irritation out of her voice.

'You really are obsessed with this . . . with this idea of . . . poking me. What possible difference could it make if I did let you sleep with me?'

I had no good answer to this, but I said stupidly,

'I think that it's just that you may be making too big a thing of going to bed with me. You could sleep with me and then we could still be Platonic friends or whatever. I just think that you may be obsessed about losing your virginity.'

'And who said that I was still a virgin?'

Her voice was suddenly hard and she pushed my head off her lap and stood up.

'For your information, I'm not a virgin. And I'm not sure, but I think that I may be pregnant. That's what I was coming round to ask for your help about, but I can see that you are beyond helping or hope. And now I'm not going to be interrogated by you any more. I'm going. Maybe in a few months – three or four say – we can talk about things, when you are calmer.'

She made to move to the door. I blocked her way out and held her pressed against the table, setting the pendulums of the perpetual motion machine erratically in movement.

'Kiss me at least before you go.'

She pecked me swiftly on the cheek.

'You used to kiss me on the mouth,' I protested and I held her by the shoulders. She shook her head vigorously so that most of her hair fell across her face.

'Don't go. I swear I'll commit suicide if you go,' I cried.

She shrugged herself out of my embrace and took a few more steps towards the door. I rushed round the other side of the table and threw myself on the floor across the doorway.

'Let me kiss your feet. Where is the harm in that? Let me kiss your feet at least!' And I made a lunge for one of her legs.

Looking up I saw her face stiff with hatred and contempt, before, eluding my grasp, she stepped over me and vanished into the darkness. I do not know what happened after that. I drank an awful lot, that's for sure, and at some point I left the house and wandered about. I think that I had some more drinks somewhere else. I awoke at dawn, cold and filthy, in an East London park.

Chapter Ten

After a thorough wash, I walked over to the post office to make some telephone calls and on to the bank to draw out money. Then I proceeded by train and taxi to Croydon Airport. My fellow passengers on the aeroplane were mostly men in fur coats. I thought that they might be arms dealers. Below me, England, with its tidy packets of fields and its ribbons of suburban development, fell away. I paid it and the arms dealers little attention. I sat swigging whisky from a hip-flask and thinking hard.

Obviously things had gone badly wrong, but I was struggling to decide whether the universe was so constructed that the wrong was indeed irretrievable. Ought it not to be possible for me to travel back in time and space and for me to return to a time when I still had Caroline's love, a time when, if I had acted differently, everything which followed would have been different? How far back would I need to go? Back before last night's hideous encounter certainly. And back to before the night of the Chelsea Arts Ball, when I already knew in my heart that I did not have her love any more. And though Paris was good, I already had a sense then that there was something wrong. Now I came to think of it, she was preoccupied when we returned from Brighton with the Eluards. Really, it would be best to go back to the opening of the Surrealist Exhibition in the New Burlington Galleries, back to before the hour of our walk to Trafalgar Square and her encounter with Clive Jerkin, back ideally to the moment when Caroline had me pinioned against one of the Gallery's walls and had declared to me 'I love you'.

As the aeroplane dipped and swerved over the Thames Estuary, I closed my eyes and concentrated. Was I not of the Serapion Brotherhood and dedicated to the proposition that through the power of the imagination we can transcend time and space? Surely in a moment I should find myself, wine glass in hand, standing in the New Burlington Galleries and listening to Paul Eluard recite *'Une femme est plus belle que le monde ou je vis . . .'* I should be there at the exhibition, perhaps with no memory of a Chelsea Arts Ball, or of Caroline's announcement of her possible pregnancy or of my flight from Croydon, or any of those things, but that would be a blessed sort of amnesia.

However, it was useless. I believed in it, but I did not believe in it hard enough and when I next opened my eyes the aeroplane was struggling against the prevailing winds off the coast of France.

The odd thing was that Caroline's revelation of her faithlessness had only increased my desire for her. Perhaps it was that her declaration of her capacity for independent and secret action had given her more depth. She now seemed the more fully human, precisely because she was so much less than perfect, and I found that I loved her treachery as much as I did her beautiful body. Even so, the treachery shocked me, and it challenged my view of how the universe really worked. For I had believed that it was elective affinity that had brought us together, operating through the laws of chance and desire. Caroline and I had been destined for one another.

> *'Une femme est plus belle que le monde ou je vis*
> *Et je ferme les yeux'*

I had recited those lines to Caroline in St James's Park and then, months later, their author had recited them back at us. Surely that had been an omen and a blessing conferred upon us by blind chance? It was hardly possible that I could have been mistaken. Caroline had no right to move against fate's decree.

I had anticipated some sort of trouble at the airport, an interrogation about the purpose of my visit, a thorough search of my baggage for suspect literature, or something along those lines, but there was no such thing.

'Welcome to Munich and the Reich.'

That month there were many visitors to the city, attracted by the Festival of German Art and Culture and I had some difficulty in finding a *Gästheim*, so that by the time I had successfully negotiated the rent of a room and had unpacked my things, I thought that I should like to collapse on the bed and go to sleep. But sleep was hard to come by, for on that night and the nights that followed I thought of Caroline and what she had done, and what I had done, and what we ought to have done and what we might have said about what we had done. Pushing sleep and everything else aside, these thoughts rushed on like a mill-race. It was rare that I managed to doze for more than a couple of hours.

I spent the next couple of days walking at random through the city, taking my directions from the saluting arms of the statues, the eagles' gaze and the flapping of the red swastika banners. In my memory of those weeks I spent in Munich, the sky was always blue with only a few white clouds visible, and, though it seems absurd to say so, I think that clouds before the War looked different from those that we have seen in the sky since then. So I remember that the clouds over Munich were thirties' clouds. I remember also admiring the women in the city. They were almost always elegantly dressed and as often as not they were arm in arm with officers from the army, the S.A. or the S.S. My artist's eye rested as much on the uniforms as on the dresses. 'Fascism is the aestheticisation of politics,' as I remember Walter Benjamin remarking to me once.

Munich that summer was a city of roses and everywhere I looked I saw garlands of roses, as well as the banners and the eagles alertly poised on marble columns. The city furnished an appropriately grandiose background to my personal unhappiness. I was alone. Not only was I without Caroline, but, for the first time in quite a few years, I was free and independent, able to commune with myself and plunge deep into introspection, without feeling that I had to report back to the Serapion Brotherhood on the results of my investigations.

In the evenings I drank alone in my room and listened to the distant sounds of singers and brass bands in the cafes and beer-gardens. I felt no desire for company. I resumed my exercises in mesmerism and I found some faint consolation in those monotonous eye drills. Some words of Nietzsche, which Manasseh had once quoted to me came to my mind, 'And if thou gaze into the abyss overlong, perchance the abyss will gaze into thee'. Engaged in exercises designed to build up the power of my eyes, I spent much of my time in front of the mirror, studying the reflection of my pupils trapped on its surface. Despite Nietzsche's warning, I persisted in my work in front of the mirror and then, a little later, without quite knowing why – trying I think to keep my purpose secret even from myself – I also began to study my lips and their movements. I set myself to master lip-reading.

It was only on my third day that I felt ready to set out for the avowed and arbitrary goal of my trip to Munich, the exhibition of *Entartete Kunst* – Degenerate Art – in the old Institute of Archaeology. In this building Nazi officials had assembled and put on display, all hugger-mugger, a huge collection of paintings and sculptures by avante-garde artists: Nolde, Kirchner, Braque, Chagall, Schmidt-Rotluff, Kokoschka, Mondrian and many others.

'It is not the mission of art to wallow in filth for filth's sake, to paint the human being only in a state of putrefaction, to draw cretins as symbols of motherhood, or present deformed idiots as representatives of manly strength.'

Here and there, placards on the walls bearing Nazi commentaries, like the one above, abused the paintings and admonished those who gazed on them.

'Artists who for fourteen years were duped by Jews and Marxists and accepted laurels from their hands are now being extolled as our revolutionaries by certain individuals lacking in instinct and by specific politically motivated backers. It is high time we stopped being too tolerant.'

'The Jewish longing for the wilderness reveals itself in Germany and the negro becomes the racial ideal of a degenerate art.'

'If they really paint in this manner because they see things that way, then these unhappy persons should be dealt with in the department of the Ministry of the Interior where sterilisation of the insane is performed, to prevent them passing on their unfortunate inheritance. If they really do not see things like that and still persist in painting in this manner then these artists should be dealt with by the criminal courts. (Hitler.)'

Mingling furtively with the rest of the gallery-goers and eavesdropping on their conversations, I learnt to my dismay that these exhortatory texts were not really necessary. From all directions I heard such remarks as,

'It's disgusting! How can one tell what it's supposed to mean? How can we ever have been taken in by such stuff? If you want my opinion, I should say that it is the job of the artist to produce only beautiful things and not to dredge up all this muck. It really makes one quite sick!'

And from one pretty young *Hausfrau* in a floral print frock,

'It's not the paintings that should be on display here, but the artists so that we could all spit on them!' An old woman in black, doubtless her mother, cackled approvingly.

And I, the Surrealist spy in the House of Degenerate Art, cringed guiltily. I was afraid of being unmasked. I was even more afraid that it might be possible that they were right and I wished that I was as confident of my loyalty to Surrealism as they were confident in their hatred of it. It was a dreadful thought and a preposterous one, but might it not be conceivable that these awful people would succeed in making me see modern art in the way they did?

And yet, as I walked from room to room, and attempted to study this hatefully assembled collection of Cubists, Expressionists and Surrealists, my mind rarely stayed with the pictures on which my eyes were fixed. Instead, I was

129

thinking of Caroline and her seduction by Clive. I conjured up the scene in which she yielded up her virginity to him and, having done so, I replayed it again and again like a spool of scratchy old film, all jerky movements in flickering light. Caroline, blushing, undresses before the superciliously smiling Clive. Tremulous in her nakedness, she walks towards him. She assists him to undress and fumbles eagerly with his collar-studs and cuff-links. Now Clive is naked, except for his socks and the suspenders which keep them up and he presses her down onto the bed and she throws her arms around him, as he, without any preliminaries, thrusts his prick into her and she is crying, at first a little with pain and then with joy. Finally, in languorous pillow talk, they laughingly discuss what on earth can be done about the miserable, love-sick Caspar.

But this was only part of it, for I had invested so much of myself in my love for Caroline that she had become the embodiment of my soul, my *anima*, so that, at the same time Clive is entering between her legs, he is forcing my legs apart also and, at the same time he is fucking her, he is sodomising me. Since I am so bound to Caroline in my imagination, then later when she crawls over to kiss and suck at Clive's prick, I too find my mouth in the same place.

Then, as I continued to walk among the paintings, imagining these things and worse, it occurred to me that the *Hausfrau* with the shrill voice must be right. I did deserve to be spat at, for surely I must be a degenerate to have such thoughts as these. I should go back and find that young woman in the floral print dress and I should go down on my knees before her and I should confess that I was a Surrealist artist and beg to be horsewhipped.

'*Entshuldigen Sie bitte, gnädige Frau,* excuse me please, I am a diseased and degenerate artist. I am not worthy of the love of a healthy woman. So whip me, whip me! Flog the sickness out of me!'

However, at the same time I was considering this, I also knew that I should be unable to bring myself to do it, for I

130

really loved as well as feared the monsters that peopled my brain. So I did not confess and since I did not confess, I was never found out and I was not beaten up and flogged by all these people who had queued up to sneer at and abuse the confidence trick called modern art. The thing was that these people had a very clear idea of what a degenerate artist should look like. He has dulled, drug-laden eyes. Unwashed, greasy hanks of hair fall over a low simian brow, his lower lip is slack and there is an unmistakable trace of Jewishness in the hook of his nose. Whereas I was tall and very blond and, when she first saw my hatchet face in profile, Pamela remarked that I looked a little like Buster Keaton. Among the people at the exhibition of *Entartete Kunst*, I might have been an off-duty S.S. officer. My realisation of this led on to further disturbing thoughts. If everyone gets the face they deserve, what was I doing with the face of a Nordic blond beast? And if I had the face of an S.S. officer, should I not make the rest of me join my face and apply to join the ranks of the S.S.?

I was thinking, thinking, thinking all the time and my thoughts were out of control – like a complex piece of clockwork from which the counterweights or escapements had been removed, so that the springs were flying loose and the cogged wheels turning faster and faster. A war was coming and it was clear· that Germany would win it. I agreed with Manasseh on this and I also agreed with his view that England was exhausted and effete. But if I joined the S.S., then I could be on the winning side and then when we entered London I could have Clive hunted down. He would almost certainly have become a fighter pilot or an officer in one of the smarter regiments. I would have him shot. And I could have Caroline brought before me in shackles . . . But, no, this was all too childishly mad.

More prosaically, I kept devising and discarding strategies for winning Caroline back when I returned to England. At times I thought that I should assume an air of coolness and even restart my affair with Pamela, in order to awaken Caroline's jealousy. At other times, I thought the opposite

– that I should plead my case with such fire and passion that she would be unable to withstand me and perhaps I would even be able to argue her into seeing the greatness and brilliance of my art. At yet other times, I thought that I should stop talking vaguely about getting a respectable job and that I should actually start applying for whatever was being advertised.

The pornographic film on its continuous reel still played in my head, as I went backwards and forwards between the various strategies, powerless to decide between them. Hours passed before I was really able to look at the paintings that I had come to see, and then I was only able to focus on them by pretending that I had Caroline hanging on my arm and that I was telling her about these works of art and explaining to her what the artists had been trying to do in painting them. Her ghost listened obediently to my silent words.

I was pleased to find that Surrealism was represented in the exhibition by, among other things, Max Ernst's *La Belle Jardinière*. This was a painting of a nude woman in a garden. Her stomach was ripped open and a bird pecked at her stylised entrails, while a ghostly nude gardener danced in the garden behind her. I explained to the non-existent Caroline how this painting was one of the works produced during the period of trances, when Breton, Péret, Desnos and others experimented with mesmerically induced trance-imagery. In the painting itself, the closed eyes of the two figures may indicate that they have summoned up each other's images while they are themselves in trance states. Gala Dali, the dark muse of the Surrealists, was the model for the woman in the painting – or rather Gala Eluard as she was back in 1923 when she and Max Ernst were conducting their affair. When I recalled how Gala had sat on the shingle at Brighton and how she had gazed with those deep-set, black eyes of hers on Caroline and me as we sported in the water, she now seemed to me to have been a creature of ill-omen.

La Belle Jardinière was disturbing. Max Ernst had intended it to be so. As phantom-Caroline and I contemplated the painting, I became uneasily aware of a certain kind of complicity between Surrealism and Nazism. After all, we Surrealists had set out to shock people. And now at last, here in Germany, we had found an audience which was prepared to take us seriously. They were shocked. In England, we had dressed up as deep-sea divers or gorillas and, standing on our heads on the tops of grand pianos, we had lectured gallery-goers about the power of Surrealism to outrage and we had attracted only weary smiles and polite disagreement, but in Munich at least our works were accorded their proper status and they were officially classified as 'outrageous' by the Nazi authorities. When I said that I was shocking, Dr Goebbels agreed.

There were other exhibitions on in Munich that summer. Across the park from the *Entartete Kunst* exhibition, I discovered the *Grosse Deutsche Kunstausstellung*, the Great German Art Exhibition, where the paintings were hung in a long, low, classically Fascist colonnaded building and Arno Breker's preposterously over-muscular statues of men and horses stood quite lifeless on their pedestals. Although the paintings and sculptures were of little intrinsic interest, as I inspected them I recalled how Ned had described Surrealism as having reached a dead end, and that I had also heard some critics saying that Surrealism had passed its heyday in the 1920s. Here by contrast, in the *Haus der Deutsches Kunst*, I was confronted with works made by artists who were certain that they were producing the art of the future. Much of their work was technically incompetent, and almost all of it was uninspired and tinged with vulgarity, and yet as I gazed on these works in 1936, not having the gift to see into the future, it did indeed seem possible to me that I was gazing on the art of the next thousand years.

Elsewhere – it was in the Library of the German Museum, if I remember rightly – there was an exhibition devoted to *Der Ewige Jude*, the Eternal Jew, but though Manasseh had declared everyone in the Serapion Brotherhood to be honorary Jews, I still found little to interest me in all that propaganda. From time to time in the streets, I would be surprised by fancy-dress processions celebrating two thousand years of German culture, or some such Nazi lie – great carnival floats painted gold and silver, and flanked by horsewomen dressed as Valkyries or men in the armour of the Teutonic Knights, and followed by blonde maidens in white chitons who tossed flowers at the smiling, cheering crowds. Everyone was so happy. Only I was miserable and afraid.

I realised then that I was desperate to leave Munich and so, having consulted several guide books, I took the train to Potsdam and from there made my way to a hotel on the Wannsee. It was only then that I attempted to get back in touch with Caroline. I sent her a telegram:

SORRY TO HAVE BEEN SO BEASTLY. WHEN I GET BACK THINGS WILL BE BETTER. ALL MY LOVE. CASPAR.

I had decided to spend the next two months or so in Germany before returning to England and attempting to pick things up with Caroline. In the meantime I wrote to her almost daily. I spent hours on rough drafts of these letters, sucking at the end of my pencil and fumbling for the right phrases. In the end, quite a few of the letters I sent had more drawings than words – pictures of boulevardiers, sun-bathers, chess players, members of the Hitler Youth and the League of German Maidens engaged in Strength-Through-Joy group gymnastics, yachts scudding across the lakes and, in the background, the holiday chalets and hydrotherapy clinics which fringed the shores. I was anxious to present myself in my letters as a cheerful person reporting on a long and agreeable holiday. These letters, an extended exercise in lying, were I suppose the closest I have ever got to writing a novel. In reality I was miserably and doggedly making preparations to win Caroline back by any means I could devise. (Although I had sent her a *poste restante* address, Caroline never replied to my letters.)

I also sketched out a series of possible strategies in

134

preparation for my return to England. By 'sketched' I mean to say that, since I had so little skill in putting my thoughts into words, I used to visualise them instead and I drew the key scenes on my sketch-pad; me on my knees before Caroline, Pamela and I walking past Caroline and pretending to ignore her, Clive and I fighting for Caroline's favours, me raping Caroline . . . In the end I had almost thirty sketches of alternative scenarios, and I kept leafing through them and shuffling them about.

I now look back on those weeks spent on the strands of the Wannsee as a period of *Sitzkrieg*, or Phoney War. I had the faint hope that my extended absence would make Caroline realise that she could not live without me. In the meantime I was doing everything I could think of to build up my psychic strength. I spent much of the day sunbathing and watching the phosphene image of the sun on my eyelids slowly transform itself into hypnagogic imagery, which I then blindly attempted to record on my sketch-pad. Later I would scrutinise the images I had drawn, looking for omens of my future fortune. But when I sought to study the people in the hypnagogic landscape more closely and find in them guidance as to what I should do about Caroline, they fled away and transformed themselves into rocks, trees and animals. I suppose that to them I was like a distant and inefficient God who had difficulty in understanding his own creation. The strain of these trance-like states was considerable and I emerged from them shaking and gasping for breath.

Of course, I also went swimming. I have already observed, I believe, that it is impossible for someone steeped in Freud not to think, as he plunges into the water, of that act as anything but a sort of practical metaphor for the submerging of oneself in the depths of the unconscious. But now, under the surface of the Wannsee, surrounded by so many earnest German swimmers, as I forced myself deep into the muddy depths of the lake, I felt myself to be swimming among shadowy thought-shapes which were quite new to me. The Nazi and the Surrealist have both

135

plunged deep into the dark lake of European myth and, though they have re-emerged from those depths with very different trophies, nevertheless these heroic swimmers are half-brothers, engaged in a mad struggle against reason and logic.

In the evenings I persevered with my exercises in mesmerism. I concentrated first on building up the power of my will and then on projecting it out through the eyes. Since my room in the hotel had no mirror, I actually had to go into Potsdam and buy one. The mirror was a necessary piece of equipment, but an exasperating one, for mirrors are so restrictive in what they allow you to see. In that respect they are a little like hypnagogic imagery, for when I am in one of my hypnagogic states I can only look forwards. I am unable to rotate my gaze 180 degrees and look and see what is going on in the back of my head. The Belgian painter, René Magritte, has done a painting of the millionaire, Edward James, in which the subject looks into a mirror and sees reflected there the back of his own head. I think that a mirror which could perform such a service would be of real use.

I also continued with my lip-reading exercises, conscientiously mouthing sentences into the mirror. In addition, I went to one of the cinemas in Wannsee or Potsdam almost every day and I would sit with wax pellets stopping up my ears and study the lips of the actors on the screen. I saw an enormous number of films in this way – old classics like *The Cabinet of Dr Caligari*, *Nosferatu* and *The Blue Angel*, yes, but also a vast mass of more recent films produced under the patronage of Dr Goebbels. A few were out and out propaganda exercises, like *Hitlerjunge Quex*, but more commonly Wannsee's holidaymakers were offered mountain adventure films and frothy light musicals. Films in English with German subtitles were particularly useful for practice in lip-reading and so it was that one evening I found myself watching *Mystery of the Wax Museum*. It was not until half way through the film when Fay Wray reappeared as the waxen image of Marie Antoinette that I realised that my shirt-front was wet with tears.

Finally, after some nine weeks of swimming and exercising my eyes and my mind, I realised that I was ready to carry out my thought-experiment. The following morning I went down to a secluded section of the beach and, stretching myself out on my towel, I entered the hypnagogic state. On this occasion the after-image of the sun lingered for a while as a brilliant zig-zag of purple phosphene fringed with yellow which floated in a hardly less brilliantly glowing green space. I waited and watched until the zig-zag faded and the green space began to model itself in light and dark, slowly transforming itself into a shady, leafy forest in bright summer. I was not alone in this forest, for soon I saw that a steady stream of hikers, tennis players, cyclists and anglers were passing among the trees on their way to their healthy recreations. I watched these folk for a long time before pouncing on and detaining one of them. She was a young woman. Her frizzy blonde hair was held in check by an Alice-band. She wore tennis gear and her racket was clasped anxiously across her breasts.

'What must I do to regain the love of Caroline?' I demanded of her.

She would have liked to escape. If she could have, she would have transformed her eyes into pebbles and her body into a bush, rather than be caught, immobilised and interrogated by me. The unconscious, for which she was going to speak, never yields up its secrets willingly, but the power of my mesmeric gaze had trapped her. Having thus trapped Trilby – as a temporary figment of the unconscious mind, she had no name, of course, but I thought of her as Trilby – having thus trapped her, I sent her into as deep a hypnotic trance as I dared. Then I tested the strength of her trance by using one of the standard hypnotist's tests, the postural swaying test, in which I had her lean forward against my hands, my phantom hypnagogic hands, until her body was rigid at an angle of 45 degrees to the ground.

Only when I was satisfied in this way that I had her completely in my power, did I ask the question again,

'What must I do to regain the love of Caroline?'

Her answer, when it came, was of course silent, but it had been precisely for this moment that I had been training myself as a lip-reader. Trilby spoke distinctly and I had no difficulty in reading her lips. I only had difficulty in believing what she was saying.

'You must love Clive. You must love Clive in the same way that Caroline loves him. Only by loving Clive in the same way that Caroline loves him, will you be able to see what she sees in him and only then will you be able to remake yourself in such a way that she will see the same thing in you. You must love Clive. You must love Clive in the same way she loves him.'

'But that is impossible!' I expostulated.

'It is hard.' Trilby seemed to breathe her reply. 'It is very hard, but you must love Clive.'

Then a group of Trilby's sporting companions came up. They were determined to bring my dialogue with her to an end.

'You must let her go,' they said. 'She has given you our answer. Now we want her for our game of tennis.'

Well then, since I had had my reply, I released Trilby from her trance and allowed her to sink thankfully back into the shadows of the forest and I in turn returned to a normal state of consciousness on the shore of the Wannsee.

I lay gazing up at the sun and, though it was hot, I found that I was shivering uncontrollably. So I must love Clive Jerkin. I must be able to run laughing into his arms. I must love his name, and his public school reminiscences and his humming of the old school song. I must love his bassoon-playing and must even love his cock in my mouth, while he continues to play the tune of his old school song on his bassoon. I must be tremulously eager for all that and then when that climax is over I must go off and darn the holes in his socks for him. And, of course I must love that baby of his whom Caroline may be carrying in her womb.

I must love it as if it were my own child. What Trilby had commanded me to do seemed to me to be mystical in its self-abnegation and mortification. However, since Trilby was the oracle of the Forest of the Unconscious, I could not dream of disputing her pronouncement.

I picked up my towel and my sketch-pad and walked back to the hotel. At last I felt ready to return to England. You see, when I had flown out from Croydon Airport I had been in a terrible state, half mad and frightfully confused about what I should do next. Now I felt much better. I was rested. I had dived to the bottom of the lake and then returned to its surface spiritually regenerated. I now thought that I knew what I should do.

For three months I had been on my own. I had had brief exchanges with hoteliers, waiters, ticket-collectors and people like that. Apart from such trivial encounters, I had spoken only to the invisible spirit of Caroline and of course to Trilby. In general though, I had found the unwonted solitude refreshing.

Chapter Eleven

I had hoped that there might be a letter from Caroline waiting for me when I returned to Cuba Street, but there was none. Towards the end of the following afternoon, I waited with a bunch of roses in my hand outside the office of the Anglo-Balkan Fur Company. Brenda and two of her colleagues emerged and walked off, then Jim the office boy and finally Mr Maitland who locked up. I had spent so many hours anticipating my reunion with Caroline and concentrating on what I should say. Now I was taken unawares. I was so astonished at not finding Caroline where I had expected her to be that I just watched her boss walk away.

The next day however, when Brenda finished work, I was waiting for her.

'Hello, Brenda. Remember me? I'm Caspar.'

'Of course I remember you.'

She sounded nervous and she started walking faster, but I easily matched my step to hers.

'Can I buy you a drink?'

'No thank you. That's awfully good of you, but I've got to get home. I'm in a bit of a hurry, I'm afraid. I've got someone waiting for me.'

'Just give me five minutes of your time then,' and I took her by the arm and spun her round, so that we were looking into each other's eyes. Her lank brown hair framed a face that was pudgy and yet still quite attractive. Her eyes were full of dull resentment.

'Where's Caroline, Brenda? Why isn't she at work?'

Her reply contained a hint of tears.

'I don't know. She didn't turn up for work some time in July. She just left without giving any notice. I really don't know. Stop looking at me like that. I've got to get on now.'

Hearing her reply, I felt my stomach drop. But my grip on her elbow only tightened.

'But you must know more. You must tell me.'

By now she was slightly hysterical.

'Let me go. You are horrible! She was my friend, but you and your lot spoilt her. If you want to know the truth I thought she must have gone off with you in a big, swank car.'

She covered her face. At first I thought that she was trying to shield her eyes from mine, but then I saw that she was really crying. Finally, when she had calmed down, she looked back up at me with those big sullen eyes of hers.

'You don't like me do you? Well, I don't like you either and, if you don't let go of me now, I'm going to scream for the police. I hate you! I hate you!'

Astonished by her display of schoolgirlish petulance, I let her go. Then, after only a few minutes of pacing about in the street, I came to a decision and I took a series of buses down to Putney. Although the day that Jorge, Oliver and I had picked her up from her parents' house before motoring on down to Brighton was still vivid in my memory, it took me quite a while to find that house again and it was late at night when I rang the doorbell.

Her father – I presume it was her father – came to the door.

I raised my hat politely.

'Good evening, sir. Sorry to disturb you, but is Miss Begley in? I'd like a few words with her if I may.'

The man's face screwed up with distaste.

'Go away.'

'I'm not a door-to-door salesman, you know.'

'I know who you are. Now just go away, or I'll do something I won't be responsible for.'

The door slammed shut. I rang the bell again, but, though I could hear the father and mother arguing inside, the door did not reopen.

I started shouting,

'Caroline, darling, if you are inside come out to me. It's

Caspar! Caroline! Caroline! I'm sorry. Forgive me. Caroline, I want you . . .'

After a bit though I gave up and I went and sat on a garden wall on the opposite side of the road for an hour or two, hoping to catch a glimpse of Caroline, even though part of me already knew that she was no longer living in Putney.

The following day I wrote letters to Caroline and addressed them to her house and to the office for forwarding. Uncertain what to do next, I went round to see MacKellar. Since I had last visited him, he had acquired one of those large padded dentist's chairs which, by pumping with one's foot, one could make rise or sink. Books had been pulled off the walls to make space for skulls. One skull had had tiny little holes drilled into it and those holes filled up with paste jewellery. Another skull had had all its teeth removed and in their place two rows of tiny light bulbs glowed in the jaw. I did not like to examine the rest.

MacKellar politely enquired about my time in Germany, but I did not tell him much. Then I asked him how *Blind Pew Looks Back* was getting on. When would I be seeing a text that I could illustrate?

MacKellar sighed.

'I'm sorry to have to say it's not going well. It's not really going at all. I can't get the pirates to walk on to the ship. I have to push them every step up the gang plank and then, since I can't hear them talking, I have to do all their talking for them. If I put them in any particular situation, like, say, a storm at sea, they just stand around waiting for me to tell them what to do. I feel more like a solitary little girl holding an imaginary tea party with her dolls than I do a real writer.'

MacKellar sighed again and continued,

'Do you remember how Oliver was always saying that every writer has only a limited amount of emotional capital, amassed between the ages of eighteen and twenty-five, from which he has to write for the rest of his life? Well, I'm afraid I've exhausted my capital.'

'How is Oliver by the way?'

'No one has heard anything. Ned's extremely worried. The death toll among the volunteers in Spain is quite high, but we just haven't heard anything about him. No, well anyway, the only thing that really interests me about my pirates is their teeth . . .'

I let MacKellar run out of steam, talking about dental hygiene, the history of dentistry and how he would like to stop being a novelist and study for dental qualifications. Only he could not see how he could possibly raise the money. And then his publisher was still showing no interest in *Dentist of the Old West* . . .

At last I was able to talk about what I wanted to talk about, Caroline, and I described the circumstances of her vanishing.

MacKellar was sympathetic, but only up to a point.

'Well, I'm sorry of course. She was charming and I did like her. Still, perhaps you are better off without her. She was a bit stupid. I remember once, when you were out of the room and the group was discussing you and her, Oliver quoted Baudelaire on the subject; "Stupidity is the adornment and preservative of beauty".'

I was surprised, though I suppose that I should not have been, to discover that our relationship had been discussed behind our backs. I was even more annoyed to hear Caroline dismissed as stupid.

'Ned said to me that he thought that she was extremely intelligent.'

'Yes, well he thinks that every woman he fancies is intelligent. He probably even thinks that Felix is intelligent. And you know, though Ned is probably cleverer than you and me put together, his judgement is extremely poor.'

'So forget all that. Whether Caroline is a moron or a genius, I have to find her. What on earth should I do next?'

'The answer is so obvious that I am surprised that you have had to come round here to hear me say it. *Cherchez l'homme*. Find this Clive Jerkin you have been talking about.'

Yes, it was obvious. At least it was obvious once MacKellar had said it. I had thought that I had been actively engaged in seeking out Caroline when the reverse was actually the truth. I had been doing everything I could to avoid thinking about the place where Caroline must be. Subconsciously I had wanted to delay the moment when I went looking for Clive. It was certain that I would find Caroline ensconced in his flat and when I did find her, then I had sworn myself to do as Trilby had instructed me. I was going to have to offer myself to them as their lover.

I talked with MacKellar a little longer, but I was depressed and he was depressed and we were making each other more depressed. So, though Bryony, his wife, did offer me lunch, I soon left.

It took me a day and a half to find Clive Jerkin. If it had not been for his slightly odd name, I doubt if I should ever have found him. I began my enquiries in the City, but I eventually located him in smart offices on the Brompton Road. I called on him towards the end of a morning. A receptionist sitting at a desk at the end of a marble-flagged hallway stopped me and asked if I had an appointment. I said no, but that my name was Caspar and that I had come about Caroline.

Within a minute of the receptionist ringing through, Clive came hurrying out of his room. He offered me his hand and I reluctantly shook it.

'So you are the Caspar I have been hearing so much about! How splendid! You sounded so extraordinary that I thought she might be making you up. Well, this is ripping! Look, I was about to call it a morning anyway and go off for lunch. There's an Italian restaurant round the corner. My shout.'

Without waiting for my reply, he gleefully ushered me out of the office and we started walking towards the restaurant. This was not at all the sort of confrontation that I had anticipated. Even more unexpected was what came next. We had only walked a few steps when he turned to me and asked,

'How is Caroline by the way?'

'What do you mean? I thought that she was with you.'

He shook his head decisively.

'No. Why should she be with me? I presumed that she had gone off with you to Paris or somewhere, months ago. No? Well then, it seems that she has diddled both of us. What a pair of chumps we are!'

It was a very long lunch. Clive actually sent one of the waiters round to his office to get the secretary to cancel a couple of appointments. First, I got him to talk about his meetings with her and the amateur dramatics. Apparently she was a damned good actress. He had admired her enormously.

'A corking girl! A real English rose! They don't make many like her any more!'

However, apart from a bit of kissing and cuddling, particularly backstage during the rehearsals of *The Vortex*, there had been nothing between them. Caroline had told Clive that she wanted their relationship to be Platonic.

A very intense young man, his eyes, bright and tiny as a sparrow's, darted about all over the place and he was interested in and enthusiastic about absolutely everything. Over the last year or so he had become particularly interested in 'long-hairs and bohos'.

'After I met all you lot in Trafalgar Square with that woman with roses all over her face, I actually went to the Surrealist Exhibition. Gosh, that was fun! I can remember looking at "Second-hand Bookshop no. 1" and admiring its technique, though at that time I didn't know it was by you, of course.'

He leaned across the table and poured me some more wine, before whispering with theatrical confidentiality,

'It's all a bit of a lark though, isn't it? Come on now, you can tell old Clive Jerkin. Just between you and me. I won't tell anyone. Surrealism's jolly interesting, but in the end it's a kind of put on. It's good because it makes chaps like me think, shakes us out of our bourgeois preconceptions and all that, seeing a floppy watch or a furry teacup, but Surrealism is just a joke, isn't it? Don't let me down on this one.'

I shook my head in vigorous denial, though if I thought about certain cases like MacKellar I would have had to admit that Clive was at least partly right.

Clive had actually been reading David Gascoyne and Herbert Read on Surrealism and he wanted to check his reading against mine. However, although he was interested in me as a representative of Surrealism, he was even more interested in me as an individual. Partly it was that Caroline had talked so much about me. But it wasn't just that.

'I find this hard to put into words,' he said. 'But when I was a boy I wanted to run away and join the circus, but I never did. When I left home, I left it for Eton and Oxford. You though are the sort of person who, when he thinks of running away to join the circus, just goes ahead and does exactly that. I'm actually grateful to people like you, for, as the years pass, I often find myself wondering what would have become of me if I had actually joined a circus, or become a painter in Montmartre, or a soldier of fortune in some South American War. Well, then I can check myself against people like you. I mean that you are the me that I might have become, if I had gone down your particular road. Oh dear, I'm afraid that I'm not making much sense.'

I couldn't reciprocate, as I had never dreamed as a child of running away to join a business broker's office and, besides, the only thing I was interested in that day was Caroline. I sat there thinking about how things might have turned out, if, when I had returned to England, I had found Clive and Caroline married. How I would have visited them in their flat. How I would have set about installing myself as the third partner, the gooseberry, in a bizarre *ménage à trois*. How I faced the practicalities of loving Clive as Caroline did and getting his cock between my lips, while he continued to burble enthusiastically about the Bohemian way of life. My imagination has always been strong, but at this point it was beginning to fail.

'Penny for them,' said Clive, who had at last noticed my silence.

'Oh nothing . . . Forgive me, but do you swear that Caroline is not with you and that you don't know where she is?'

'Oh for God's sake! I thought that we'd got all that out of the way. I really haven't the faintest notion where the dear girl is.'

Then, reaching inside his jacket, he produced a wallet and from the wallet a photograph. I found myself staring at the image of a young woman whose plump face was framed by ringlets of curly dark hair.

'That's Sally,' said Clive proudly. 'We are getting married next March.'

A thought struck him.

'Look, I'll get you an invitation to the wedding. You'll be so much more interesting for me to talk to than Sally's ghastly relatives. I love the girl dearly, but her family are another kettle of fish. Do come.'

I smiled non-committally.

'But what about Caroline? Where has she gone and how am I going to find her?' I persisted.

Clive's birdlike head moved left and right and up and down while he thought rapidly.

'Private detectives – a detective agency, that's the answer.'

'Good, but how does one set about finding a detective agency?'

'I have no idea, but I'll put my secretary on to it. Give me your address and I'll be in touch. What fun this is going to be!'

I went on from the restaurant to Ned's place and I walked in on Ned using a cut-throat razor to spread butter on to toast, while talking to a young man whom I did not recognise. I could see Felix on the bed in the next room and guessed that she was sleeping off a hangover.

'You just missed Jenny,' said Ned, pointing me to a chair. 'And Jenny ran into Monica a few days ago. You heard that Monica got involved with those Mass Observation people and has been beetling backwards and forwards between Blackheath and Bolton in that old Tin Lizzie of hers? Well, it's more interesting than we realised. According to Humphrey Jennings, the man she's working with, what they are trying to do is not just to train volunteer observers to survey political opinions and collect statistics on what people are eating and wearing and all that sort of stuff. No, the ultimate aim is to get everyone observing everyone, and everyone to be on the alert, so as to spot the subliminal flickers of imagery emanating from the collective unconscious as it manifests itself in the events of ordinary lived experience. Mass Observation will transform itself into a psychoanalysis of everyday life conducted on a massive scale. I have decided that this ought to be discussed at our next meeting and I am proposing that everyone in the Brotherhood registers with Mass Observation and starts training immediately – taking notes on conversations overheard in pubs, and recording how long the people in the pubs take to get their drinks down, and the point at which they light up their cigarettes – stuff like that. Mass Observation is going to put the quest for the Marvellous on a new and more scientific basis.'

This was absolutely typical of Ned. I had vanished months ago without any warning and during all that time I had not been in touch with Ned or any other member of the group, and yet he showed not the slightest curiosity about why I had gone away or where I had been. Instead he followed his invariable practice of talking about whatever was at the top of his head.

I nodded politely to the unknown young man and only then did Ned say,

'Oh yes, I forgot. Caspar, this is Mark. He's a new recruit to the Brotherhood. He was living in Portugal until recently. He's a – what's the word? – a *monachino*, a specialist in the seduction of nuns.'

'Hello, Mark. Do you do anything else?'

Mark's face was plump, but the cherubic look was belied by the Mephisophelean arching of his eyebrows. In response to my question he only shrugged and smiled.

'He has turned seduction into an art form,' said Ned.

'Why nuns?' I wanted to know.

'Their skin smells nice,' said Mark at last.

Then, having decided that I was going to find Mark difficult to talk to, I turned to Ned.

'I've just been to Germany, Ned, and I have seen the future and it does not like us.'

And I told him about the Exhibition of Degenerate Art and what I had observed of the growing militarisation of Germany, the anti-Jewish laws, the Strength through Joy Movement and so on.

Mark silently left soon after I had started my analysis of how things were in Germany. Ned was interested in the 'degenerate' art of course, but he did not want to hear about the politics and, though he did hear me out, he looked uncomfortable.

'Dark entities that hitherto existed only in gruesome fairy tales are now transforming themselves into real things. The Nazis are similar to us, Ned,' I concluded. 'We and they are both trying to encounter the Irrational, but shake hands with the Irrational and you may not get your hand back.'

All Ned said to this was,

'Come on, we are going on a pub crawl. Tonight I want to drink enough to be able to forget everything I have ever thought.'

While he was out of the room, foraging for some drinking money, Felix sleepily padded in and gave an affectionate peck.

'You sodding arsehole Caspar, where the fucking hell have you been? Still I'm glad you're back. Maybe you can talk to Ned. This orgy business – it seems like it's been

149

dragging on forever – it's becoming an obsession with him. First, he had Adrian researching Dionysian rituals and Bacchic festivals, but now this creep Mark has turned up and it's getting sinister. Ned and he are studying the Marquis de Sade and Antonin Artaud and the two of them are working out how the orgy we are going to have will fit in with the philosophy of the Theatre of Cruelty. Talk to him, Caspar. He listens to you. I don't like the way things are going.'

I nodded absently and when Ned reappeared, jingling coins in his pocket, I went out with him. I did intend to pour cold water on the great orgy project, but first I wanted to talk to him about Caroline and once we were seated with our drinks in the Pillars of Hercules, I told him some of what had passed between Caroline and myself before I left for Germany and how, now that I had returned, she seemed to have vanished into thin air.

'When I lost her love, I failed in the only thing in life where failure really matters. I can't live without her, Ned. Now that I have been without her for three months, I know that I can't live much longer without her. I'll die if I can't have her. I'm considering committing suicide.'

Ned took this pretty calmly.

'Well it might be an option, I suppose, but are you sure that there really is an exit out of this world?'

We gazed into our beers and I pondered Ned's image of life as a sealed nightmare with all ways out locked and bolted. Then I continued,

'I can't understand how she can do this to me – I mean how she can have had such a powerful effect on me, how she obsesses all my thoughts. Half of me can see that she is perfectly ordinary; the other half wants her more than money, fame, happiness or life itself. I spend all my time thinking about how she speaks and moves. I can't understand it.'

'Oh, but that's easy,' said Ned. 'It's all a matter of sexual recognition signals. Your unconscious mind has been responding to Caroline's breasts and buttocks. Thought

150

doesn't come into it; only hormones do. It's like white mice responding to a certain sort of sexual smell or the peahen's desire which is automatically triggered by the peacock's spreading of his tail. And with Caroline, her responses will be unconsciously determined by her reproductive drives and her need to find both the right mate and the right nesting place before she starts producing children. Now the case of the Californian fruit-fly, *dropsophila pseudo obscura*, is really interesting. Scientific observation, conducted on a massive scale, on the breeding habits of the fruit-fly has shown that the female fruit-fly prefers males with rare markings over fruit-flies with markings that are statistically closer to the average. Now you, Caspar, are definitely unusual in looks and everything else; so in principle I would have thought that you had a very good chance.'

'But it's not a Californian fruit-fly that I'm trying to attract.'

I would have liked to have talked more about Caroline, but then we were joined by John Gawsthorne, the eccentric bibliomaniac and horror-story writer. Having been eavesdropping on our conversation from his seat by the bar, he decided to join us. I remember that we talked a bit more about suicide and Gawsthorne quoted Marcus Aurelius: 'Nothing happens to any man that he is not formed by nature to bear'. And then Gawsthorne wanted to talk about my Secondhand Bookshop cycle of paintings and how I decided what titles to paint on to the shelves. Then Ned started to urge Gawsthorne to sign up for the Serapion Brotherhood's orgy,

'Caspar has come back to England just in time. We are holding it at the Dead Rat Club on Thursday next week. At last Mark and I have got it all organised.'

'Is it really necessary, Ned?' I objected.

'Of course it is – and it's just what you need, Caspar. One thing it will do is make you realise that in sexual terms, when you come right down to it, Caroline is just a hole with a lot of flesh around, above and below the hole.

151

She's no different from any other woman. One cunt's the same as another. The cunt is the main thing and all the rest of the body is an optional extra.'

I wanted to object, that if this was really his opinion, why did always he choose to sleep with women with pretty faces, Felix being a case in point? But, turning back to Gawsthorne, Ned continued,

'The orgy will be a major assault on rationality, a return to the power of primitive ritual. The event will have its own destiny, so that all the participants will be caught up in it. Besides, I have a surprise planned, something that will ensure that no one who participates will ever forget the event.'

Then talk drifted on to the other members of the group and Ned was worrying about Oliver and whether he was still alive or not.

Suddenly Gawsthorne jerked his thumb to point to a man drinking alone at the far end of the bar.

'That man's back from fighting for the P.O.U.M. in Spain. Maybe he can tell you about Oliver. I'll introduce you, if you like.'

Nowadays everybody has heard of George Orwell, but in those days before the War and before the publication of *Animal Farm* and *Nineteen Eighty-Four*, he was less well known. Even so, he was quite well known, I suppose, but, since Ned and I only read Surrealist novels and since we were not interested in politics, we had not heard of him. He for his part, on being introduced, gave no sign of ever having heard of us either. Orwell's face was gaunt and craggy – a bit dog-like. Like Clive, he had been to Eton, but unlike Clive he certainly did not look ex-public school. His voice was deep and monotonous. It reminded me a bit of Jorge's manner of speaking. Later I learned that in Orwell's case the way he spoke was the after-effect of a wound in the neck received on the Aragonese front.

He seemed perfectly affable and Ned asked him if he had come across Oliver Sorge anywhere during his time in Spain. We were in luck. Orwell had indeed encountered

Oliver in a bookshop in Madrid. He remembered him well.

'He was looking for an English – Spanish dictionary. He seemed a bit clueless – didn't even have enough money for the dictionary. I met him just the one time. I was with the Trotskyists in the P.O.U.M., while he was in the Anarchist F.A.I. He seemed pretty clueless about Anarchism too. I couldn't make him out. He was all right, I suppose, but terribly nervous and pale, gabbling a bit about a woman he was escaping from. But I wasn't in too good a shape myself. None of us were. You've no idea what it's like out there. It's not just the Fascists who are killing people. The Communists are also killing Trotskyists and Anarchists. Your friend will be lucky to get out alive. You don't know what war is like. But you will learn, for the war we are fighting in Spain will come to England soon and German bombs will rain down on London's scruffy streets and snug little pubs. The bombers will always get through. But everyone in England is trying to pretend we can avoid it all by doing nothing.'

Suddenly Orwell gestured violently upwards with both his hands, as if he was hurling an invisible table into the air.

'This place is asleep! Wake up, England! Wake up!'

Everyone in the pub looked round to see what the shouting was about and then, embarrassed, looked away again.

When Orwell had calmed down, Ned pressed him for any more information that he could give us about Oliver and his present whereabouts. He shook his head.

'I don't thinks so. I've been back in England since June and a lot has happened since then. I just remember thinking what a strange man he was – rather effete.'

Suddenly a look of acute dislike crossed his face.

'I've just worked out who you two are,' he said. 'You're Serapion Brothers. And you,' prodding at my chest aggressively. 'You do those foul paintings. What the fuck do you paint like that for? It's diseased, disgusting, phosphorescent in its putridity. But you call it art and expect us to treat you like an artist. I saw "Secondhand Bookshop no. 4" in a gallery only the other day and it turned my stomach.'

(In 'Secondhand Bookshop no. 4' rivulets of blood and sperm dribble down from the spines of the books to form pools on the dusty floor of the shop.)

Orwell continued,

'It reminded me of some of Salvador Dali's vile stuff, things like the totally repellent "The great Masturbator" and the filthy and diseased "Sodomy of a Skull with a Grand Piano". You and your Surrealist cronies are aesthetic gangsters and parasites. You prey on rich degenerates like Edward James and Jorge Arguelles.'

In response, I was shouting as loud as Orwell,

'I've just come back from Nazi Germany. You'll be pleased to hear the Nazis share your views.'

'Don't talk to me about Nazism or Fascism. I've just come back from Spain. What the hell have you done in the fight against Fascism?'

And now Ned was shouting too,

'If it comes to it, we'll fight against puritanical authoritarians like you, as well as against the Fascists. People like you think that everybody has to be drab and dour like you. A good comrade never laughs. You take it for granted that politics, which is a sort of racket run entirely by people like you, is the be-all and end-all of life, and you have never taken notice of love or mystery as they appear in the world. Your sort of politics represents the death of the soul. Come on Caspar, we are going.'

Two pubs later, we were in the Wheatsheaf in Rathbone Place and I had got around to describing to Ned my struggles to control my hypnagogic images and communicate with them and my ultimate failure in this enterprise.

'I thought that I had her under my power, but that girl, Trilby, lied to me – by omission at least. She should have warned me that, when I returned to England, I would find that Caroline had vanished. Also she should have told me that there was nothing serious between Clive and Caroline. Trilby has to be punished – Trilby and the whole crowd of imagery in my unconscious which she was speaking for. However, I can't work out how to do it. There must be some way of torturing the truth out of my hypnagogic images. The trouble is that they are so elusive and, having no real bodies, I suppose that they are immune to pain.'

'Don't rush things Caspar. I don't think you are being very rational about this. After all it would be crazy to actually punish Trilby, since she wasn't really lying. She was giving you the best advice your unconscious mind could provide on the basis of the information that was available. But your unconscious mind isn't actually an infallible oracle and you can't treat it like that. No, to get better information on Caroline and where she is, you'd have to tap the collective unconscious.'

'Sounds wonderful, but how the hell do I do that?'

'I suppose you must think less and concentrate harder.'

'I don't think that I can concentrate harder than I have been doing in the last few months. And concentrate on what, for God's sake? And where is the collective unconscious when its at home?'

Ned was silent. I hoped that he was casting about for some sort of solution, but I feared that he was so drunk by now that he was simply trying to remember what it was that I had just said. However, eventually he did produce an answer of sorts.

'No, you are not thinking about this the right way. You as an individual don't have a collective unconscious. It is a shared thing. You share it with all the people in this pub and with all the people in London and in the whole world even. What you need to do is conduct a kind of Mass Observation of the collective unconscious.'

Ned was enthusiastic about the prospect that he was now envisaging:

'Obviously you can't interrogate the whole world's unconscious thought processes, but what you can and must do is take as large a sample as possible. Members of the Brotherhood will naturally help, but you will need more than that. You'll have to stop people in the street and offer

155

them money, so that they will let you hypnotise them and get them to communicate under hypnosis with their hypnagogic imagery and answer your questions. It will be pioneering work. You'll be a Magellan or a Pasteur of the collective unconscious.'

I could not share Ned's enthusiasm. It was obvious to me that his scheme was quite impossible. For one thing, he did not realise how utterly exhausting the process of mesmerism was for me. Every time I attempted to hypnotise someone, I could feel my natural electricity draining out of me, leaking out through the eyeballs. A project that demanded the hypnotising of hundreds or even thousands of people would certainly kill me. For another thing, by no means everyone is an hypnagogic subject. Only about a fifth of all adults regularly experience hypnagogic imagery. And surely people in the streets would be suspicious if I went and offered them money if only they would submit to being hypnotised by me? Surely they would say no. MacKellar was right. Ned, for all his brilliance, did not have good judgement.

'I think perhaps I've had enough to drink,' Ned said.

I was startled for, once Ned had embarked on one of these pub crawls, he usually did go to the limit. However, seeing the expression on my face, he continued,

'I'll be sick if I have any more alchohol. I want something else. Let's go to Cable Street.'

On our way out of the Wheatsheaf, Aleister Crowley, whom I had not noticed before sitting by the door, sought to detain me.

'My dear boy! How are you getting on with Dr Aczel's *Exercises in Practical Mesmerism*?' he said with an evil chuckle. However, I escaped his grasp.

Nothing can be more squalid than Cable Street, but within Scrupulous Chen's opium den, as it was in pre-War days, everything was lavish in the oriental manner. Chinese servants in traditional dress glided silently across the thick carpets bearing the long pipes and the rolled and heated pellets of opium, and cups of tea to the clients who sprawled about on cushioned and curtained bunks. '*Les vrais paradis sont les paradis artificiels*'. The stuporous customers that night were an odd mixture of Mayfair socialites and sailors from the docks, plus, a scattering of East-End Chinamen. A couple of women in red satin dresses were dancing together, but no one paid them any attention.

I spoke no more with Ned, but I lay on my bunk and contemplated my hypnagogia, while I pondered the mysteries of Caroline: her first manifestation in a pub on her own, her secret visit to the waxwork museum in Paris, her skills as an actress, her decision to go the Chelsea Arts Ball dressed as Marie Antoinette, her insistence that I wear dark glasses, her real or imagined pregnancy, her vanishing. Surely at some deep level there was a pattern to it all? But before I could find that pattern, my thoughts had taken another tack, for it came to me that it was not she who had decided to hide from me, but I who had driven her away from me, for had I not by my increasingly strange behaviour forced her to reject me? I, only I, was responsible for my failure to control the vast electrical forces that surged through me. I was the master of and sole originator of my misery. Although I had not realised it at the time, it was now obvious to me that the moment that I had begun to study Dr Aczel's *Exercises in Practical Mesmerism* I had entered into a Satanic pact. I recited quietly to myself 'I am counted among them that go down to the pit. I am become like a man without help, free among the dead. They laid me in the lower pit in dark places and in the shadow of death.'

The effects of opium are subtle and they took some time to act on me that night. But eventually I closed my eyes and prepared to set out through the opiate shadow lands in pursuit of Trilby. No sooner had I closed my eyes than I found myself looking on a procession of brides, robed and veiled in white, who followed one another down a wooden spiral staircase. It occurred to me that one of them might have been Trilby, but, with those veils over their faces, it was impossible to tell. At the bottom of the staircase, I found myself in a Chinese theatre. A mandarin stood on stage and, as I looked, at every instant his robes changed shape and colour. Once outside the Chinese theatre, I conceived the plan of visiting the Musée Grevin in order to discover what it was that Caroline had gone to see there. Why I might even encounter Caroline there among the waxworks! However, I was unable to find the entrance to the Musée Grevin and indeed, though I walked amid tall apartment blocks, none of the buildings had doorways. The brides reappeared, walking down the doorless streets and through the French parks and formal gardens. They seemed to be talking amongst themselves, but my lip-reading skills were rendered useless by their veils. Finally I gave up the attempt to find the entrance of the Musée Grevin and composed myself to sleep on the grass in one of the formal parks.

In the morning Ned and I emerged from Scrupulous Chen's Place of Restful Abode and bade each other bleary farewells.

'See you at the orgy,' Ned said. 'Nothing matters more to me than that you should be there.'

Back in Cuba Street I found a postcard waiting for me from Clive. It read:

'The game's afoot! Messrs Meldrum, Franey and Hughes, Private Detectives, 39 Great Portland Street, are the people you need. Keep in touch and let me know how you get on.
                    All the best,
                              Clive.'

Clive seemed to regard the whole thing as a great lark, but I was seriously worried, for I thought it possible that Caroline might be in danger. I did not bother with break-fast. Opium destroys the appetite. I was still feeling rather strange. Even so, I hurried straight off to Great Portland Street.

The legend on the frosted glass door informed me that Messrs Meldrum, Franey and Hughes were chartered members of the British Detectives Association. I knocked and went in. A small man with long dark hair and drooping Dundeary whiskers sat at a desk surrounded by radio equipment. The desk was covered by three telephones, three ashtrays and a sporting paper. Maps and press-cuttings covered every available inch of wall space. One cutting from the *Evening Standard* announced in large letters 'DONALD MELDRUM. THE MAN WITH A THOU-SAND FACES'. The place made me think of what I had heard about the old *Bureau central des recherches surréalistes*, which used to have its office in the Rue de Grenelle, Paris. Reports were brought in by members of the Surrealist movement. These reports, which concerned dreams, strange adventures, striking coincidences and messages from the subconscious, were collated and studied. However, that was back in the 1920s and the whole enterprise had only lasted a year or so.

I stood lost in reverie. Finally, I turned to the man at the desk.

'Which one are you.' I wanted to know.

'Meldrum,' he said softly and gestured me into a chair on the opposite side of the desk. He fumbled about for his cigarettes and lit one, before offering me one as well.

'And you are?'

'Caspar. Just Caspar.'

'Ah.' Meldrum looked apprehensive. He must have thought that 'Caspar' was some sort of criminal alias, adopted to preserve anonymity in my dealings with him.

I asked him about the sort of work he undertook and he said that it was mostly fraudulent insurance claims, but of course there was also the serving of writs, divorce work, checking out the real backgrounds and financial circum-stances of prospective brides and bridegrooms, the detection of pilfering in shops and warehouses and the odd missing person. Meldrum kept laughing nervously as he talked about his work.

I said that the case I was bringing him concerned a missing person and then told as much as I judged it necessary for him to know about Caroline, the circumstances of my meeting her and of her vanishing. Meldrum took notes as I talked. He frequently interrupted to find out how to spell words like Serapion, Surrealist and Eluard and he kept muttering and quietly laughing in nervous amazement, as if he could hardly believe the story I was telling him. When I had finished telling him all that I wanted to tell, he still had questions of his own.

'Was your lady friend . . . er, ah ha ha! . . . a clean thinker?'

'What the hell does that mean?'

'Ah ha! ha! Well, it's not important . . . Was she perhaps a Roman Catholic?'

'No, she wasn't. Why?'

'It saves me having to check the convents.'

'Now, tell me, did she frequent dressmakers and clothes shops?'

'Yes, she did. Quite a lot actually. Is that significant?'

'Ah, ha ha ha! Yes. No. Probably not . . . only there are rumours you see. Ah ha ha, yes!'

'What sort of rumours?'

'Oh you can imagine the sort of thing. A pretty young woman visits a dressmaker. She goes into a cubicle to try on a new dress, but she never re-emerges. A pad of ether is slipped over her face and she is taken out of the shop in a packing case. A well-organised team of white slavers ensures that she is smuggled out of the country and put in a locked cabin on a slow boat bound for Macao or Shanghai. From Macao or Shanghai she will be shipped up country to be sold to one or other of the Chinese warlords. They are said to particularly esteem English ladies and they make use of drugs to turn these ladies into sex-slaves. Ha ha ha! It is of course a remote possibility, but it will need to be investigated. Then again since the Nazi persecution of the Jews got under way, the Jewish fur-traders of Leipzig have moved lock, stock and barrel to London and competition between the various fur companies has become pretty cut-throat. Your Caroline may have become the victim of a trade war. Then – another thing I must ask you – did she take drugs?'

'No, not to my knowledge.'

Then suddenly it strikes me that he is talking about Caroline in the past tense.

'You think that she is dead don't you?'

'Oh! Ah ha ha ha! No, not necessarily. There's no need to get down in the mouth quite yet. But, as you read the papers you will have read of the Torso Murders. I shall certainly want to check the mortuaries.'

(In those days I never read newspapers and, of course, I had not heard of the Torso Murders.)

'In confidence I may tell you that the police are seeking a certain Captain Willoughby who has fled to the Continent, but there is no definite evidence that he is indeed the perpetrator of these ghastly crimes.'

Then Meldrum sat in sober thought for a few moments before asking,

'And in all the time you knew her, did anything strike you as odd about her behaviour?'

'Only two things. First, when we were in Paris, she paid a secret visit to the waxworks museum and, second, in the last few months that I was seeing her, she insisted that I wear dark glasses.'

'And, from what you tell me, you may well have been the last person to see her alive? Ah ha ha!'

That thought had not struck me before. Meldrum seemed even more nervous than usual as he said this. I for my part was nervous too, for I was conscious of all the electrical equipment in the office and of the electricity seeping out of my eyes. Then it came to me as I gazed on Meldrum, twitching and softly giggling to himself on the other side of the desk, that he was entertaining the possibility that I had killed Caroline in a fit of jealous rage. Presumably in this scenario, I had come to him either to throw suspicion off from myself, or because I was genuinely an amnesiac and had no memory of how I had slaughtered

161

her and disposed of the body. Seeing my gaze, Meldrum looked hastily up at the ceiling.

'The Case of the Vanishing Typist! Ah ha ha! Yes. It certainly sounds intriguing. A guinea a day plus expenses and ten guineas in advance. Have you a photo of Miss Begley?'

I passed one to him, together with the money.

'What a doll! Why she really is as beautiful as you said she was!'

Then, as he hurried me out of his office,

'You'll get my first report within the next ten days.'

On Thursday I met Clive. He treated me to an expensive fish luncheon at Wheelers and, after getting every detail he could out of me about my experience in the office of Meldrum, Franey and Hughes, he wanted to talk about art and politics. He was disappointed to find out that I was not a Bolshevik, for he had rather assumed that all avante-garde artists were Bolsheviks and that long-hairs were united in believing that Russia was the country of the future. Not only was I not a Bolshevik, but I refused to talk about politics. So Clive was forced to confine himself to art. As was apparent from our previous encounter, Clive was intrigued by Surrealism, but he did not take it altogether seriously. He kept trying to get me to agree that the way forward lay with abstract art, with the work of people like Ben Nicholson, Henry Moore and the members of the Unit One group. I told him that I was not interested in ways forward or the sort of mechanical progress he was envisaging. I was really more interested in movement backwards and downwards.

For reasons that will soon become apparent my memory of events in those last few weeks in 1937 has suffered and luncheon with Clive was the last thing of the slightest significance that I can remember happening before the evening of the orgy in the Dead Rat Club.

Chapter Twelve

There is no need I think to give a full and detailed account of the orgy at the Dead Rat Club. It features in all the social histories together with other scandals of the inter-war years: the Stavisky affair, the manslaughter of Billie Collins, the kidnapping of the Lindbergh baby, the Philipino egg scare, the defrocking of the Rector of Stiffkey and the Chu Chin Chow murder. At this point I have only to give my own personal impressions of what happened that night and explain how it in turn led on to the strange things which followed.

A backroom at the club had been commandeered and a thick black carpet laid specially for the event. The room was not particularly large, barely large enough, even with all its furniture removed, to accommodate the thirty or so people who assembled that night. Norman at the bar served oysters and champagne while we waited for everyone to assemble. Almost every member of the Brotherhood was there. Since we were a bit short of women, Ned and Jorge had brought up the numbers by hiring some high-class prostitutes for the night. There was a lot of smoking and joking, but no one was really listening to the jokes. Everyone was nervous, but the prostitutes were especially nervous – and also very suspicious. Apart from the prostitutes, there were a few surprise appearances; Pamela and Norman had both decided to participate. The man from the BBC whom MacKellar had talked to at the International Surrealist Exhibition was there together with his girl-friend. Most unexpected of all, Scrupulous Chen was also present, freely handing out cocaine and benzedrine on a first come, first served basis. Chen was a handsome man and a smart dresser and I caught several of the women gazing at him with interest.

Some odd bits of apparatus had been brought along for

the event. Jenny Bodkin arrived brandishing a dildo shaped like a long black rat. MacKellar and Bryony came with a tray of tea cups which they said would do for a sperm-tasting session. However, the idea of purchasing sleep masks and prosthetic limbs had been abandoned as silly. Instead the lights in the room with the black carpet would be switched off and we, after stripping outside, would blindly make our way into the darkened room.

Ned gave us a pep talk beforehand about the liberating power of group sex in the dark. It was the democratic way of making love, a way which gave the fat, the thin, the ugly and the old equal chances in the sexual lottery. But Ned went on to make it clear that he was not all that much exercised by thoughts of erotic democracy. His ambition went beyond that and he looked forward to the divine madness that would be unleashed by our couplings and which would make itself manifest to us in the room. Ned was shaking as he talked and I thought that he was excited as never before by this demonstration of his power over us.

Then we all stripped and leaving our clothes in nervous, untidy bundles all over the floor, one by one we passed behind a heavy curtain and entered the pitch-black room. (As I stepped beyond the curtain, I remember thinking that it felt a little like dying.) I went in just after Pamela, for my first thought was to catch up and tangle with her if I could. However, once inside the room she seemed to vanish and so I began to edge my way around with my back to the wall. I had not gone very far before a hand caught at my ankle and then two hands reached up at me pulling me onto the floor. I made no attempt to resist, but fell awkwardly and found my face pressed against what was evidently a soft, smooth woman's thigh. I began to kiss and lick at this thigh, working my way up in a leisurely fashion. But I had not got very far with this arbitrarily chosen task, before a shrill screaming rose from the far side of the room. I remember that my first response was a feeling of irritation at some stupid bitch who'd lost her nerve, but the screaming continued; its shrilling filled the darkness and seemed to ripple back from the walls, and soon I could hear that more than one voice was screaming. Several people were shouting for the light to be switched on.

The light came on. I looked across the room and, having looked, closed them instantly, but the horrific image was still there trapped on my eyelids amidst clouds of phosphene; Ned sat slumped against the wall and women knelt at either side of him. His head was at odd angle and blood jetted out from his neck, drenching his torso and spraying the naked women and the walls.

When I opened my eyes again, I discovered that it had been Felix's thigh which I had been kissing. She was now shakily trying first to get to her feet and then stumble across the sprawled bodies towards Ned. She was wailing,

'Oh, the fucker! Oh the poor fucker!'

Of course the thing I now lament more than anything else in life is losing Caroline, but, after that the thing I regret most and the thing I am most ashamed of is my failure to stay with Felix as she wept over the corpse of Ned that night. However, I did not and I cannot go back and relive that night – and thank God for that. Norman was shouting that everyone who could get out should get out, put some clothes on, any old clothes and run for it, for Pamela had gone to phone for the police.

There was such a scrimmage at the door, I feared that none of us might escape in time, but in only a few moments I was dressed and out in the night air. I walked vigorously for a while, until I found myself at a tea stall in Convent Garden and I rested there a bit and idly listened in to the conversations of the porters and taxi drivers. Then I walked back towards St James's Park and paced about the park until the dawn came up. Although the park at night appeared to be empty, I could not allow myself to be deceived. There were eyes everywhere – the eyes of Mass Observation and in more recent months, as the threat of war came closer, the eyes of Nazi spies as well. Everyone knew that the Nazis already had their spies in place in

London. I was alert to the dangers of their gaze and yet not afraid, for my eyes too were powerful. Why just by looking at a mirror I could make smoke rise from its surface! By the time the sun rose I knew what I should do. Ned's scheme for sampling and interrogating the collective unconscious was just screwy, like so many of the poor man's now aborted ideas. Even so, I thought that it might be possible through the power of my gaze to force someone close to Caroline to reveal either something that they were deliberately concealing from me or even something that they were not conscious of knowing.

Brenda arrived early at the office of the fur merchant and stood waiting for someone to come and unlock the door. I arose from behind some dustbins where I had been hiding.

'Hullo Brenda. Remember me?'

She shrieked, so I attempted to calm her.

'I'm not going to do you any harm. I just want you to look into my eyes. Look into my eyes Brenda.'

The stupid girl would not listen. She just kept struggling to escape from my grasp and she was still shrieking. I had had enough of shrieking.

'I conjure you to look into my eyes, Brenda. Don't be unreasonable, Brenda.'

Although I was trying to keep my voice soothing and monotonous, I was conscious of its jagged quality. Anyway, before I had made any progress at all with my attempts to mesmerise her, I was attacked from behind. It was Mr Maitland. He was quite old and I might have fought him off, had he not been joined shortly afterwards by a policeman.

I was taken to Bow Street and charged with assault and resisting arrest. When I came before the magistrate and the question of bail was raised, it seemed wisest in the circumstances not to mention the name of anyone in the Brotherhood, and the only other person I could think of was Clive. Clive arrived with a lawyer and a little later he had a doctor round at the police station too. Naturally I am a little confused about the sequence of events around this time and I'm not sure whether the bail was ever paid.

I remember travelling up to Hampstead in a limousine with Clive and the doctor. Clive was flushed and excited. Perhaps this was the next best thing to running away to join the circus? He said that we ought to move fast, before my name was connected with 'The Outrage at the Dead Rat Club'. So, on his doctor's advice, I signed the committal papers which authorised my confinement in the Milton Clinic.

At this point in my narrative I have taken a break. I have just been downstairs in my house in Waterloo on my hands and knees in the bathroom sniffing the linoleum floor. If I ever have need to remember how it felt in the clinic, then I only have to sniff some linoleum. Its smell has the power to take me back across the years – better yet if its smell is coupled with that of urine – then I am back there, walking down those lime-green corridors. There seemed to be more corridors than rooms in the clinic and often a door, when opened, opened not into a room but into yet another corridor.

I was not at first aware of the corridors, for I spent the first few weeks of my confinement under heavy sedation in a room, or cell I suppose I should call it. I was in a straitjacket, though I can't really think that there was any need for that. The doctors and nurses used to confer on the far side of the cell, whispering about my case, quite unaware that my skill as a lip-reader allowed me to read on their mouths the strange things that they were saying about me. The word 'paranoiac' came up quite frequently and this made me think of Salvador Dali's famous paranoiac-critical method of painting and his way of transforming swans into elephants with only a few brush strokes. I recalled Dali saying that 'the only difference between me and a madman is that I am not mad'. Well it was like that with me also, for I could see that, as far as the doctors were concerned, I had all the symptoms of madness, and yet reflecting on myself objectively I was sure that I was not mad. Indeed, it struck me as somewhat unjust that I, a mesmerist of indubitable talent, should be confined and humiliated in a straitjacket, while over in Germany another great mesmerist, Herr Hitler, was not only at large but was being saluted and cheered by huge crowds.

My earliest trips out of the cell were on a trolley which took me to an empty ward in the clinic where electro-convulsive therapy was administered. The first time that it happened I was actually looking forward to it, for I was aware how much electricity I had lost through leakage from my eyeballs in the past months. Electro-convulsive therapy seemed a good way of getting myself recharged. Perhaps it was, but after those sessions I became aware of great holes in my memory – of windows looking out on to emptiness, of people without faces and of street-names without streets to go with them. (I should have called this, my book, *Memoirs of an Amnesiac*, only the musician Eric Satie took that title for his own.) I felt that I was losing electricity rather than gaining it and very soon I began to dread my visits to the empty ward. I was supposed to be unconscious when the shocks were applied, for I was strapped down and gassed before the electrodes were at-tached to the head, but in reality there was always some part of me deep inside that was conscious of what was happening, so that I felt the electrodes attached to the skull, the rubber gag placed between my teeth, and my body convulse under the straps as the searing, skull-shattering pain raged through me. I would have confessed to anything to end that torture, but I was not quite conscious enough to be able to do so and, besides, my torturers were not interested in confessions.

Apart from electro-convulsive therapy, the other thing that I was afraid of was Dr Aczel. My reasoning was as follows: it was trouble with my eyes and my study of Dr Aczel's *Exercises in Practical Mesmerism* which had led to my hospitalisation. What could be more likely than that, as the clinic came to grips with my strange case, they would get in touch with Dr Aczel, the leading authority on mesmerism as well as, in a sense, the author of my misfortunes? I could imagine Dr Aczel sitting in an office, in some part of the hospital which was inaccessible to me, and letting his burning eyes range over my case notes. When he was ready he would come for me, entrance me and gaze deep into me as one gazes into an abyss.

During my confinement in the Milton Clinic I had to abandon my own exercises in mesmerism. When I wrote a little way back of 'reflecting on myself', I meant this metaphorically, since for over a year I never saw a mirror. There were no mirrors in any part of the hospital I was allowed into. I suppose the fear was that a patient might smash one and then use a broken shard to slash at his wrist. I tried instead to use my reflection on the surface of my bathwater as a substitute, but, since my baths were always supervised, I was unable to concentrate.

After only a few days, I was released from the straitjacket and then, three or four weeks later, I received my first visitors. The very first was Clive and then, after I had told him how to get in touch with her, Jenny Bodkin, and later yet, as the weeks turned into months, Clive sometimes came with his new wife, Sally. Through Clive and Jenny, I was able to follow the aftermath of the gruesome affair at the Dead Rat Club. The police had arrived about ten minutes after the departure of most of the participants, but they detained those who remained on the suspicion of being accessories to murder. The evening papers on the day after speculated wildly about the ritual sacrifice of a Surrealist philosopher-artist by drug-crazed orgiasts. However, the cut-throat razor beside Ned's body had belonged to Ned and a search of Ned's flat and an examination of his papers soon revealed that Ned had been planning the manner of his exit from the world for over a year.

Ned's jottings showed how, influenced by his study of the Theatre of Cruelty, he had envisaged his suicide as a kind of educational tableau. One notebook in particular began with a quotation from André Breton blocked in large red letters: 'THE WORD SUICIDE IS A MISNO-

MER: THE PERSON WHO KILLS IS NOT THE SAME AS THE PERSON WHO IS KILLED'. During my confinement, I thought a great deal about this verdict of Breton's without ever really feeling that I understood it. Also, in the statement which Felix made to the police, she said that she thought that Ned had committed suicide because he was afraid of death. I had difficulty in understanding that too, but I think that perhaps his was a fear akin to vertigo – the latter being an affliction whose sufferers are not afraid of the heights as such, but rather they are afraid of themselves and their potential readiness to hurl themselves off from those heights. One thing that did emerge from Ned's rambling writings on the subject of suicide was that he considered it to be, as it were, built into the philosophy and practice of surrealism – the natural end towards which all Surrealists tend. The earliest writings of the French group reveal that Breton, Aragon and Eluard were morbidly fascinated by the sinister bridge of suicides in the Parc des Buttes-Chaumont. In his *Paris Peasant*, Aragon speculates that some who hurled themselves from that bridge to their death had had no previous intention of killing themselves, 'but they found themselves suddenly tempted by the abyss'. A little further on in the same chapter, Aragon begins to speculate on the mysterious affinities between vertigo and desire . . .

As early as 1919 Jacques Vaché had killed himself with an overdose of opium. Then Jacques Rigaut shot himself through the heart in 1929, in 1933 Raymond Roussel committed suicide in curious circumstances, and two years later René Crevel, after leaving a note on his desk, saying 'I am disgusted with everything', gassed himself. Then in 1937 Ned Shillings's long affair with the Marvellous had ended in a blood-boltered *acte gratuit*. So it seemed at first glance, but thinking back on things and particularly on our conversation in The Pillars of Hercules, it has crossed my mind, that perhaps Ned really did believe that it was impossible to leave this world simply by committing suicide and perhaps he envisaged himself spending the rest of eternity with thirty naked and copulating people in a darkened room from which there was no exit. Who knows?

Of course, I in my cell in the clinic had a somewhat different perspective on the history of Surrealism from the one which I think that Ned had ended up with. My vision was perhaps unduly solipsistic, but I saw Surrealism's beginning and end as both being in the madhouse, for Surrealism's precise origins were in the mental asylum in Saint-Dizier where André Breton had worked as a medical orderly during the First World War. It was there that he first became fascinated with the insanely beautiful utterances of the mad. This in turn had led Breton on to study the theories of Dr Janet on hysteria and prepared the way for the elaboration of the aesthetic of convulsive beauty as well as foreshadowing Breton's celebrated love affair with the madwoman Nadja.

Anyway, to return to the aftermath of the orgy, Norman was charged with keeping a disorderly house and sentenced to two years. Scrupulous Chen, most unfairly, was found guilty of drugs dealing and got ten years. A couple of prostitutes were bound over. Although Felix was one of those who had stayed by Ned's body, she did not appear in court. Her father was something senior in the Air Force and she was taken back to the family home in Northern Ireland. I never saw her again.

Apart from Clive and Jenny, the earliest of my visitors was Donald Meldrum. I did not recognise him at first.

'Why you've shaved your moustache off!'

'It was a false moustache in the first place.' He smiled apologetically. 'I got in by pretending to be your cousin. Don't let me down on that one. I thought I owed it to you to make a report — not that I really have anything to report. Neither of Caroline's parents would talk to me, nor would that hysterical young woman, Brenda, but I was successful in interviewing Jim and Enid from the office. I also impersonated a civil servant from the Ministry of Labour and talked to Maitland on the telephone. I talked to the Begleys' neighbours, but Caroline's parents seem to keep themselves pretty much to themselves. I paid a lad to watch their house for a few days, but that produced no leads. I've covered the morgues and, though one can never be sure, it does not seem that any body corresponding to Caroline's has turned up. I also did the hospitals and I've put an advertisement in the *Chronicle* asking for anyone with information to get in touch with me. No one has. There are other possible lines of enquiry, but in the circumstances I think that we must consider the Case of the Vanishing Typist closed.'

I learned later that Meldrum had returned my deposit of ten guineas, leaving it with the clinic's registrar for safekeeping.

There were other visitors. Jorge came accompanied by Jenny. Jorge was horribly uncomfortable and he seemed to think that madness might be infectious, something that could be caught from inadequately scrubbed linoleum. He had come to say goodbye.

'I am going back to Argentina. England is no bloody fun anymore.'

I was sorry to hear this, for Jorge had been the best customer for my paintings. It was from Jorge that I learned that Antonin Artaud, friend of the Surrealists and pioneer of the Theatre of Cruelty, had also been confined in a lunatic asylum, only a few weeks after me. The rumour from Paris was that he was being given electro-convulsive therapy, also just like me. I wrote to him first to a hospital in Rouen and then to Rodez, but I never received any reply. My letters to him have been published in a long article in the *Times Literary Supplement* and I do not need to repeat their contents here.

The strangest visit was from MacKellar. He staggered in smelling strongly of cider.

'Hail Caspar!' he said. 'I hand you bananas.'

And he presented me with a bunch of bananas.

'MacKellar! It's good to see you. How are you? How are the others? Is there any news of Oliver?'

172

'Information about I is not good.' he said. 'Post-orgy. Bryony said *adios*. As for my books, a man who is publishing books says my books not good. Our pals all *kaput* or not around and our conjuring pal is still in Spain I think.'

After only a few seconds of this, I was wondering if the reason for MacKellar's presence in the ward was that he had just been admitted to it as a patient. Alternatively, had someone told him that the only way to talk to lunatics was in lunatic language?

'Thanks for the bananas.' I said. 'But why bananas?'

MacKellar's forehead creased in anguish, as he struggled to answer.

'I go to a man who has fruit which I want to buy. I want not this fruit, but . . . but a fruit which is small and which *vino* contains. *Vino* is of this fruit. Robin Hood's colour is this fruit's colour. But I could not say it to any man who has fruit, so I buy bananas for you. I could say bananas.'

'Jolly good of you. Thank you.' I said. 'Do I gather that *Blind Pew Looks Back* is not getting anywhere and that you are writing something else?'

He nodded enthusiastically.

'I am. I hail it *Irrationality's Triumph*. It is about a mandarin in China who cannot say particular words for, if that mandarin says particular words, mortality triumphs. With this book about a magic mandarin, I will be rich, oh so rich. A man who is publishing books will buy it. But Caspar, your insanity, how is it? And this hospital, how is it?'

While MacKellar was vigorously and excitedly clawing the air for more words, I was dopily baffled. Sedatives and electro-convulsive therapy had made me stupid, and it took me almost half an hour to work out that, after his failures with *Blind Pew Looks Back* and *Dentist of the Old West*, MacKellar had embarked on another project, to write a full-length novel set in Imperial China which would be composed entirely of words which did not contain the letter 'e' – that is to say he was going to write a

173

lipogrammatic novel. In order to get in practice for the writing, MacKellar was trying to go about not using the letter 'e' in conversations as well. The reason that he had purchased bananas from the fruit-monger was that he had not been able to ask for grapes. By the time I had worked all this out, the strain of conducting conversation in this manner was taking its toll on MacKellar and his initial vigour was quite exhausted. Soon afterwards he bade me a bleary farewell and shuffled out of the ward. Not only had he smelt of cider, but his overcoat, which he never took off, had been heavily stained.

'I will visit again soon,' had been his parting lie.

He never reappeared. I wish I had better memories of my last sighting of him, for this was pitiful. Our leader and teacher, Ned, had died violently by his own hand, but MacKellar, fooling about and fenced in by his self-imposed 'e'-lessness, had been quite unable to talk about it.

Finally, there was the visitor who did not come. Whenever I was told that some one was coming to see me, I became excited, thinking that it might be Caroline come to see me and take me by the hand and take me back to bed in Cuba Street. But with this excitement, there was also fear – fear and shame that she should ever discover me reduced to such a strait.

I forgot to mention that after a couple of months I was moved from my solitary cell into a ward with six other patients. Although I was encouraged to play ping-pong and cards with the other patients, I found that I preferred a solitary card game, my own special version of patience which took a very long time, for before I turned each card over I tried to will its suit and value and to force the random order of the pack to conform to my will. I would sit at the card table and imagine my will bearing down on the next card and compelling it to become, say, the four of spades.

At other times I would stare out of the window and I would try to use my mental forces to form the clouds into the shapes I wanted. Cloud-sculpting might be the art of the future, I thought. In principle, these sorts of exercises were no different from my interior drills in which I marshalled and shaped my hypnagogic imagery. (Indeed I had long thought that hypnagogia's fundamental message was that, contrary to superficial appearances, the real world was in fact just as fluid and submissive to manipulation by the enlightened mind as hypnagogia was.) In practice however, I found that I was rarely successful with my drilling of cards and clouds. They were disobedient and regularly slipped out from my control. Indeed after some months I was forced to conclude that I had not really been having any success at all. At the risk of repeating myself here, I must emphasise that Surrealism is not, as most people think, an artistic movement; it is a scientific method of investigation in which experiment plays a leading part. My experiments in the clinic and their failure led me to the objective conclusion that the universe was not after all constructed around me, as my presence at its centre had at first led me to surmise. It was a blow and it took me a long time to recover from this discovery.

The clinic's staff also encouraged me take up art therapy and here they had more success. Just the smell of turpentine and oils had the power to lift my spirits. I had not painted at all since before I left for Germany. The last painting I had completed had been my miniature portrait of Caroline. Since then my mind had been on other things and besides my hands had been shaking too badly for me to think of handling a paintbrush. In the clinic, however, sedatives slowed the tremor down.

Now that I picked my brush up again after so long an interval I found that both my style and my technique had altered. My brushwork was much looser and impressionistic and there was a naive, almost childlike quality to the pictures. Although the meticulous Flemish brushwork technique was abandoned, I still worked in miniature, filling the picture surface with tiny emblems and scraps of writing. Most of the work I did during this period is in the Prinzhorn Collection today.

The best known work is also by quite a long way the largest. When I started 'How to Get About in London', I crazily thought that I might be able to sell it to London Transport and that it could be reproduced on posters in the Underground stations and that this would help me get work as a commercial artist. However, as I toiled over this huge canvas, other preoccupations took over. 'How to Get About in London' is a vast pictorial map, at the centre of which, located in a maze of streets filled with billowing fog, one beholds the face of Caroline. Her face is situated roughly in the area of Holborn. I have painted myself behind bars in the clinic in Hampstead, but then there is another me whom I have painted smoking opium in Cable Street and who is dreaming the rest of this autobiographical map. The spine of London runs up from Trafalgar Square, up Charing Cross and on up Tottenham Court Road, to Euston and beyond. Those streets which are not filled with fog are filled by quotations in tiny, tiny writing and these quotations intersect at crossroads. For example, Aldous Huxley's 'An intellectual is someone who has found something more interesting to think about than sex' runs along Oxford Street to the top of Charing Cross Road at which point it shares the last word, 'sex', with a quotation from André Breton which runs up Charing Cross Road and across into Tottenham Court Road. 'I wish I could change my sex as I change my shirt'.

Again, 'It' is boldly lettered at the centre of Seven Dials and from this 'It' run a whole series of quotable streets: 'It is certainly true that my ideal was simply to become a husband, to live solely for being married. And lo and behold, while I despair of attaining that goal, I become an author, and, who knows, maybe a ranking author' (Kierkegaard); 'It is necessary to think in opposition to the brain' (Gaston Bachelard); 'It is not worth living if one has to work' (André Breton) and so on, round the dial. I have also painted in some of the Tube stations, but in place of the legend 'London Underground' I have written over the entrances 'A dream is a tunnel running under reality' (Reverdy).

The purpose of these quotations is to help the foreign visitor find his way about the city. I am proud of this my masterpiece, for it is an innovative blend of cartography, literature and personal reminiscence. As far as the latter element is concerned, one sees the pub in Soho where De Quincey met the prostitute Anne and where I met Caroline. Caroline's house in Putney shut up and barricaded, Aleister Crowley standing outside the Wheatsheaf waiting for someone, a female vampire looking out of the window of Oliver's garret in Tottenham Court Road, the New Burlington Galleries in Bond Street, Clive waving from his office in Brompton Street, Meldrum, Franey and Hughes conferring in their office in Great Portland Street, and Jorge's 'Chariot' parked beside Green Park. The city as a whole is dominated by two features; first a vast Madame Tussaud's Waxwork Museum to the north of Caroline's face and, secondly, to the south, on the site where the Dead Rat Club should be, one sees a barren hill surmounted by an empty cross round which weeping women kneel. Then, beneath Soho's Golgotha, one sees that St James's Park is circular and can be rotated to facilitate chance encounters. Finally, at each corner of the map there is an archangel with puffed-up cheeks. The job of these creatures is to blow people together and to blow them apart again.

There is a smaller companion picture, 'London After the Bombing' in which I am accompanied by a woman veiled in white and together we contemplate a similar map of London, but one in which everyone else is dead, most of the buildings are ruined, and the sayings on the streets have buckled and become jumbled-up word-salads. Other works produced in this period include 'Thought-Forms Copulating', in which naked human forms cover every square inch of the picture surface in a perfect sort of organic tesselation and 'Mr Sorge Fights Against Fascism', in which Oliver, in a top hat and opera cloak, stands on the battlements of a castle and confronts a great billowing cloud of darkness, from out of which one can dimly discern a veiled woman emerging. Finally, I should mention 'The Eyes of Dr Aczel' in which men and women are shown trapped in the huge, hemispherical eyeballs of the mad doctor.

Once the electro-convulsive therapy had been discontinued, I found that I was neither happy nor unhappy in the clinic. I made no attempt to escape, though I am sure that I could have used my mesmeric powers to do so. By the end of my first year, I was allowed a great deal of freedom to wander about in the building and the grounds, but it was only some way into the second year of my confinement that I secured access to a mirror. What I saw in the mirror was disturbing, for I saw a face that was exactly like my face, but I knew that it was not mine, not the real me. It lacked my identity. I did not know whose face it was, so I left it, my double's face I suppose, trapped in the mirror. This was not the disaster it might have been, for by then I had abandoned all thought of developing my mesmeric powers any further. Instead I painted, played patience and, for the first time in my life, read the newspapers. I followed the developing situation in Europe with growing anxiety – the Spanish government's retreat to Barcelona, the formation of the Axis, the Anschluss with Austria, the Czechoslovak crisis, Munich, the collapse of the Spanish Republic, the Danzig crisis, the German invasion of Poland, Britain's declaration of war and the Phony War period. By the winter of 1939–40 I had become desperate to leave the clinic, for I could imagine what would happen when the Germans came marching into London. Doctors attached to the S.S. would tour the city's hospitals and asylums and all the degenerates, cretins and madmen in those places would be rounded up and killed by injections of cyanide. Notoriously that was Nazi policy.

In a panic, I started painting studiously ordinary portraits of hospital staff and pictures of flowers and trees in the grounds. On occasions when I thought I was not being observed, I used to walk about talking to myself and practising being normal.

'How are you?'

'I am well, thank you.'

'What weather we are having!'

'Yes. The weather interests me enormously – no, I mean to say that I am only quite interested in the weather.'

And so on.

I need not have worried. Early in 1940, we heard the news that the Milton Clinic was being requisitioned for wartime purposes. Everyone who could conceivably be discharged from the hospital was being discharged. I was among those judged fit enough to be returned to society.

Chapter Thirteen

The Milton Clinic was a time machine. When I had stepped into it, England was at peace, but when I walked down from Hampstead into central London in the spring of 1940, I found that I was walking through a city many of whose features were quite strange to me: barrage balloons like dinosaurs stranded in the air, parks dug up for vegetable gardens, and Georgian terraces stripped of their railings. Indeed, so strange was the city, in which all the street names and sign posts had been removed, that I occasionally lost my way.

To look at things in more personal terms, I had admitted myself to the clinic in 1937, on the day after my participation at the last ever meeting of the Serapion Brotherhood. In my years as an artist before my hospitalisation, I hardly ever spoke to anyone who was not of the Brotherhood. Now, however, I emerged into a world in which Ned was dead, Oliver missing presumed dead, Manasseh in the United States, Jorge in Argentina, Felix in Northern Ireland, and MacKellar, after his divorce and the sale of his home, gone God knows where, but possibly to the doss house. Others like Mark and Jenny had been called up and dispersed to barracks and airfields in the provinces. So one could say with Malory's King Arthur, 'such a fellowship of good knights shall never be together in no company'. Surrealism was on the run all over the world. Breton and Tanguy had escaped to New York, but after the Fall of France other Surrealists were reported to be held in concentration camps and there was no certain knowledge of Paul and Nusch Eluard. Born in the wake of one World War, Surrealism had expired at the onset of the next.

The lease on my house in Cuba Street had been surrendered soon after my admission into the clinic and the kind and efficient Jenny had supervised the storage of most of my possessions in one of the Harrods warehouses. Having nowhere else to go, I went to stay with Clive and Sally in their big house near Woking. I was there for a few weeks while I sorted myself out and looked for somewhere to rent. It was really Sally I stayed with, for we saw little of Clive. He had succeeded in his aim of becoming a millionaire before the age of thirty, but, when the war came, he had thrown up his business-broking with alacrity and wangled himself into the R.A.F. I think that Sally was actually relieved at seeing less of her husband, for, when he did appear, his indiscriminate enthusiasm for absolutely everything and his curiosity about anything was exhausting. He would turn up burbling about the aerodynamics of the Spitfire and rudders, flaps and aerodynamics and about his other recent enthusiasm, *Finnegan's Wake* and, after a few hours on these topics he would drop them and cross-question me about the hospital. What was it like to be a mental patient? What were the doctors like? What had the other patients been like? I was vague and my answers disappointed him. The trouble was that I had paid very little attention to the other inmates of the clinic, for I had found them dull and ordinary by comparison with my old companions in the Serapion Brotherhood.

A few weeks after my release from hospital, I came before a call-up board. The result was a foregone conclusion and the whole thing should only have taken ten minutes, only no one on the board could understand how it was that I had no surname and we spent hours going round and about the issue. The end of the matter, however, was what it always was going to be. I was categorised as grade 4 – unfit for service in any military capacity whatsoever. But, if I was not to become a soldier, what was to become of me?

I could not pick up where I had left off, producing Surrealist canvases and hunting for commissions to illustrate books. Artists' materials were now very hard to find and almost the only place where one could buy brushes of any sort was in ironmongers's shops. My best patron, Jorge

Arguelles, was now living on the other side of the world, as was Edward James. There was hardly a gallery left open in London, and, even if there had been, people were not buying paintings any more. That was unpatriotic. You were supposed to buy war bonds or something. As for books, the production of books had been seriously cut back and those which were being produced were being produced in conformity with wartime economy standards.

In the end, I found work through chance meetings in pubs. The War was a great time for chance meetings. It was as if all the cards on the table had been thrown up in the air and then, for the first time ever, they were thoroughly shuffled. Everyone was on the move – service-men in transit, couriers, refugees, evacuees – and people were always meeting one another in unexpected contexts. I lived in daily expectation of re-encountering Caroline serv-ing in a soup kitchen, or in a darkened railway carriage or an air-raid shelter. In wartime, such a meeting was possible – no, even probable. Surely, it was likely that I had already just missed her vanishing round a corner or climbing on to a bus? Of course, I longed for such a meeting, but there was also a part of me which dreaded it, for I had emerged from hospital impotent. It might have been the shock of the orgy, in which death and sex had been so indissolubly fused together, that had desexed me, or it might have been all the electro-convulsive therapy and the sedatives. I do not know. By contrast, the excitement of war, the feeling that one did not know where one would be tomorrow or even if one would be alive tomorrow, had heightened the sexual temperature of most of those around me and I would often stumble across lovers copulating on bomb sites. In my asexual state, I would contemplate them with a sort of scientific detachment before walking on.

Though I did not find Caroline, I did find employment by hanging around in pubs. I ran into Roland Penrose in a pub in Charlotte Street and he found me work with a film director friend of his. Originally I was taken on to paint the flats, but my face was my fortune. With my blonde hair and hatchet-faced profile, I was the very man they needed to play a sinister S.S. officer. *Darkness Over Lublin*, a film about the German occupation of Poland and the Polish resistance, was shot at the Ealing Studios. The sets swarmed with Polish and East European Jewish actors and advisors. A film is so like a dream – or, in the case of *Darkness Over Lublin*, a nightmare – and I found a peculiar pleasure in impersonating a creature of nightmare. The director loved the way I could make my eyeballs bulge and glitter.

Rehearsals and shooting lasted only six weeks and that was the beginning and end of my career as an actor. However, by then I had met Paul Nash, also in a pub, and he remembered me from pre-War exhibitions. He very kindly provided me with an introduction to Kenneth Clark and Clark in his turn got me taken on by the War Artists' Commission. Thus I became one of a group which included Graham Sutherland, Henry Moore and Edward Ardizzone. Our job was to make an artistic record of the War. I received maintenance, £1 a day for each day spent away from home, a warrant for third-class rail travel and a small sum for each painting completed, this sum being fixed in advance according to the size of the canvas.

My commissioning by the W.A.C. coincided with the beginning of the Blitz in 1940 and this coincidence provided me with my artistic mission. I became a painter of ruins and firestorms and I thought of myself as the heir to Piranesi and Mad John Martin. I left my Surrealist box of tricks unopened for the remainder of the War. The Blitz provided its own Surrealist effects – a white horse galloping around inside a burning meat market and displaying all its teeth in a panicked, mirthless grin, a girl in a blue dress emerging with her skipping rope from clouds of black smoke and skipping calmly by, and the facades of buildings curving and distending like the sets of *The Cabinet of Dr Caligari*. Everywhere I walked I saw staircases which led nowhere, baths suspended apparently in mid-air, brick waterfalls flowing out of doorways and objects jumbled incongruously together in conformity with Lautréamont's aesthetic prescription; 'Beautiful as the chance meeting of an umbrella and a sewing machine on a dissecting table'. Long tongues of flame would leap out of every window of some great office block, like demons being expelled from a disenchanted castle. I was not really very aware of the Germans or their bombers: I felt rather that it was the fire that was our real enemy while water was our ally. At times I toyed with the notion that Britain had entered the War on the wrong side and that we should have allied with the glamorous fire against the dull and squelching water.

The W.A.C. was keen that I should get to ruins as soon as possible, while they were still burning and collapsing if I could, and in any case before the salvage and demolition teams had begun their work of tidying up. Since I took this mandate seriously, I worked by moonlight and by firelight, to the sound of tinkling glass and trying to shield my drawing board as best I could from the descending dust and soot. When subsequently people have asked me what I did in the War and I have replied that I was a War Artist, I am conscious that this may sound rather effete. It conjures up an image of me finicking away, mixing my paints to get just the right shade of beige to match a shadow on some general's uniform. However, my work was genuinely dangerous. I was nightly under threat from falling bombs, unexploded bombs and collapsing buildings. And these were not the only dangers. The East End got the worst of the bombing and, when I drew and painted there, I tried to do so from a place of concealment in the shadows. Eastenders, bombed out of their homes and perhaps with relatives still buried in the rubble, if they spotted me at work, would mass against me and chase me through the ruined streets. I think that, if they had ever caught me, they would have driven a stake through my heart, in order to bring my ghoulish career to an end. Even in the West End I was several times threatened with death.

With part of my mind I could sympathise with such attitudes, for I felt strange to myself, as I sat breathing in the acid smell of explosive and that of scorched and rotting flesh, calmly sketching heads and hands sticking out of the rubble, while all around me people were rushing about, clawing away at mounds of bricks, operating stirrup pumps and forming bucket chains. I had left the madhouse for this. Everyone used to dread the cloudless nights and the bright full moon, the 'Bombers' Moon' – everyone except me that is. I used to sleep in the daytime in anticipation of such nights and then at around six o'clock, when the first sirens were sounding, I would emerge with my drawing board, hungry for new visions of the Apocalypse.

So I loved my work. I could have been born for it. But what I hated about the War was the enforced mateyness and that feeling of we're-all-in-it-together. I hated being offered 'a nice cuppa' and, whenever anyone muttered anything about 'tickling the ivories', I used to slip out of the room, for fear lest I be caught up in renditions of 'Run Rabbit, Run, Run, Run' or 'Heil Hitler! Ja! Ja! Ja!'. It was inevitable that all sorts of things should become compulsory in wartime. However, I did not want my participation in sessions of 'Knees Up Mother Brown' to become one of those things. My long hospitalisation had left me unaccustomed to lots of people and chatter. I even had to force myself to go into pubs and I had to learn how to drink again.

At first, I tried to pursue my vocation as the artist of ruins in strict solitude, but, as I came more closely to grips with the nature of my work, I began to realise that this was not really possible. To get to the scenes of disaster swiftly enough I needed good intelligence and this could only be gained from the firewatchers, despatch riders and emergency services. As the weeks passed, I even found myself talking to gangs of looters and attaching myself to them as they raced towards the latest bomb site. The looters did not mind. After a while they came to regard me as a friendly neutral. So it was then that I was drawn into close relations with the thieves as well as the A.R.P. men, stretcher bearers, demolition teams and others and, as

I worked, I would listen to them talking about the progress of the War. Their version of what was going on was quite different from what one got from the wireless.

I heard the most extraordinary things. Huns disguised as nuns were at work surveying our coastal defences. The Germans had already attempted a sea-borne invasion and failed. Their bodies were still being washed up on the beaches. The Royal Family had been evacuated to Canada and a troupe of actors were now impersonating them in Buckingham Palace. A kind of werewolf preyed on the bomb sites, looking for fresh bodies to eat. Most people said that he looked like a fireman and some said that there was a whole crew of werewolf firemen operating in the East End. What the werewolves did not eat themselves they sold at the back doors of posh restaurants on the Strand and Piccadilly. Then again, the foreman of one salvage crew told me how he had been chatting up a foreign girl in uniform – a green uniform he did not recognise, perhaps of something like the Free Latvian Forces – when the air-raid siren went off. They were in the vicinity of Chancery Lane, but instead of going down into the tube station, as everyone else was doing, the girl took him by the arm and made him follow her. They passed through the nondescript-looking door of some official-looking building and descended a deep and dimly lit spiral staircase. At the bottom, the salvage foreman found himself in a shelter the like of which he had never dreamed of. All the other people sheltering there were female officers in the green uniforms of their foreign army. There were beds with clean white sheets, champagne in ice buckets and great piles of tinned foods. The foreman spent a night of ecstasy in that shelter. However, though he did his best to memorise the exact location of its exit, he told me that he was never able to come back at that place again.

I was fascinated by the proliferation of rumour and the elaboration of wartime folklore and I started to keep a record of the things I heard. Then, feeling that I might be

186

wasting my time doing this on my own and hoarding my records to myself, I got in touch with Roland Penrose again and enlisted in Mass Observation. This in turn led to a fateful meeting.

I had, for once, been painting in daylight. Madame Tussaud's had been bombed the day before and I could not resist the visual opportunities presented by its partial destruction. Framed by collapsed walls, one could see waxwork bodies, in charred rags spread across the rubble-strewn floor and melting and flowing into one another. My painting of the scene accurately reproduces the uncanny effect and even today I can hardly bear to look at it. Having finished that day's work, I walked down to Portland Place and met Penrose at the BBC's Langham House. He was attached to the army as an advisor on camouflage, but he had got leave to come to London and do a broadcast on modern French art. He was going to take me to a Mass Observation meeting where he would introduce me to some of my co-workers. The blackout was, of course, in force, but a 'Bomber's Moon' lit our way towards Soho Square. Then, just as we were crossing Oxford Street, Penrose grabbed my arm and made me wait. Just behind us was one of the Mass Observers, also on her way to the meeting.

'Let me introduce you two,' he said.

'There's no need,' I said as I turned to face the young woman in W.R.N.S. uniform. 'We know each other.'

'Indeed. Ill met by moonlight, Caspar.'

It was Monica. The angular planes of her face were set hard in apparent anger. Then suddenly she softened.

'I heard what you've been through, Caspar. I'm so sorry.' And to my surprise, she kissed me full on the lips.

'Well, this is a coincidence!' said Penrose.

'Not really,' replied Monica. 'There has to be a degree of improbability in the re-encounter of two people who know one another for it to qualify as a coincidence, but this encounter really was inevitable.'

At the meeting, Penrose, Harrison, Monica and one or

two others spoke briefly about Mass Observation's own philosophical and aesthetic goals, before new assignments and questionnaires, mostly emanating from the Ministry of Information, were dished out to those present. Most of the questionnaires had to do with the assessment of civilian morale. Drinking with the others at the Pillars of Hercules, Monica and I discovered that we now lived close to one another in Chelsea. Together we travelled back by tube to Sloane Square and from there we started walking and, as we walked, we started talking seriously.

'I miss the Brotherhood,' she said. 'London now seems full of their ghosts. It's good to see you again, even if you too seem a bit like a ghost. I watched you sitting so sad and quiet in the pub. Whereas before the War I remember you as always roaring and racing about, almost always with a different woman on your arm and you never seemed to care what they looked like or anything – until that typist girl, that is. And you and Oliver were always larking about, and MacKellar of course.

'What's happened to MacKellar?' I wanted to know.

'No one knows.'

I now learned that the time MacKellar had turned up at the clinic carrying a bunch of bananas must have been the last time he was ever seen by anyone in the group. I had expected him to visit again but he did not. I wish I had known. Just as I wish I had watched Ned more attentively before I entered the darkened room at the Dead Rat Club. There is a last time for meeting with and talking with everyone one knows, but one never knows when that last time will be. There will be a last time I go to Paris, a last visit to the cinema, a last breakfast, a last breath, but it is unlikely that I shall identify these 'lasts' for what they are.

'What do you do now, Monica? I mean what are you doing in the W.R.N.S.?'

'I thought the colour of the uniform would go with my eye make-up,' she replied.

'The uniform does suit you, but what do you do in it?'

'I'm a cook.'

Monica did not want to talk about the W.R.N.S. She wanted to reminisce about the Serapion Brotherhood.

'Now that Ned is dead, you are the leader of the Brotherhood,' she said.

'The way things have turned out, it seems that I am the Brotherhood.'

'Well, I could rejoin,' and she smiled at me mockingly. 'But I'm not sure that there's much point,' she added and went on to expound her theory that the function of the Serapion Brotherhood had been predictive. It was a Cassandra among art movements. Its imagery of nightmare, naked bodies and severed limbs foretold the war that was to come. Having fulfilled its prophetic role, its day was now past.

By the time she had finished explaining all this, we stood outside the door of her house in a mews off the Kings Road.

'I'd invite you in for a cup of coffee, only of course I haven't any coffee. But come in for a cup of hot water anyway.'

'At least it isn't tea,' I replied. 'I loathe tea.'

And, though I was apprehensive about what was coming next, I followed her in anyway. I really did feel like a ghost, all pale and hollow. Perhaps after all I had left the real me trapped in the reflection of the mirror in the clinic.

Inside the flat, Monica produced not hot water, but some carefully hoarded brandy. We sat in facing chairs. Covering most of the wall behind her was a huge hand-drawn chart. A maze of annotated arrows ran all over the place. At a distance, it could have been mistaken for some elaborate battle plan in which tanks, infantry and artillery were all made to manoeuvre according to the intricately devised plotting of a master strategist. More closely examined, it proved to be Monica's famous Coincidence Chart, a graphic layout in which who knew who was indicated by an intricate criss-crossing of differently shaded and dotted lines with authentic coincidences marked by red stars. For example, a few years before the Serapion Brotherhood was set up, Oliver and Ned met as they worked one summer as deck-chair attendants in Hyde Park. Neither of them at that time had any interest in Surrealism. Monica and Felix were in the same Latin class in the same posh school before they re-encountered one another at a meeting of the Serapion Brotherhood. That was another coincidence. Monica had chosen to put Ned at the centre of her vast map of the workings of chance.

In conversation that evening Monica kept coming back to Ned. She had slept with him of course. I think every woman in the group had. She looked back on the experience without affection.

'He treated me as a child-woman – or a doll, something which opens and closes its eyes when tipped backwards and forwards. We – Jenny, Felix, Jane, Pamela and the rest of us – weren't really expected to do anything. If one of us did produce a painting or a poem, that was just O.K., an unexpected bonus, but the women were really expected to be muses to you Brothers of Serapion. Jenny and I sometimes talked of defecting and founding a Sisterhood. Then that night in the club when you hypnotised me, that was the last straw – not that I minded you . . . it was the others. I admit hypnotism is rather fascinating.'

She paused, stuck for words. Then she shrugged and walked round the table to come and sit on the arm of my chair. There was something oddly sensual in the severity of her uniform and the fall of her heavy blue skirt. In an entirely abstract way I thought she looked very attractive. From her superior vantage point she looked down into my eyes.

'Hypnotise me stupid.'

'Monica, I can't. I can't do that any more.'

'Oh just kiss me then.'

'There's not much point even in that. You said I was like a ghost. Well I am. I hardly seem to have a physical body. I'm not capable of sex and I can't respond to women any more.'

190

She dropped to her knees in front of me and set to unbuttoning my flies.

'Let's just see shall we?'

She worked on me with her hands, determined to prove me wrong, but at first it was as I had predicted. So she broke away from this and stood up. Then slowly, very slowly and with her eyes focussed on nothingness, she began to undress. It was as if she were indeed stripping under hypnotic compulsion. Monica with her broad Slavonic face, big bones and long broad hips looked nothing like Caroline, yet, to my surprise, I found that I was attracted to her. My head was still telling me that the attraction was aesthetic only, with nothing of the erotic in it, but lower down I had thoughts that the head knew nothing of. When she had finished undressing, she refocussed her eyes upon me and, having seen that her performance had had some effect, moaning as if she hated what she was doing, she threw herself down upon me, so that her head was between my legs and her mouth kissing and nipping at my balls. A few minutes later we were rolling around on the floor with Monica fighting for the superior position, her breasts slapping against my face as she thrashed about. A few minutes later yet and I re-entered the state of manhood.

I gave up my rented room and moved in with Monica. The stuff about her being a cook in the W.R.N.S. was nonsense. She said that to everybody in order to discourage further questions. She eventually admitted to me that she worked in Naval Intelligence, but she never gave away more than that. 'Careless talk costs lives.' Since she could not or would not tell me about her work, I would lie on the bed beside her and invent her days for her, rich, satisfying days full of excitement: a rendez-vous with a submarine off the Isle of Dogs, a villain with a foreign accent neatly disposed of by being pushed into a bath of acid, a secret zeppelin hidden by camouflage discovered in Epping Forest, a spy at the very heart of Admiralty Intelligence unmasked by the intrepid Monica. As for my work,

I might just as well have invented my own days also for all the interest she took in them.

I introduced Monica to Clive and Sally, but their meeting was not a success, for Clive, on being told that Monica was a cook, had bombarded her with questions about economic menus and kitchen hygiene and he could not be made to take an interest in any other subject that day. We saw quite a lot of Roland Penrose and his companion at that time, Lee Miller. Lee had been Man Ray's photographic collaborator and mistress in Paris and now in London she was amassing an impressive portfolio of photographs of the Blitz. She and I happily compared notes on the art of ruins. Roland had given Lee a pair of golden handcuffs and Lee had shown these to Monica. Monica had promptly gone out and bought herself a pair, though she could not afford them in gold. In bed we played at what was I suppose a mild version of the Theatre of Cruelty. I was her hulking great slave-master and she was the slave-girl in bondage. I was never fond of these games and in time I grew heartily sick of them. However, since Monica insisted that she must submit and be degraded, I passively acted out the masterful role that she had assigned to me. It seemed that what made her attracted to me was my assertion of mesmeric power over her in the Dead Rat Club all those years ago.

The last great bombing raid over London was in May 1941 (though at the time of course we did not realise that it was the last of its kind). The Blitz had ended, though not before it had punched great holes in my memories. The old Dead Rat Club, which had served briefly as a recreation centre for the Free French, was destroyed; so was the office of the Anglo-Balkan Fur Company in Soho; so was my former home in Cuba Street. Once the Blitz proper was over I switched to painting in the daytime and my ruins, though they still had not acquired 'the true rust of the barons' wars', were no longer absolutely new ruins and my canvases registered the spread of willow herb and nettles over the brick and stone. Large parts of London now reminded me of the enchanted sleeping palace all over-grown by briars. I also painted Monica asleep, Monica as Titania, and Monica as a sex slave.

Our affaire lasted for two more years after the Blitz. I think that the reason we were together for so long was because we were so rarely together. We both worked long hours according to patterns that rarely matched and Monica was sometimes absent on mysterious missions. Since Jenny and the rest were now untraceable, we thought of ourselves as the last of the Serapion Brotherhood and in bed together we comforted each other as its orphans. But then one day Monica came home excitedly brandishing a book. Since I never go into bookshops that sell new books, I would not have spotted it, but Monica had. It was a pristine new copy of *The Vampire of Surrealism* by Oliver Sorge.

My excitement at this evidence of Oliver being still alive was swiftly overtaken by disappointment that the book gave no clue whatsoever as to Oliver's present whereabouts. The inside dustjacket merely listed his previous publications. We took turns in reading the novel in bed. When Stella made her first appearance in the story, I patted Monica's rump and smiled inwardly, for I remembered Oliver saying that Stella's broad bottom was going to be modelled on Monica's.

As for the novel as a whole, it was much less experimental than his earlier works (or for that matter, than the pieces he was later to publish). It was obvious to us that, for all its trappings of gothic fantasy and its references to ectoplasm and etherial spheres, the story was heavily auto-biographical. The hero (Oliver had rechristened himself Robert), having broken some sort of interdiction and summoned up Stella, a vampire from Hell, nightly makes love to this beautiful but sinister spirit on a red divan. As the nights pass, he realises that he is being drained of his psychic energy and that he must escape her clutches. While he still has strength to do so, he flees to Spain, where he enlists in the International Brigade and goes off to defend Madrid. Despite many hair's breadth escapes from death,

Stella is never far from his thoughts. Indeed, she is most on his mind when he is closest to death. Robert comes to realise that it is only death that will finally free him from thoughts of Stella. He becomes increasingly foolhardy, the one who is the last to retreat and the first to volunteer for suicide missions. He is seriously wounded on one of these missions and brought back to a hospital in Madrid (a vast and gloomy eighteenth-century pile, formerly run by monks). He thinks that he is certain to die and for the first time he is at peace. As the novel ends, a nurse is standing with her back to him, filling the syringe with what is presumably a pain-killer. He cannot see the face of the nurse, but the reader can. It is Stella's face.

The Vampire of Surrealism is prefaced by a quotation from Baudelaire: 'To love an intelligent woman is a pederast's pleasure'. As one would expect of any novel by Oliver, it is an intensely misogynistic book. We are to understand that not only is Stella a vampire, but so are all women. The novel is an allegory of fear of women. For a man to love a woman is to surrender his male identity; to surrender his identity is death. Uniquely among Oliver's books, *The Vampire of Surrealism* was published by the long-established and rather stuffy house of Barrington and Lane. The day after Monica's discovery I hurried round to the publisher's address given opposite the frontispiece, even though I already knew what I would find. Where the office of Barrington and Lane should have stood in Paternoster Row there was only a crater. It was one among the many publishing premises destroyed by the bombs that fell around St Pauls.

Monica's massive collection of file cards recording the conversations of friends and acquaintances proved to be even more interesting than Oliver's novel. At first she denied me access to them, but I nagged away at her until she indulgently gave way. Though I spent months immersing myself in that amazing archive, it is hard to say what I learned from it. I learned a bit about Monica certainly. She had joined the Serapion Brotherhood after 'a chance meeting' with Ned. Subsequently, she had spent weeks and months in the intensive study of the meaning of such a chance meeting. What were the objective odds of their meeting then? Or earlier? Or later? In what sense was their meeting significant? What material criteria had to be fulfilled before such a meeting could take place? Monica's notes were copious and filled with references to Pascal, Fermat, Freud and Jung. I could not see that she had got anywhere.

Anyway, at the time she met Ned, her researches into the nature of objective chance were in the future. Ned had discoursed grandly about convulsive passion, tracking the Marvellous, primal matriarchy and all the other things he used to discourse so grandly about. Monica had been mesmerised – I use the metaphor advisedly – by his talking. It was not so much that she fell under his thrall as that she threw herself under it. Straightaway she resolved to become Boswell to Ned's Johnson. She started attending meetings of the Brotherhood and committing to memory everything that Ned said, holding it in her head until she was able to faithfully transcribe it onto paper. At the same time she became Ned's mistress. She replaced Jenny Bodkin and lasted three months before being replaced in her turn by Felix. There was a wonderful file card dating from one of the last days when Ned and Monica were still living together. They were queueing behind some old women in a fishmonger's and Ned was talking, blah, blah, blah, about woman's manifest destiny as muse, when Monica impatiently cut him short.

'Woman's manifest destiny! What woman? What about this woman just in front of you with her pebble-lens glasses and her weight problem.'

The woman in question turned round angrily. Ned bent towards her, thoughtfully inspecting her as if he was indeed considering her candidacy as a muse.

Monica continued.

'I'm tired of being your muse. Why don't you let this one have a go? Or what about the old bag in front of her?'

''Ere, stop being so personal,' screeched the one with the pebble glasses and grabbed hold of Ned's jacket by its lapels. 'You want to give that woman of yours a damn good hiding.'

Then the fishmonger ordered Ned and Monica out of his shop and told them not to bother coming back again.

At about the time she was expelled from Ned's bed, her interests began to broaden and, since she had become familiar with Ned's repertoire of intellectual tricks, she decided that her own ideas were at least as interesting. She started to keep cross-classified records of what everyone in the group and the world at large said. Crawling over her records, I was amazed to find how often I spoke and how seriously what I said was taken by other members of the group (though not as it turned out by Monica). But of course I did not spend so long working on Monica's mighty card-index because I was interested in her history, or Ned's, or that of the Brotherhood as a whole. No, all that was incidental. What possessed me was the desire to learn more about Caroline. She, of course, had a whole series of cards dedicated to her, even though she and Monica had met on only a few occasions: at Gamages, at the cinema, at the New Burlington Galleries and on the outing to Brighton. (I should say here that, in writing this anti-memoire, I have occasionally supplemented my failing memories by drawing on Monica's file cards for the details of what was said on certain occasions.)

I was disconcerted to find on the cinema card, besides an objective précis of what Caroline had said and done that evening, the pencilled annotation 'A typical middle-class, tight-lipped, tight-arsed bitch'. Turning to one of her group cards which recorded meetings of the Brotherhood, I found a further record of our outing to *The Mystery of the Wax Museum* and its aftermath. Included was the record of a conversation between Monica, Jenny and Oliver as they were walking from the pub to the Dead Rat Club. Jenny was puzzled about the circumstances of my first meeting with Caroline. Surely it was unusual for a respectable girl to enter a pub unaccompanied and then to strike up an acquaintanceship with a complete stranger? Perhaps she was not what she seemed? Monica suggested that she might have had someone with her, but Jenny thought that Caroline was less innocent than she appeared. Oliver closed the conversation by declaring that he was bored with everything to do with 'that little miss'.

Monica's record of the Gamage's meeting was entertainingly supplemented by her speculations that I was an indiscriminate, bisexual erotomaniac, who was cheating on Oliver by sleeping with Caroline. I now learned that without quite saying it, Oliver, behind my back, had been giving the impression that he and I were sleeping together. On the other hand, nowhere in Monica's notes was there any glimpse of an inkling that Caroline and I might not have been sleeping together. As far as Monica could see, I slept with everyone without giving the matter a moment's thought. Monica's record of what had happened at Brighton matched my memories fairly well, though the archive additionally provided an account of conversations in her car to and from the seaside. Oliver was in a funny mood on the way back and he seemed to be trying to goad Monica to such a point that she would throw him out of the car. He had mocked her determination to pursue a career as a journalist, as well as her abilities as a driver. More nastily, he had needled her about her tendency to sit on the edge of the group, never making any proper friendships within it. He had quoted Nietzsche's *Also Sprach Zarathustra*: 'As yet woman is not capable of friendship: women are still cats and birds. Or at best cows'. Monica had wondered how Oliver was ever going to manage if his ghostly woman should turn up. Wouldn't it be more appropriate for him to attempt to raise the ghost of a beautiful boy?

In part it was my insistence on being allowed access to Monica's records and my obsessive study of them that precipitated our break-up. Monica slowly came to realise the depth of my obsession with Caroline. I made love to

Monica with my eyes shut and eventually she rightly guessed that it was the image of Caroline's face that flickered and burned on the inside of my eyelids. But that was only half the story, for slowly I came to realise that Monica loved my body and only my body. I was her 'gorgeous hunk'. She also called me 'Casparkins' and her 'teddy-bear'. I was intellectually negligible. She loved my torso and muscular legs, but my clothes had more of interest to say than I did. The more she told me that my body was gorgeous, the more I became ashamed of it. I was beginning to fear that I might be buried alive within my own body. So we started to drift apart while still sharing the same bed. Then, without rancour, we agreed to separate and I moved out to the house I still rent in Waterloo. We continued to see each other for a while and then stopped.

Not long after we separated, the War on the Home Front entered a new phase, as the Germans started firing V-weapons from bases on the Pas-de-Calais. I found that I had new ruins to record and I was busier than ever. The pilotless flying planes and the noises that they made in the air prior to their silent descent attracted a new wave of folklore, such as the belief that the *Vergeltungswaffe*, or reprisal weapons, were guided to their targets by the ghosts of dead Luftwaffe pilots. I collected as much information of this sort as I could and forwarded it on to Mass Observation.

The last V-rockets fell towards the end of March 1945 and a few weeks after that my career entered a new phase as I was sent to join the British troops who had crossed the Rhine. I eventually succeeded in catching up with the unit I had been posted to in the suburbs of Bremen. Then I was told that I was being sent on to Bergen-Belsen to make an artistic record of a concentration camp that the Nazis had maintained there.

I was excited in advance by the visual possibilities in such a commission. One of the officers who briefed me had already visited the camp and thus I was able to conjure up an image in my mind's eye – a huge muddy expanse with wooden walkways surrounded by barbed wire, matchstick men with pale bird-like faces walking amidst the chimneys, huts and makeshift tents. Something rather grand and even romantic in the manner of Caspar David Friedrich's canvases might be appropriate. The corpses would not trouble me. I had seen plenty of death in London.

I arrived in Belsen. Another war artist, a young man with dark, deep-set eyes, called Mervyn Peake, had got there before me. We walked round the camp together, hardly speaking at all. After throwing up a couple of times, I made a few desultory sketches. I think that he may have done the same. Even after the camp's liberation hundreds of inmates were still dying every day. I abandoned all plans of painting in Belsen. Hitherto I had taken it for granted that art and literature covered everything in the universe, or at least in principle they could cover everything. There were no forbidden zones. I now felt that this was not true. So I painted nothing in Belsen and I have nothing to say about it as a writer. Indeed, I would not have mentioned it all, were it not for the fact that I returned to England in a very strange state of mind. My visit to Belsen may have contributed to that strangeness.

Chapter Fourteen

I did not return to England immediately. Instead I was seconded to an American Denazification Commission with special responsibility for paintings and sculptures and it was under these peculiar auspices that I returned to Munich, the city where I had made such careful preparations for the conquest of a woman who, as it turned out, was no longer around to be conquered. Large parts of the city were now rubble and U.S. military engineers were adding to the rubble by blowing up selected Nazi monuments. I joined a small group of American and British artists and art historians who advised on the works of art discovered concealed in shelters and mines all over Bavaria. We adjudicated on what was and what was not Nazi art. Paintings of the Nazi leaders, the Wehrmacht and the Hitler Youth obviously. But what about Siegfried slaying the dragon? A trio of naked women whose bodies all conformed to the Aryan ideal? Traditional peasants sitting down to a traditional pot of stew? And was there such a thing as a Nazi style as well as Nazi content? Wherever we drew the line, some things would be on the wrong side of it. We argued, and fiercely, but on the whole we did not incline to mercy and thousands of paintings and sculptures were condemned by us to be confined in storage cellars by the U.S. Defence Department. The art which had proclaimed itself the art of the next thousand years was locked away after thirteen.

I was still in Munich on V.E. Day, when I gather all London exploded in huge and rapturous celebration. So soon after Belsen, I would not have been capable of celebrating. And several of the European Surrealists had perished in the Nazi death camps, most notably Robert Desnos, the pioneer of automatic writing in trance states. Sessions of 'Knees-up Mother Brown' would certainly not have sufficed to keep the horrors away from me. Forces radio and magazines told me that Europe had been 'liberated'. It gave me an odd turn, seeing that word 'liberated'. Liberation had been an important word in Surrealist vocabulary before the War. Liberation had implied the setting free of a kind of wildness imprisoned in the individual and the unleashing of the unsuspectedly vast powers of the imagination. De Sade, Freud and Artaud had given us the courage to transgress beyond the frontiers of the normal. It was they who seemed to point the way towards the liberation of mankind. But now having spent so many months with the British and American forces in Germany, I could plainly see that the 'liberation' that had been achieved had been achieved by meticulous organisation and strict discipline.

I was not decommissioned as a War Artist and allowed to return to London until November 1945. One evening, only a week or two after my return, I was walking down Oxford Street. London's street lighting had not been properly maintained during all those years of blackout and when the moon came out from behind the clouds it provided better illumination than the occasional yellowing street light. A fog was beginning to rise and the more distant buildings faded into it. Most shop windows were still boarded up and there was little to be seen in those which were not. I was walking along thinking about how before the War I had walked here with Caroline on one of her shopping trips. I felt her absence physically and it was actually painful for me now to walk alone in streets where we had once walked together. Nevertheless, I actively sought out this pain. The pain, like a strong fist, squeezed my heart and I staggered on the icy pavement. Then suddenly, I glimpsed something out of the corner of my eye. As I recovered my balance, I turned to face a gang of emaciated, shaven-headed figures of indeterminate sex and dressed in pyjama-like garments. They stared impassively back at me. Behind the gang, another similar figure was hanging by his neck from a barren tree. I threw up my hands to protect myself from them and, as I did so, I recognised my ghostly reflection caught in the glass of the shop window. I went down on my hands and knees on the ice before this window, the only one to be lit up in the whole of Oxford Street. From my kneeling position on the pavement, I looked up at the wax tableau in the window and at the sign above which read 'All the Horrors of the Concentration Camps. Admission 6d'. As soon as I could recompose myself, I staggered to my feet and hurried away from the scene, reflecting as I did so that it has been my fate in life to be haunted, not by ghosts or vampires or anything of that sort, but by objects, solid things of wood, wax, glass or paper, which dispose themselves to torment me and which gnaw at my conscience.

It is one of the curious features of hypnagogia that it is not necessary to close the eyes in order to be aware of the play of its imagery. It is only necessary for the room to be dark and then with open eyes I will see the inevitable swarm of men, women and things cavorting in the blackness. God help me, I think my hypnagogic imagery is active even when I am not looking at it. Only by staying wide awake in a well lit room can I avoid entering the hypnagogic landscape. Curiously, it was the Oxford Street waxworks, rather than the Belsen victims on which they were modelled, that precipitated a crisis in my private mental world. Emaciated men, women and children now began to parade on my closed lids and on darkened walls. I saw them in theatres and galleries, on beaches and in beds. Silently and reproachfully they were everywhere. I used to try to lie awake fighting off their visitations, but as soon as my concentration dropped and I began to nod off, they would be upon me again. If I had thought that I could be free of these visions if I cut out my eyelids, I would have done so.

After sticking it out for a few weeks, I went to a doctor and got him to prescribe me tranquillisers and sleeping pills. I supplemented what the doctor gave me with alcohol and opium. I was amazed to discover that the House of Serenity in Cable Street had survived the trial of Scrupulous

Chen and his imprisonment and I frequently visited the place. I relished the bitter-sweet smell of the heated opium and the increasingly tatty look of the silk and satin decor, for the memories it brought back of better times before the War.

On my return from Munich, my employment as a War Artist, 'temporary and non-pensionable', came to an end. If by 1945 Nazi art could be seen to have had its day, the same thing seemed to be true of Surrealism. The Ministry of Information and the W.A.C. had wanted representational artists for the purposes of records and propaganda, but once the war was over, gallery owners were favouring abstract painters. Although the Serapion Brotherhood had proposed to conquer all time and space, it could now be seen to have been something that was peculiar to its time – like the crazes for mah-jong, the Lindy Hop and other defunct enthusiasms. A couple of my paintings were exhibited at the small 'Surrealist Diversity' exhibition at the Arcade Gallery, in the company of works by Max Ernst, Man Ray, Magritte, Picasso and Tanguy, but my stuff did not sell. Having fallen upon hard times, I barely kept myself alive by doing odd jobs. I found occasional work as a painter of 'flats' at the Ealing Studios and, even when there was no work for me to do there, I hung around for the sake of the warmth. I also got work sometimes at the Royal College of Heralds, painting armorial blazons. Occasionally I worked as a house painter and during the bitter winter of 1946–7 I was employed by the Post Office one day a week to answer letters, most of which were addressed to Father Christmas, but I also occasionally ghosted replies for Sherlock Holmes, Charles Dickens and the Tooth Fairy.

When I could afford the materials, I continued to paint out my obsession. I did a series of canvases, imaginary portraits of Caroline – Caroline at thirty, forty, fifty . . . Even at fifty she still looked attractive, if a little raddled. However, in the last of the portraits, Caroline at ninety, she is shown standing behind me, while I toil over a canvas on the easel. She has become cadaverous; there is no longer enough white hair to cover her scalp; the liver-spotted skin is stretched to tearing point over her projecting bones and the beginnings of a wispy beard sprouts from the chin. I also resumed work on my main cycle of paintings. 'Secondhand Bookshop no 32' has hands coming out of the shelves and showing the books to women customers and pointing them to interesting illustrations.

Clive bullied friends of his to buy some of my work. He and Sally moved from Woking to Chertsey and a larger house with swimming pool, squash courts and peacocks on the lawn. Clive, who had returned to his previous career in business, was teaching himself Serbian as well as bird's-nesting for rare eggs. He also lectured me on the merits of Gilbert and Sullivan and illustrated their genius with selected extracts on the gramophone. There was an air of desperation in his musicological gabble. It was as if he did not want to give me space to speak. I saw little of Sally, but soon deduced that she was having an affair with one of the neighbours.

Apart from Clive and Sally, the only people I saw more than once or twice were Roland and Lee Penrose. Lee, who had been attached to the American forces in Germany, had taken photographs of the opening up of Buchenwald Camp, but whereas what I had seen had terrified and oppressed me, Lee was angry and bitter. From the Penroses I learnt that Paul and Nusch Eluard had survived the War, though Nusch was now looking frail and emaciated.

Slowly my fortunes as an artist took a turn for the better. Taking my initial inspiration from the hack work I did for Bluemantle Pursuivant, I now began to produce a series of smallish paintings of luridly Surrealist blazons. I devised armorial bearings for the Marquis de Sade, Sacher-Masoch, Baudelaire, De Quincey, Cagliostro, Lewis Carroll, Sacco and Vanzetti. It may have been a hangover from the wartime obsession with military insignia, I don't know, but these works proved remarkably popular. The heraldic paintings were given a show at the Dedalus Gallery. Sir Alfred Munnings visited the show and then denounced my work at a well-reported after-dinner speech in the Royal Academy as 'disgusting daubs' and 'an insult to human decency'. The owner of the Dedalus Gallery said that being denounced by Munnings was 'the winning ticket' and 'like money in the bank', and so it proved.

One evening, while urinating in the public lavatory at the bottom of Charing Cross Road, I was startled by a voice issuing from one of the cubicles.

'Is there anyone there?'

After a brief hesitation, I called back.

'Yes.'

'Are you alone?'

'Yes.'

'Then you had better take this. It is destined for you and for you alone.'

Something slid out from under the door of one of the cubicles. Having done up my flies, I walked over to pick it up.

It proved to be a pamphlet printed on yellow paper, entitled *What Have We Been Fighting For?*, produced under the joint authorship of the West Ealing Phalantasery.

'Go now and take what you have been given and study it carefully,' commanded the voice. 'We have finished our business here.'

I took the pamphlet back to Waterloo and only when I got home did I open it. The argument of *What Have We Been Fighting For?* was that we had been fighting to implement the theories of the French Utopian socialist Charles Fourier (1772–1837). His theories were expounded with touching enthusiasm by the Fourierist comrades of West Ealing. In the ideal post-war Britain, 'a land fit for the sexually obsessed', the country will be divided into phalantaseries; no one will have to work for more than a couple of hours a day at any particular task, so no one will become bored or alienated from their work. Sex counts as work. Garbage will be collected by children in brightly coloured uniforms. These children, the Little Hordes, will ride about on zebras and blow trumpets, so of course they will enjoy their work enormously. People will travel to work on the antilion, a creature which condenses and replaces the lion and the motor car. Oceans will be crossed by people riding the antiwhale. For recreation one may visit museums filled by living men and women, all of whom proudly display their best features. All of society will be geared towards the unrestricted expression of the passions. The pamphlet, after roundly abusing the Beveridge Report, urges its readers to attend the regular Thursday meetings of the West Ealing Phalantasery. Alternatively, one could write to a certain Miles Midwinter.

I was tempted. Clearly chance had put me in the way of a sort of post-war, austerity substitute for the Serapion Brotherhood and it was even possible that in Miles Midwinter I should re-encounter Ned Shillings, reincarnated in a different but still recognisable form. After much hesitation, however, I came to the conclusion that I was too depressed to face a new gang of people and that I would be unable to engage in the profound frivolities of Fourierism with any real conviction. Mischievously I posted the pamphlet on to Clive.

It shocked me nevertheless that I could have been so seriously tempted and it made me realise how lonely I was. Loneliness played a large part in my decision to submit myself to psychoanalysis. So did the fact that I could only fall asleep by drinking myself silly and passing out. Above all though, I still felt that at any moment I might re-encounter Caroline in the street and then we would go to a tea-house or a pub and I would recount to her everything that had happened to me since we parted – my exercises in mesmerism and lip-reading in Germany, my attempt to trace her through a detective agency, my sojourn in the Milton Clinic, my work as a War Artist and (perhaps) my affair with Monica. But first I wanted to practise my life story on someone else. I wished to be judged and exonerated. No, more than that, I wanted to see myself through another's eyes. I wanted to walk about outside myself and then look back and see me. As it was, I was trapped, buried alive in my own body, and no matter how hard I screamed, no one would ever hear me.

Dr Wilson's consulting room was on the ground floor of his house in Swiss Cottage. The walls were lined with prints of Hogarth's 'The Rake's Progress'. There was a bag of golf clubs in the corner of the room and his first disappointment in me was learning that I did not play. I visited him twice a week in the afternoons. I would lie on the sofa and look at the trees out of the window and while I talked, he would sit on a chair behind my head and scribble in a little notebook. Dr Wilson looked like a moustacheless Donald Meldrum, except that he did not have Meldrum's sideburns, and he was not as tall as Meldrum, and he did not have the latter's bluffness of manner. So he was like the grin without the cat. Except that Dr Wilson never smiled. Not that I could be quite sure of that, with him sitting behind my head.

'What do I do?' I said at the first session. 'What am I supposed to say?'

'You must say whatever you feel the need to say.'

'But I don't feel like saying anything.'

A long silence. After only ten minutes I capitulated.

'Aren't I supposed to tell you about my dreams?'

'If you wish.'

On the face of it I had lost that round. However, after several sessions of me relating my dreams and saying what I thought about them, it was evident that I had the upper hand after all and Dr Wilson was forced to give way. The problem he faced was that, as I believe I have mentioned earlier in this anti-memoire, my dreams are very boring – dreams of shopping, catching trains, sitting in waiting rooms preparing for interviews, things like that. Speaking for myself, I found the shopping dreams faintly interesting in a dry sort of way, for over the years I had found that a sort of repetitive dream topography had built up, which I could remember from dream to dream. So as I was walking up one dream street, I might recall that in the parallel street and a little to the left that there was an excellent ironmon-gers with an outstanding range of ironmongery – all sorts of things which were hard to find in post-war Brit-ain. I found the consistency and dullness of my dreams rather fascinating. Also I was curious about how it was that I was never quite able to purchase anything in the shops that I visited. The elusive widget glimpsed in the window of the dream shop remained forever beyond my grasp.

Dr Wilson did not share my fascination. After a few weeks he banned me from talking about my dreams. So I started talking about my hypnagogic imagery. This also proved not to interest him. Again, as I have already noted in the prologue to this book, he regarded this as some sort of anomalous optical phenomenon. Instead, he started to probe me about my earliest childhood memories of my parents. Here again he was frustrated, for my earliest memories concerned my guardian and his enthusiasms for horse racing, harlots and operetta.

By now we were six weeks into analysis and already the phenomenon of transference was taking place. Transference is the development on the part of the patient of a strong feeling towards his or her analyst, which creates an emo-tional charge between them. After only six weeks we had reached this vital stage in analysis. And it was mutual. We loathed each other. Part of the problem was that, like most Surrealists, I was well up in psychoanalytical theory and I had read more of Freud than Dr Wilson had. I was wise to all his mind games.

He was still trying to confine himself to comments like 'And how do you feel about that?' and 'Is there anything else you would like to say?', but he was finding this pose of neutrality increasingly difficult and again and again he was betrayed into impatience. Having failed to get me to talk of my parents, he got me to talk about Caroline. This I was willing to do in great detail. After a few weeks I had only got as far as describing how I was feeling while I stroked her knee in the cinema while it was showing *The*

Mystery of the Wax Museum, when he exploded with impatience:

'Stop it! Stop it! Enough! I can do nothing for you. Psychoanalysis is definitely not for people like you. Analysis is a remedial treatment for neurotics, but you ... you are ...'

He fell cautiously silent.

'I am what?'

I swear that he was about to denounce me as mad. However, to have done so would have been to have lost the game according to the rules he was accustomed to play by. He would probably have been drummed out of the ranks of the Psychoanalytic Association by other Freudians.

After a careful pause, he replied.

'You have not come here in good faith. You do not want to be cured. You do not want to be returned to society as a properly functioning member of that society. Instead, you have come to me for confirmation of your fantasies. Now I want to hear no more about this Miss Begley. It is possible that she may once have existed, though personally I doubt it. Whatever was once the truth of that matter, she now is merely the creature of your mind and has no existence outside your imagination. So no more of her if you please. I cannot, and psychoanalysis cannot give you back this phantom of desire. All psychoanalysis can do is treat people so that they can function ordinarily in society –'

'But that is what I want! I want to become ordinary! Make me ordinary, please!'

'No ordinary person would have said what you have just said. The fact is that you have come to me to make you more exceptional than you already are and to make your life all wonderful. You expect life to be colourful, marvellous, with exciting things happening all the time. But life isn't like that and, if analysis can teach you anything, it is how to compromise. Life is hard for everyone. It's something you'll just have to buckle down and accept. A first step in this necessary process would be to drop your fantasies of the perfect woman, the so-called Caroline.'

I let the silence build up, before asking,

'And how do you feel about what you have just said?'

But, it was foolish to bait Dr Wilson and, my question having alerted him, he retreated back to the games-playing mode of the professional analyst.

'Would I be right in detecting hostility in your question?' he wanted to know.

'Why do you ask?' I replied.

And so it went on with question parried by question. But Dr Wilson's querying of the reality of Caroline had disturbed me more than I let on to him. When I came to think of her, I realised that she had become so much a creature of my mind that she was now hardly more real to me than Trilby. It then occurred to me that a partial answer might be to put some flesh on my memories of Caroline.

The very next day I went round to the Royal Academy of Dramatic Art in Gower Street and asked to see the Principal. Had I an appointment? I had not. What was my business? I wanted to hire a young, female drama student for a day. Eventually I was brought before one of the Principal's deputies and I explained my needs to her. Quivering with indignation, she heard me out before shaking her head decisively.

'Quite out of the question. We are not an escort agency.' And eagerly ushering me out of the office, 'If you don't mind, we'd like you to leave the premises now.'

This was a set-back. However, the woman's remarks prompted me to ring up an escort agency with an office in Chelsea. The woman at the other end of the line, once she had managed to grasp what I was seeking, told me that my demands were too bizarre and specific. Her young ladies were not equipped to offer the sort of service I was demanding. At this point I briefly abandoned the project.

But the next session with Dr Wilson was especially stormy. It ended with me asking.

'You hate me don't you?'

His chair creaked uneasily.

'Yes.'

'You are not supposed to say things like that.'

'Why not, if it is true?'

'You think I murdered Caroline, don't you?

'I am so far from thinking that, that I do not believe she ever existed.'

The session terminated early. I stormed out of the consulting room. I went to a newsagent, close to the tube station and bought a little notebook and then sat in a cafe, writing in it until the notebook was more than half full. Then I took the tube to Leicester Square and from there I walked into Soho.

The prostitute I picked out in the end was chosen because she looked the most respectable. She wore a calico print dress and might have passed for a young housewife. Indeed, I had thought when I picked her out that she might be in her mid-thirties, but there was an odd sheen to her face and inspecting her more closely in the pub, I saw that make-up had been skillfully applied in a pancake layer and she was probably in her late forties, or perhaps even older. Still she was quite a handsome woman.

Over drinks in the pub in Greek Street, she told me that her name was Martina. I told her that from now on, as long as I was paying her, her name was Caroline. Then I passed the notebook over to her and explained how I wanted her to learn Caroline's half of the dialogue. In a few days' time, once she had memorised Caroline's part, we would meet again in this same pub and I would have a sleep-mask over my eyes and she would take me by the hand and lead me out of the pub and we would walk towards St James's Park. Step by step and word by word, we would re-enact my first meeting with Caroline all those years ago.

Pseudo-Caroline opened her mouth to refuse, but I pressed five pounds into her hand. That was in advance. There would be another five pounds when we next met in the pub and yet ten pounds more, if she performed as well as I hoped.

'You will be the star of this production,' I said. 'You are quite good-looking.'

'I bet you say that to all your popsies,' she said, patting her hair self-consciously.

'I'm offering you a terrific part. You have the chance to give the performance of your life. Have you seen *Brief Encounter*?'

Silly question. Everybody has seen *Brief Encounter*.

'You will be Celia Johnson to my Trevor Howard,' I continued. 'This is one of the great love stories of our time. I don't want you just to memorise your lines in a mechanical way. I want you to feel your way into your part, like method actors do. It's difficult, I know, but you must draw on your own past insofar as it is possible, so as to help you understand what it would be like to be Caroline – a young typist, still innocent and virginal and with little experience of life.'

Pseudo-Caroline looked baffled. I wished I had succeeded in getting someone from R.A.D.A., someone who really could have put Stanislavsky's theories into practice in recreating the role of Caroline, but 'Needs must when the Devil drives'. I was in a hurry. I was in a fever of impatience.

Pseudo-Caroline doubtfully said she'd do her best. Then she skimmed the notebook, mouthing some of the dialogue to herself, until she came to the last page.

'It says here "IMPROVISE". What does that mean?'

'What it says. At that point we'll play it by ear and the better you perform, the better I'll be pleased and the more I'll pay you.'

Pseudo-Caroline was still puzzled and suspicious, but it was true. I had no idea what would happen when we reached the park and sat down on the grass. I had stopped short in the notebook at the point where Caroline had said she was going to get us some ice cream and then vanished. I wanted to see what would have happened if she had not disappeared in that way. There was a fluttery feeling of excitement in my stomach as I looked forward to the mysteriously uncertain ending of our little play.

At last Saturday came. I was early in the pub. Jorge's broad-brimmed gaucho hat had gone back with him to Argentina, so I had purchased a bowler hat instead. With such a hat I can imagine myself to be a man in a Magritte painting. Extraordinary things always happen to men who wear bowler hats. I was wearing the hat and clutching the Indian sword-stick (for though Oliver had come round several times to Cuba Street to collect it, he had invariably forgotten to take it away). As soon as Pseudo-Caroline came through the door, I donned the sleep-mask and I called out impatiently,

'MacKellar? MacKellar?'

Pseudo-Caroline replied in a low, artificially sexy voice.

'Was that the name of your friend?'

I nodded.

'Well, he's gone out just now, but he wrote a message which he pressed into my hand.'

And she pretended to read the note which began.

'Dear Miss –,

'You have a kindly face. I beg you take care of this tragically afflicted young man . . .'

And so we continued. Pseudo-Caroline had not thoroughly mastered her lines and it was fairly obvious that she was consulting the notebook from time to time, but I did not mind that. What was more of a problem was that as we emerged from the pub, my hand trustingly in hers, I realised that not only was it bitterly cold, but a thin drizzle was falling. The pavement was wet and I was concentrating on my feet and worrying about what we should do in the park if we could not sit on the grass. Nothing was quite right. Her perfume was too strong and it reminded me of rotting gardenias. One of her nails scratched sensuously across my palm. On my eyelids, in place of the luridly coloured wild rout of the old days, I could see gaunt and spectral men in striped jackets and

213

trousers, who seemed to wish to usher me on towards the front of a queue whose end was invisible.

Distracted by these matters, I did not at first realise that she was not in fact leading me towards St James's Park. This only became obvious when she began to coax me downwards, down a staircase of stone or brick, which in its lower half seemed to disintegrate into a heap of dusty rubble. The descent was narrow and she pressed her body against me as she continued to mouth words from the notebook and to coax me slowly downwards. Finally, after what seemed a long time, we reached the bottom. There was a squeaking and a slithering behind me – perhaps a rat. I was about to ask Pseudo-Caroline what was going on, when I felt something cold against my neck and heard a man's voice close to me.

'Your money, where is it, chum? Hand it over. I got a knife at your throat. And drop your walking stick.'

He should not have reminded me of the stick. Without appearing to do anything, I surreptitiously turned the silver top of the stick and pressed a stud inwards to release the Indian blade. I brought it up with a flourish to flail in the empty air. At almost the same moment I lept blindly forward and staggered a bit and felt as I did so a stinging sensation on my neck.

'Look out, Arnold! He's got a fucking sword!' cried Pseudo-Caroline.

At last I could pull the sleep-mask down from my eyes. It was twilight and, under the heavy cloud cover, the darkness was coming on fast. The three of us faced one another in the water-logged crater of a bomb-site, shielded from the surrounding streets by large advertising hoardings. Arnold wore a duffle coat, scarf and a fisherman's woolly hat and he was rather hopelessly brandishing a flick-knife. Pseudo-Caroline stood close beside him wringing her hands. I blocked the only exit across the the heap of bricks and rubble up to street level. My neck was bleeding a little, but it was only a nick. As I gazed at Arnold's pale and startled face, it suddenly occurred to me that stupidity is not morally neutral, not always anyway. There are certain kinds of stupidity that are actively evil.

'Drop the knife,' I said.

He did so.

'On the ground, both of you. No, not like that. I want you kneeling, facing each other.'

They knelt in the mud facing one another and shivering. I was shivering too. It was very cold.

'She betrayed me. I want you to hear her confession, Arnold. I am going to stand back a bit so that you have some privacy. Caroline must pay the penalty for her treachery, but before I behead her, she should be allowed to make her confession. That is only right and proper. After that I'll want to use your scarf to cover up her eyes.'

Holding my sword raised before me like a royal executioner, I walked backwards a bit, till I was close to the ruined staircase. They faced one another and talked in low tones. It did not look to me as though he was shriving her soul. Never mind. All of a sudden they rose to their feet and ran in opposite directions round the site. Arnold had spotted another way out, a precarious track which wound its way up to a gap between the hoardings. He started to climb. Then Pseudo-Caroline changed course and stumbled in her high heels towards the way up that he had found. It was not going to be possible for me to detain them both. I barred Pseudo-Caroline's way with my sword. She was moaning horribly. She was quite unable to speak. But it was never my intention to execute her. Dr Wilson was right. I was not a murderer. However I had no idea at all what to do next. We had reached the improvisation stage much sooner than I had expected.

Then, fast as the snap of a finger, it came to me what should happen next. A grown-up can re-enact the dreams of youth, if only he is bold enough. I forced her up the brick staircase at sword's point. The bomb site we emerged from was one of those between Leicester Square and the National Gallery. I hailed a taxi and told it to drive to Swiss Cottage. I pushed Pseudo-Caroline into the cab ahead of me. She was still moaning, but I smiled reassuringly at her and said,

'Behave yourself and you'll still get paid.'

The volume of her moaning abated somewhat, though only somewhat. The taxi driver, however, was quite oblivious to her distress.

'Swiss Cottage. That'll cost you. People complain about how expensive taxis are,' he said. 'That's because petrol is so expensive. They don't realise that. And why is petrol so expensive? It's because we are still at war. We should never have got involved in the Korean War in the first place. Two World Wars in one century are enough. We've no business fighting the Koreans' wars for them . . .'

While the taxi driver favoured us with his views on the Koreans, the Chinese, the Japanese and the Russians, I was using the point of the sword-stick to make eyeholes in the sleep-mask. Then I redonned the mask and the hat and, as I did so, a mysterious feeling of pleasure swept over me. It took me a while to track down the hidden source of this pleasure. Then I recalled how as a child I used to sit in solitary splendour in the nursery which also doubled as a cinema, while my guardian screened for me episodes from the matinée serial. *The Adventures of Zorro*. That was it! With my bowler hat, eye-mask and flashing blade, I am the very incarnation of the masked avenger, the English Zorro! Hurrah! Romance and adventure were still to be had for the asking! Hurrah!

When we reached our destination in Swiss Cottage, while I was still fumbling for some money to pay the driver, Caroline murmured beseechingly to the taxi driver,

'Help me, please help me!'

But he did not hear.

'I told you it would be pricey. And you mark my words, we'll be hearing from the Chinese again. Been a pleasure talking to you, mate. Cheerio.'

I hammered on Dr Wilson's door with the pommel of my sword. By now the thin drizzle had turned into something more like real rain. We had to wait a long time on the doorstep while the lights in the house came on and finally Dr Wilson opened the door to us. It was not late and I was astonished to see that he was already in pyjamas and dressing gown.

'Good evening, Dr Wilson. Sorry to get you out of bed. This is Caroline, the woman you said does not exist. Caroline, this is my analyst.'

Pseudo-Caroline looked to Dr Wilson in despair, but then she did a nervous bob and said,

'Charmed I'm sure.'

He ignored her and looked thunderously at me.

'May we come in?' I said, brandishing my sword. 'It's rather wet out here. Caroline is going to agree to marry me after all. I think some drinks would be in order. We have come to bring a bit of colour and a touch of the Marvellous into your drab life.'

I was going to say some more about the Marvellous, but at this point Dr Wilson's wife, her hair in curlers and her body in a heavily quilted dressing gown, appeared at the top of the stairs and, seeing me masked and armed at the door, she started screaming. Pseudo-Caroline started screaming too. I had never seen Dr Wilson's wife before. It had not even crossed my mind that he was married. Lights came on in neighbouring houses. Someone must have phoned for the police. They arrived just as we were settling down with our drinks and I was prodding pseudo-Caroline to tell Dr and Mrs Wilson about what it was like to work as a typist for a fur company.

I was charged with a whole string of offences, most of them beginning with a, like abduction and assault, and I was remanded in custody. However, my lawyer said that since I had not been charged with arson in a naval dockyard (which is a capital offence), I would probably get off with a fine. He was wrong. I was sentenced to three months in jail. My one big consolation was that the psychiatrist who examined me before sentencing found me to be perfectly sane. When this was announced in court I favoured Dr Wilson with a big smirk.

I served out my sentence in Brixton. It was while I was there and I had a little time to think that I conceived of this project, my anti-memoire, which is also an open letter to Caroline. In it I have held nothing back. I stand naked before her – no, more than naked, I have taken the knife to myself and flayed myself alive.

Caroline. 'There is no name, with whatever emphasis of passionate love repeated of which the echo is not faint at last.' So said the Victorian poet and essayist, Walter Savage Landor. Caroline, Caroline, Caroline, Landor was wrong. The old gent was a fool. The power of your name still burns fiercely within me. In writing this book, I have attempted one final act of sorcery designed to entrance you and bring you back to me. Caroline, Caroline, Caroline, I am nothing without you and without you my life has been a meaningless story.

Chapter Fifteen

When this book – a book which really wrote itself – came out in the autumn of 1952, it received mixed and confused reviews. Cyril Connolly in *The Observer* characterised me as 'a lonely figure left stranded by the ebbing tides of the Surrealist movement' and as 'a charmless blend of Peter Pan and Captain Hook'. According to Connolly, 'Caspar combines the egocentricity of the first with the lack of moral principles of the second. However, he has succeeded in capturing the ethos of a particular group dedicated to experiment in art and literature, as well as the flavour of a certain period. Fortunately, both the group and the period are now behind us'. The best review I received was from an anonymous reviewer in *The Times Literary Supplement*. That review was not so different from Connolly's, but it did praise the book for its startling frankness and for the insights it gave into a certain kind of distorted sensibility. Apart from a clutch of lesser reviews and a card from Clive severing all contact between us there were at first no other responses to my book.

I continued to paint and sales continued to improve and I even noticed that paintings that I had sold before the War, if they came back on the market, were now reselling at higher prices. I learned from one gallery owner that quite a few of my paintings were being bought by another dealer acting on commission and then being shipped off to Argentina – presumably to Jorge Arguelles. Items in my Surrealist Roll of Arms continued to be in hot demand, but I abandoned the series after a while, feeling that I was getting stale.

To coincide with the appearance of my book, I worked on what can only be described as a nonself-portrait of myself as writer. In this painting I show myself seated at a desk, pen poised over a notebook and gazing into a large mirror that is propped up on the desk, but in the shadowy background we can also see Caspar, the writer's *Doppelganger*, the painter who stands with palette and brushes behind the canvas on the easel, and this second Caspar also gazes into the mirror. Their faces are the same, yet it is evident that the man who paints the portrait is not the same as the man who is writing about the painter.

Once the nonself-portrait was completed, I commenced on a new phase of experimentation. After so many years, both lean and fat, of hardship and success as a painter, I knew where I stood and it was not in the same rank as Picasso, Magritte and Max Ernst. I was a second-rate artist. Of course, second-rate is not at all bad, but still . . . For a long time I had been feeling that I wanted to go back to basics and make a fresh start and try to master new skills. However at my age and with my reputation it would have been ridiculous for me to go along to the Slade or Camberwell and apply to be taken on as a student. Then it came to me how I could procure a teacher without having to stir from my room in Waterloo. Over the last two or three years Belsen's visual after-effect on my hypnagogic imagery had been fading and, though there were occasions when I would lie awake, gazing on long shuffling columns of concentration-camp victims, those occasions were now less frequent.

I determined that I would summon up an hypnagogic art teacher. I gave him a trim white beard, beret and blue blouse, called him Marcel, and provided him with canvases, paints and an easel. I believe that William Blake followed a somewhat similar procedure and received instruction from such a master in his dreams. Blake even produced a pencil-portrait of his teacher. Anyway, day after day I close my eyes and concentrate on producing Marcel and his equipment. Once he is firmly established, I set him to work, painting on the backs of my eyelids. The rhythm of Marcel's brushstrokes is quite soporific and I have to struggle to stay awake and concentrate. I have a pencil and sketch-pad to hand all the time and, though my eyes are closed, I attempt to reproduce in sketch form, but as accurately as I can, what Marcel is painting in my head. Marcel's face is turned away from me, so I cannot see what he is saying, if anything, but that is unimportant. I learn by looking over his shoulder and copying him. It is like Surrealist painting by numbers. Not only do I not know what I shall be painting from day to day, but I have no firm grip on it from minute to minute. Marcel always starts at the top of his canvas and works methodically down to the bottom without going back to retouch anything. However, if for example he is painting a landscape, that landscape is changing constantly while he paints. A picture which begins at the top as a distant view of Chinese junks in a harbour at sunset may end up in the foreground as a pile of wreaths laid in an English cemetery, and yet the transition from harbour to cemetery is seamless. The same is true of still-lifes, insofar as one can speak of still-lifes in the ceaseless flux of hypnagogia, so that a bowl of fruit rests on a field of fire and a vase of flowers descends into the mouth of a dolphin. Under Marcel's patient tuition I feel that I have taken on a new identity as an artist. My control over my hypnagogia is increasing and I find that what I want to see always appears before my eyes and the colours are brighter too. Childhood bright. There can be no colour without light. Marcel is silently teaching me how to locate and make use of the inner sun of hypnagogia.

Six months after the publication of *Exquisite Corpse*, I received a long letter from Sweden. It was from Monica. For the last three years Monica has been lecturing in the Department of Social Sciences in Stockholm, while also working on a social history of Surrealism. She wrote of course in response to the publication of my book. The letter's tone was characteristically mocking. It began 'I have only myself to blame I suppose, as I never thought that you had a book in you . . .' Monica went on to lament the fact that people could not take out a copyright in their own lives, but she took comfort from the thought that, since her colleagues in the Social Science Department had not seen my book, they had no idea that they had a nymphomaniac in their midst. However, the chief burden of her letter was that I had misunderstood and misrepresented the nature of her researches into coincidence, so that I had made her out to be some kind of crank. She insisted that her approach to the subject had a sound philosophical basis and she quoted Schopenhauer on the subject. According to the German philosopher, all events in man's life 'stand in two fundamentally different kinds of connection: firstly, the objective, causal connection of the natural process; secondly in a subjective connection which exists only in relation to the individual who experiences it, and which is thus as subjective as his own dreams, whose unfolding content is necessarily determined, but in the manner in which the scenes in a play are determined by the poet's plot. That both kinds of connection exist simultaneously, and the self-same event, although a link in two totally different chains, nevertheless falls into place in both, so that the fate of one individual invariably fits the fate of the other, and each is the hero of his own drama while simultaneously figuring in a drama foreign to him – this is something that surpasses our comprehension and can only be conceived of as possible by virtue of the most wonderful pre-established harmony ... It is the great dream dreamt by that single entity, the Will to Life ...' Then Monica continued 'Dearest Casparkins, don't worry if you can't understand all this. You never were cut out to be an intellectual and I fancied you just as you were.'

I scratched my head. Certainly I could make very little of this stuff by Schopenhauer. I suspected that beneath her pose of intellectual aloofness and irony, Monica was actually rather offended by my revelation that Oliver made free with her bum in his novel. Monica had signed herself off affectionately and then added a postscript. 'God knows what Caroline will make of all this – if she is still alive'.

I was still debating how to reply to Monica's letter when, two weeks later, I received a postcard. I recognised the handwriting before I had succeeded in deciphering a

word and I had to put the card down and wait until my
heart had stopped racing madly, before picking it up and
reading;

'Dearest Caspar,
'If you would like to see us, come to the Pavilion Tea Room
in Battersea Park next Tuesday at 4 o'clock. It would be super to
see you there.

Lots of love,
Caroline.'

So after all these months my long anti-memoire had
succeeded in giving birth to this tiny postcard! There were
four days to go and, once I had received the card, I could
neither paint nor draw. My hands shook all the time and I
could not even keep the image of Marcel steady on my
retina. I smoked and paced about the house, preparing and
discarding emotional positions. Having, after so many ef-
forts and so many years, lured her back to me, I surely
could not afford to let her slip her away from me again.

On the Tuesday I was unable to face lunch and I set out
early, walking along the river from Waterloo towards
Battersea Park. It was a desolate journey. The Festival of
Britain had been concluded in September 1951 with Gracie
Fields singing 'Auld Lang Syne' to a great crowd on the
riverside. A couple of weeks after that the workmen went
in and set to demolishing the pavilions and restaurants. The
Festival Hall itself and the great funfair in Battersea Park
were the only parts of the Festival to be left untouched by
the demolition teams. Walking westwards from the former
site of the Festival, now a sea of mud and rubble, one
entered into a nightmare territory of craters and curiously
shaped ridges, gullies and towers. During the War, the
glittering moonlit surface of the Thames had guided the
German bombers into London and the damage they had
wreaked on the southern edge of the river was spectacular.
I liked what I saw. Though I walked amidst ruins, yet I felt
no grief about what had vanished. In my opinion the Blitz
had done London a favour by thinning out our ghastly
legacy of dark and depressing Victorian architecture.

As I picked my way through the rubble, I tried to rehearse things I should say to Caroline, but since I had no idea what sort of person I should be speaking to, where she had been or what she had been doing, this was difficult – like preparing the defence in a trial where the state was refusing to let the defendant know what he was accused of. Lines from sentimental old films came and went in my head, lines like, 'Well, we'll always have Paris'.

I was also worried about whether I would recognise Caroline. Would she appear in a nun's habit? Or in a wheelchair? Would some obese lady, overladen with pearls, step out of a Rolls-Royce? And what was the 'us' the card referred to? I entertained fantasies of two Carolines, or even twenty or thirty Carolines, holding hands in a neat little crocodile and proceeding across the park towards me.

I entered the park over two hours in advance of our appointed meeting time. I had the mad idea that she might be similarly impatient and arrive early too. In the meantime I wandered round the fairground and admired everything: the Giant Caterpillar, the Big Dipper, the Tunnel of Love, Moggo the Largest Cat Alive, Sleipnir the Eight-Footed Horse, Mr K the Hunger Artist, the Punch and Judy Show, the Girl Kept Alive in a Block of Ice and the Hall of Mirrors. All of London should look like a fairground and the red and gold horses with distended nostrils and flared lips would career round the carousel and the women pinned to the walls of the hurtling rotor would be unable to prevent the billowing up of their skirts and the ping-pong balls in the rifle range would dance perpetually on their air-jets. Always faster and madder. London moves too slowly. But I loved the fairground. The gold-framed scrollwork on the fronts of the booths and rides was as gaudy as a mandrill's arse and my eyes were saturated in their colour.

Even so, though I lingered drunk with brightness and movement, for as long as I could in the fairground, I was still almost half an hour early when I settled under the brightly striped canopy of the Pavilion Tea Room. As I sat trying to get a waitress to take my order, the fairground began to disappear in the gathering dusk and mist. The air was very damp, not quite drizzle. Sitting in the cafe, sipping tea (which I hated) I felt a little like a secret agent who pretends to be merely idling while he is in fact waiting to receive vital intelligence. Any one of the people now approaching the Pavilion Tea Room might be my hitherto unidentified contact. That man in a Homburg and a thick dark overcoat might be Caroline heavily disguised, or that batty looking woman with her hair still eccentrically in curlers, or that park warden in a stiff serge uniform . . .

In the end she surprised me by coming up from behind. Before I quite knew what was happening, she kissed me swiftly on the cheek and lowered herself warily into the chair opposite me.

'Hello Caspar.'

I had to catch my breath. She is so beautiful. It is strange to say, but for an instant I did not recognise her and I think that was because, contrary to my expectations, she had hardly changed at all. She was bigger than I had remembered her. That is true. But this was not because she had put on any weight, but only that over the years she had been shrinking in my memory, as if I had been remembering her down the wrong end of a telescope. She was still slim and there were only the faintest traces of wrinkles at the corners of her eyes. She wore a heavy tweed jacket and skirt. A large gold brooch was attached to her white blouse, yet, despite this somewhat matronly dress, she could still have been taken for a young girl. She uneasily crossed and uncrossed her legs.

'Well, aren't you going to say something? Like "Hello Caroline?" I got the impression from your book that you wanted to see me and talk to me.'

'Hello Caroline,' I said. 'You are alone?'

'Yes, well, Oliver is here somewhere, but he thought that I should talk to you first. He's a bit frightened of you, you know. He thought that you might have brought the swordstick along. He's taking Ozzy round the funfair.'

'Ozzy?'

'Yes. Ozzy is our son. Oliver hopes that Ozzy will become a conjuror too. Ozymandias is a good name for a conjuror.'

'How old is Ozzy?'

'Oh, I can't remember,' she said vaguely. 'Fifteen or sixteen, I think.'

'All these years . . .' I began, but I couldn't think how to finish the sentence.

'Yes, it's been a long time,' she said. She tilted her head at that characteristically quizzical angle. Then looking at me intently.

'Your book hurt me, you know. It was like that first painting you did of me, "Striptease". I felt – still feel – as if I had been undressed, as if I was dirty, even a bit of a bitch. If you loved me, I can't think why you wrote it.'

'I wanted to see you again, Caroline.'

'Yes, well . . .' Then her expression softened. (It hurt me that afternoon to see how her expression softened whenever she thought of Oliver.) She smiled.

'Oliver thought your book was very good. He thought it was a hoot. He just lay back and roared. What Oliver says is that you have always been a literary sort of painter. He thinks that you shouldn't have become a painter at all. You should have been a writer. He says that *Exquisite Corpse* is more like a novel than anything else. It's not just you. Oliver says that all Surrealist painting is like that – awfully literary. What do you think?'

But I did not reply and very soon Caroline gave up trying to get me to talk. I just sat there, feeding on her beauty with my eyes, while she related the story of her life without me. As she talked, I found myself anticipating what she would say next. It was all so inevitable. I might have guessed. Perhaps I did guess, but, if so, I had kept that guess secret from myself.

At first, when she met me Caroline had been fond of me – no, more than fond, she had indeed loved me. Then there was that trip to Brighton with the Eluards, Gala,

226

Marcia, Jorge and Oliver. Oliver had sat on the shingle madly talking about his love for an imaginary vampire called Stella. It was nonsense of course — or rather not nonsense but a kind of code, couched in the form of a fantasy story. Oliver had fallen in love with Caroline. Perhaps he had done so the first time he saw her, but if so, he only became aware of his passion for her that morning on Brighton beach when she recited Baudelaire. Then, as he sat talking on the beach about Stella, Caroline intuited that he was talking to no one but to her and about no one but her and something in her responded to Oliver's bizarrely couched declaration of love.

At first she had tried to resist, but Oliver had deluged her with notes and flowers and, on evenings when he knew I would be elsewhere, he had waited for her outside her office. It was not long before she realised that she did not really want to resist. One evening, without warning, she went to visit Oliver in his flat in Tottenham Court Road and there on the red divan, supposedly reserved for the visitations of the vampire woman, Oliver and Caroline, both of them virgins, made love for the first time.

'Did you really not spot it?' said Caroline at this point. 'Stella's face might have been pinched from Felix and her bum from Monica, but Stella, the essential Stella, was and is me. I am Oliver's vampire and I feed on his amazing passion and energy. *The Vampire of Surrealism* is one long love letter from Oliver to me.'

'I thought he was homosexual,' I said stupidly. 'We all did. He was always talking about how he hated women.'

Caroline shook her head sadly.

'He does hate women. It's true that he's a misogynist. But the reason he hates women is that he feels that they make him love them too much. He senses that his vulnerability to the beauty of women threatens his masculinity and his pride. For him, going to bed with me really is like lying down with a vampire. If anything, Oliver's a hyper-heterosexual. He is like a flamenco dancer. Have you ever seen flamenco dancing? Oliver snarls and shouts and he arches his back away from me, but he still has to dance with me.'

Caroline's story continued. By the time she went away with me to Paris (too late to get out of that), she had given herself to my oldest and best friend, but she was still very fond of me, maybe she even sort of loved me a bit in a different sort of way. She did not want to break with me, but she could not tell me the truth. She did not know what she wanted to do, nor could she imagine how things would work out. Oliver, who could not bear to be parted from her for a whole week, had followed us over to Paris and secretly delivered notes to her, begging for a meeting. Things had to be decided one way or another. If she would not agree to meet him, then he would confront me with the facts. Finally she had agreed to meet him in the only place he knew about, the Musée Grevin.

'The Musée Grevin isn't just a waxworks museum,' said Caroline. 'Who gives a fig about waxworks? I certainly don't. But inside the Musée, there's also an amazing room whose walls are all covered in mirrors, so that everything and everybody in it is reflected on and on into infinity. Also there's a dinky little theatre where conjurors perform all day long. Oliver used to go there and study the form of his French colleagues and rivals. Anyway, that day Oliver and I sat there for quite a while, holding hands and watching the tricks and kissing a bit. We also talked about what to do next, but, as usual we couldn't decide anything. I felt terribly guilty. I'm sorry we deceived you, but the thing was that I wasn't sure at that point whether I was going to leave you or what I was going to do. I still did love you then, but it seemed to me that you didn't want me so badly as Oliver did. I wish you had been a bit more forceful – as he was. I don't know. I was just confused.'

'Then, when we returned to England I still didn't know what to do. You were very demanding. Also you were becoming a bit strange – I'm not sure you realised how strange you were becoming. And Oliver warned me that you were studying hypnotism, apparently in the hope of turning me into some sort of mesmerised sex slave.' She paused. 'Please don't blame Oliver for what happened. He was feeling terribly guilty about stealing me from you, but I told him I wasn't 'your woman'. All the same, I was frightened what you'd do to him or to yourself if you ever found out. In the end, Oliver, who was suffering terribly from the uncertainty, thought it would be best if he went abroad and we tried to see if we could live apart from one another for a bit. Maybe we would even be able to forget one another . . . Of course, Oliver didn't give a hoot about the Spaniards or the Popular Front. He's never been political, but he sort of thought it would be a good thing to do, particularly for a writer. All the writers were going to Spain that year. But I think that part of Oliver was sort of hoping to get killed in Spain.'

She fell silent and sat scanning the park in the gathering gloom, doubtless hoping to find her husband and her son in its shadows. The fairy lights, which trailed over the Pavilion and the nearby trees, had been switched on and a loud speaker relayed big band music from the Light Programme. From time to time couples would rise from the Pavilion's tables and, heavily muffled in scarves and overcoats, they danced to the music.

At last Caroline felt able to resume her narrative.

'It was only a month later that I discovered I was pregnant. In the meantime I had been seeing a lot of Clive and the other Putney Thespians. Clive didn't know anything about Oliver or the baby. You were always moody and sulky at that time, but Clive made me laugh and kept me sane. He certainly knew how to treat a lady. A perfect gentleman, Clive. How is he by the way?'

'I'm afraid he has taken strong exception to the book and is refusing to see me ever again.'

'Oh dear. Poor Clive. Anyway I was going to tell him and you about everything and ask one of you for help. I really had no other idea about what to do next. In the end, I decided not to tell Clive. He was so chivalrous that he would probably have insisted on marrying me and rearing another man's child. So it was going to be you. That evening when I came round to Cuba Street (that was a lovely house by the way – I'm sorry it's gone) I was going to tell you everything, but you were in an exceptionally strange mood that evening and you'd been drinking rather a lot. I could smell it, not just on your breath, but on your clothes as well. And I simply couldn't stand it and I walked out and ran away from you as fast as I could.

'I took a taxi most of the way to Putney. It was a long ride and by the time I reached home I had made my mind up. I was going to Spain to look for Oliver. Stealthily I packed a case and left a note for Mummy and Daddy telling them not to worry (though of course they did frightfully) and I crept out of the house. When morning came I took my savings out of the Post Office . . .'

Caroline continued describing her adventures as she crossed France and Spain, but I found it increasingly difficult to concentrate on the details of what she was saying, for the beauty of her mouth muffled the words that came out of it. I was thinking mad things like; she is beautiful. A Piero della Francesca painting is beautiful. But I don't want to go to bed with a Piero della Francesca painting. Whereas I do want to go to bed with Caroline. Why?

Caroline described her train journey through France, her meeting with a pair of deserters from the French army who'd befriended her, the smuggler's trail across the Pyrenees, the rough bus journey to Madrid and the hopeless days spent trailing from the headquarters of one anarchist organisation to another. ('It's funny. You wouldn't have thought that anarchists had organisations. But they do. Lots of them!'). Meanwhile the city was repeatedly attacked by German and Nationalist bombers. Eventually Caroline had tracked Oliver down in a military hospital outside Madrid. He had got dysentery and nearly died from it, but, by the time she found him, he was recovering. He was just about strong enough to think about resuming work on *The Vampire of Surrealism*, while he recuperated. Although Caroline had no experience of nursing, the times were such that she got taken on as a kind of nurse-cum-cleaner-cum-cook.

By the time Oliver was recovered, the Spanish government, for some reason or other, had agreed to repatriate all foreigners in the international brigades. But Oliver and Caroline, plus a couple of German anarchists also from Oliver's platoon decided that they did not want to go back to their own countries. Instead they went to Barcelona and there they boarded a cargo ship bound for Mexico.

As Caroline continued to talk about her adventures in the Americas, a terrible sadness came over me. For most of my adult life I have thought of my story as being the story of Caroline and me and my love for her, but, as I listened to her, it was absolutely clear that she thought of her life as having been the story of Oliver and her and their love for each other. I am only a secondary character in her story, a kind of spear-carrier, whose chief function has been to introduce her to the real hero of her story. She will always be grateful to me for that. I thought of the great story as taking place in London, Paris and Munich, but these places were only settings for the subplot. The real story took happened in Mexico City, Lima, Buenos Aires, New York and Toronto.

Ozymandias was born in a sleeper-car en route for Buenos Aires. Oliver found reasonably well-paid employment as a conjuror working in the entertainment palaces and smart night clubs of Latin America. When it was possible and when Caroline could find a nurse for the child, she would appear with Oliver on stage.

'I used to wear spangly leotards and a crown of ostrich feathers. I've kept my figure,' she said complacently. 'I had to.'

Then a characteristic *moue*.

'Well, as work goes, it certainly beats typing.'

Later they moved to the United States and she tried to fulfil one of the dreams of her girlhood, by setting up as a dress designer, but without much success. Oliver was still writing stuff that was still getting published, but not for real money. It was fortunate that he was in such demand as a conjuror.

'Oliver's real talent is in making things vanish. He's a genius at that. Even other magicians say so. He says that it is just a matter of misdirecting the attention.'

Once the war was properly under way, they moved to Canada and Oliver went to the British High Commission to ask about enlisting and going back to Britain, but somehow he ended up being assigned to the Canadian equivalent of E.N.S.A. and he travelled about from one barracks town to another entertaining the troops who were preparing to cross the Atlantic.

Since the War, Oliver has continued to work as a conjuror and still with Caroline as his assistant. He is a well-respected man. Not only is he President of the Canadian version of the Magic Circle, but he is also leader of a sort of Surrealist literary group in Toronto. When Oliver saw my book reviewed in *The Times Literary Supplement*, he ordered it from England and they read it and talked about it and they decided they ought to have a holiday in England. It was silly never to go back just because they were afraid of me. It was time I learned the truth.

At last Caroline was finished with her life story and she looked at me.

I just said,

'Caroline, why?'

'Oh Caspar dear, it's difficult, but in a way the answer is in that awful book of yours. It's all about how you are — how you look at the world and then you sort of rework it so it looks weird and then you go and sell the weird thing you have created to a gallery and you earn a living from this. The point about it is that you compromise with reality all the time. You were even talking at one time about becoming a commercial artist. Anyway, you never quite leave the world of the ordinary. You are too logical. Whereas with Oliver . . .'

(That smile again!)

'With Oliver there are no compromises. There never

232

can be. Since his books don't sell, he lives on magic. Rather that than make the books more commercial. So he's like you, but he's more like you than you are yourself. From the earliest weeks of our affair I loved his ruthlessness and his readiness to lie to and cheat on his best friend, just for love of me. I literally worship Oliver's intensity and his sheer energy and I always will. He makes things happen just by concentrating on them. I really believe that by concentrating he can will himself to think that water runs uphill and then, when he looks, he sees that water does indeed run uphill.

She paused,

'Do you remember that evening in Paris when we were over at André Breton's flat with Jacqueline and the Eluards and we were looking at André's photo album?'

'I don't remember ever being in André's flat.'

'No? I wondered about that. There are all sorts of gaps and distortions in your book – like the way you make it seem as though we two were alone almost the whole time in Paris. It just wasn't so. Anyway, in the flat I was looking at photos of Jacqueline Lamba, Nusch Eluard, Valentine Hugo, Leonora Carrington, Lee Miller and the rest of them and thinking 'Gosh! The Surrealists get all the beautiful women, don't they?' Then it occurred to me that that was possibly what you wanted me for. No male Surrealist was complete without a beautiful woman hanging on his arm. If I stayed with you, I should become a piece of Surrealist equipment – like your paintbrush, only not as important as your paintbrush.'

'Caroline, it wasn't like that and it never would have been. I swear.'

'No, I suppose not.' She reached across the table to take my hand. 'I was very fond of you, you know and I now know how much you loved me. But it's not enough. You might paint me as a goddess, but your grip on reality is strong enough for you to know that I am not one. But Oliver . . . Oliver knows for certain that I am a goddess, one of those special people who has taken human form and walks about on Earth in the guise of a woman –'

She let go of my hand and looked at her watch.

'You have to forget me, you know. I'm giving you permission to forget me. Come on now. We've talked long enough. It's time to go over and meet Oliver.'

I put my hand over hers.

'Stay a while. You are so beautiful.'

But she took her hand away again.

'Oh come on now! Don't be such a cowardy custard! Oliver is impatient to see you and I want you to see Ozymandias. Oliver will be waiting for us outside The Hall of Mirrors.'

I paid the waitress. Caroline pulled me to my feet and linked her arm proprietorially in mine. The park was staying open late that evening. There was to be a firework display – something to do with the imminent coronation of a new monarch. Together we walked through the gathering dark towards the faint music of the fairground and we talked of less important things.

Caroline told me that she had liked Monica and was glad that she and I had got together eventually. But Oliver thought that Monica's theories about coincidence were rubbish, for she paid too much attention to statistics and not enough to the power of love to discover coincidence in the operations of chance. Then Caroline was talking about the hotel they were staying in somewhere outside London. They would be moving on soon, as Oliver had a phobia about being trapped in the ordinary.

And I was thinking about Oliver. I had thought he was dead. This would be like a resurrection. Should I kill him now? What good would that do? I felt too sad and empty to hate him.

As we got closer to the fairground, Caroline stopped talking, unwilling to compete with the full-throated mechanical music of the steam driven calliopes and carousel organs.

Oliver was standing, waiting outside The Hall of Mirrors. He had grown a neat little Anthony Eden-ish moustache and he was wearing an American-style suit with broad lapels. Unlike Caroline, he did look tireder and gaunter – even a little ghostly. As he saw me coming, he extended a hand and then, thinking the better of it, he pressed the hand against his heart in an oriental form of salutation.

'Hello again, Caspar. Am I forgiven?'

He did not actually say these words, but, remembering my skill as a lip-reader, he mockingly mouthed them.

'I forgive you, curse you!' I mouthed back.

'Where's Ozymandias?' shouted Caroline anxiously.

Oliver smiled at me exultantly and pointed over the roof of The Hall of Mirrors to the Big Dipper. A ride was coming to an end and the carriages were slowing to a stop. In the third of the carriages a boy – a young man almost – with jet black hair and large eyes rode alone. He was smiling too. This was unmistakably Ozymandias. I watched the carriages rattle to a final stop and the boy step down, before turning back to Oliver and Caroline. But they were no longer with me. The boy had also vanished. Once again I was left alone with the images on my eyelids.